ABOUT THE AUTHOR

LISA L HANNETT lives in Adelaide, South Australia—city of churches, bizarre murders, and pie floaters. In just over two years, she has sold more than 20 stories to venues including *Clarkesworld, Fantasy, Weird Tales, ChiZine, Electric Velocipede, Shimmer* and *Steampunk II: Steampunk Reloaded.*

Her work has appeared on *Locus*'s Recommended Reading List 2009, *Tangent Online*'s Recommended Reading List 2010, and in the *Year's Best Australian Fantasy and Horror* 2010. "The February Dragon", co-written with Angela Slatter, won an Aurealis Award for Best Fantasy Short Story 2010. She is a graduate of the Clarion South Writers Workshop.

Bluegrass Symphony is her first collection. Her second collection, *Midnight and Moonshine* (co-authored with Angela Slatter) will be published by Ticonderoga Publications in November 2012.

You can visit her online at www.lisahannett.com.

Bluegrass
Symphony

Also by LISA L. HANNETT

Midnight and Moonshine (FORTHCOMING 2012)

Bluegrass Symphony

T≋
p≋
Ticonderoga
publications

Bluegrass Symphony by Lisa L. Hannett

Published by Ticonderoga Publications

Cover designed by Lisa L. Hannett and Russell B. Farr
Designed and edited by Russell B. Farr
Typeset in Sabon and Vladimir Script

A Cataloging-in-Publications entry for this title is available from the National Library of Australia.

ISBN   978-1-921857-00-3 (hardcover)
       978-1-921857-01-0 (trade paperback)
       978-1-921857-98-0 (ebook)

Ticonderoga Publications
PO Box 29 Greenwood
Western Australia 6924

www.ticonderogapublications.com

10 9 8 7 6 5 4 3 2 1

Thank you so much to everyone who helped see this collection through to publication, particularly: Russell B. Farr for showing such unswerving enthusiasm for these stories (and for being so gracious when I pestered him about the cover); Ann VanderMeer for giving my first book the coolest introduction I could ever have imagined; Alisa Krasnostein for giving me the impetus to begin writing several of these pieces; Katrina Burge for introducing me to Gillian Welch's music, especially "Elvis Presley Blues"; Professor Graham Tulloch for believing that writing speculative fiction is indeed a valuable way to spend my time, regardless of impending thesis deadlines; Faye and David Gilliland for agreeing to read only the stories I earmark as safe for parental eyes; my sisters (Kelly, Terri, Amy, Sara, and Rachel) for their encouragement and support; Nick Prescott and Rebecca Vaughan for inspirational conversations and reading holidays; Katie Cavanagh for being the first person to read my work (and the first to buy this collection!); Danielle Shane and Heather Montgomery for putting up with my flights of fancy for the past two decades; Tully Barnett for treasured discussions about spec-fic, writing, and everything in between (and for understanding my ideas even when they're presented as caffeine-fuelled rambles); and Catherine Crout-Habel for being a fantastic storyteller in her own right. Thanks also to Diane Walton and Robin Carson at On Spec: The Canadian Magazine of the Fantastic.

My deepest thanks go to dearest Brain, Angela Slatter, for her expert advice; for reading every word in this book (and many others besides) and offering pitch-perfect insights and comments; for brandishing the flensing knife with enviable skill, and showing me how to wield it myself.

Finally, my love and endless gratitude are dedicated to Chad Habel; for without him, none of this would have been possible.

Contents

Introduction

Ann Vandermeer

I was first introduced to the work of Lisa Hannett when she sent me a story to consider for *Weird Tales*. It was about a talking mechanical crow at a strange carnival, beautifully written and hard to forget. I didn't take that story but I knew she was a writer to watch. She continued to send me stories and then I had the good fortune to work with her in closer circumstances at Clarion South (remotely from home while my husband had the good luck to actually *be* in Australia). Eventually we connected on a story that fit *Weird Tales* and we've worked together on various other crazy yet inspired projects ever since.

I've always enjoyed Lisa's fiction because her characters are alive with passion and fury and her worlds are teeming with excitement and movement. Her use of language can make even the most horrifying scenes beautiful, so that you won't, you can't, turn away. That's a rare talent.

The stories in this collection are no different. Bound together by a common environment, they tell the tales of a land that brings to mind the American South. But make no mistake; these aren't your familiar back roads of Tennessee or Alabama. It's not even a trailer park way down in Mississippi. Instead we're transported to towns like Alabaska, Two Squaw and Plantain, which reside somewhere deep in the wilds of Tapekwa County. People live and work and love there just like we do, except . . . that they don't. Not really.

This is a land of wolf boys, minotaurs and shifting (yes shifting, not shiftless, although there's quite a bit of that, too) redneck people who are just trying to get ahead in the world. Mothers who only want to protect their daughters and daughters who cherish their mums. A brother who thinks he can save his beloved sister from a fate she's running toward as fast as she can. Reverends who perform special magic ceremonies with the help and the sacrifice of willing flesh. And you know, it's all for the good of the community, of course.

The relationships between fathers and daughters, the lengths each will go to redeem the other, play an important role: "It's a strange kind of love, what they share. I knowed its like meself, so it's easy enough to recognise. One what makes folk sacrifice anything to get what they's yearning for. One what makes a little girl reckless enough to go into the forest alone, just to save her daddy. One what makes that daddy suffer all manner of indignities, if it means she'll always be his. His alone."

And yes, some of the superstitious country folk have mysterious ways and some of the cowboys would just as soon hold a shotgun on you as raise a can of beer with you. There are menfolk who treat their womenfolk like worn out possessions. There are womenfolk who use magic to get what they want (or at least what they think they want) from their men. But there's also something very strange going on. Stranger than you might think.

These stories are about more than people just trying to get something from one another. These stories are about power and redemption, transformation, and sacrifice.

♪

Where does that power come from anyway? Sometimes from the "usual" ways: from eggs that the special hens lay, or blood soaked towels or tentacles sprouting from a young man's chest. Just the usual, right?

Did I mention the twiggy folk? They are there to help you get your heart's desire. Right? Of course they are. You've just gotta trust them. Because they know better than you what you really need. And they will make sure you get it. Hesteh says, "But paths don't jest go one way: what you lost gotta come back to you some day, sure as spring follows winter."

As for what you might think is an "all-too-often used" subject, Hannett has included the most provocative, unusual take on a vampire tale I've ever read. Lisa has a way of twisting and turning all the usual conventions. "In his mouth I tasted the incoherent feathers of our unborn baby's thoughts. I sampled my agony, distilled in his venom." She makes them her own. She's good at that, she is.

This collection of stories will make you think twice before taking a walk in the woods. It's full of twisted magic and talking squirrels. Rodeo shows that happen in less than ten seconds. A Beauty Pageant that ends in an impossible way. And as Ada says in "From the Teeth of Strange Children", "There's so many dangerous critters in this land . . ."

But what about those talking squirrels anyway? Go read—and you'll find out.

ANN VANDERMEER
MARCH 2011

Bluegrass Symphony

Carousel

Carousel

The moths delight in the iron tang soaking the front of the silent girl's dress. Their proboscides suck at calico fabric flowers; no longer all blue, some have bloomed red across the grey cotton field. The nectar from these new blossoms engorges their bodies, fills them with power and confidence. It makes them stronger than birds and their beaks just as sharp. Nothing but time can stop them.

They work quickly.

While swarms of larvae nibble at the thin material covering the girl's twisted chest, which is rising and falling unsteadily, the adults crawl over her face, licking salt water from her eyes. Not so much to drink now as there was this morning. Everything in her, around her, is drying in the shed's close quarters. They redouble their efforts, hairy legs skimming dirty blonde hair, sun-darkened skin and beige cardigan at a blurring pace. Scales of brown, black, taupe chitin fall from their wings as they fly, as they land, leaving her coated in iridescent dust.

The light in her eyes is fading. They must catch it before it goes out.

Too shocked to feel fear, the girl doesn't enjoy but doesn't quite mind the sensation of tiny feet brushing her forehead and eyelids, the bridge of her freckled nose. Their touch is as gentle as Isaac's; he who'd always stopped pushing whenever she asked, no matter how worked up he'd got from their sweaty-palmed fumblings. With Isaac, hardness didn't have to mean pain. Ever since his troupe came to town, he'd been convincing her, kiss by kiss, that this was God's truth. Last night, she'd finally let him prove it.

Her breath comes short and fast now, as it did then. Air rushes in across cracked lips then gets too heavy to push back out. Consciousness keeps afloat on lilting gasps and thoughts of Isaac's embrace. She tries to cry out for him, but only manages to exhale, launching a dozen moths from her ribcage. She can't feel what they're doing down there, can't lift her head to look. The hum and flutter of wings encourages her slowing heart to keep up if it can.

It can't.

The fall was too great, the angle unfortunate. Bodies are meant to sit on carousel horses, not topple from them head-first. She blinks, but the rest of her remains still, lying on the sawdust-covered floor of her Pa's shed, arms and legs akimbo. She wishes she could pull down her skirt, so Pa won't find her with her knickers showing. So he won't see the cherry blood Isaac left there.

𝄞

Where you been, Cassie? Pa's voice had snapped out of the darkness; it lashed a welt of guilt across her soul, froze her creeping footfalls halfway across the back porch. The moon had set and the sun was only a suggestion of pink on the horizon, but as Pa had butted his cigarette and moved out of the shadows, Cassie could see his face whiten with fury. It went deep red as she blundered through her cover story. Spit punctuated his hollered accusations.

Sneaking around with them carnie boys, wasn't you? Lifting your skirts for a spin on the Ferris wheel, for a lick of pulled taffy, for a chance to win a dime? His grip had been unbreakable as he dragged her by the arm, pulled her a hundred metres or so along fields gone fallow behind their weatherboard farmhouse. She'd dug her heels in the dry soil, scuffing her best boots and grazing her bare knees.

It ain't true, she'd cried. *It ain't.* She did her best not to look at the carnival lights, glowing like salvation in the distance. She'd kept her eyes down, tried to persuade with body language as much as speech. Pa knew better than to listen to her mouth or believe her penitent figure; he'd trusted lies like hers once too often.

Pa had hauled Cassie to the shed. Inside, he'd towed her back and forth, ten steps in and twenty across, clearing away any equipment she might use to escape. Hammers, circular saws, drill bits, chisels, nails—everything sharp was removed and tossed onto the brittle grass. When he'd finished, only the outlines of tools remained, gaps in the thick dust coating workbenches, shelves and three-legged stools. New afterimages of work he had long since abandoned.

You ain't coming out 'til you fess up, he'd said, shoving her to the floor.

All Cassie had to hand was a rubber-headed mallet. It was too blunt to do any real damage but its heft was reassuring. It was the perfect weight for throwing. Gripping its worn handle, she could still picture how it used to look in her Pa's calloused hands, gently tapping a chisel groove into patterns he'd pencilled on blocks of yellow poplar or Appalachian pine, raising curls of spicy-scented wood in its wake. When she was little, she'd loved nothing more than watching her Ma and Pa making carousel horses.

As a team, they were unmatched; demand for their creations kept food on the table even when the harvest was poor. Unlike the straight-legged ponies other artisans made, Pa could carve horses in all sorts of poses—prancing, leaping, tossing wavy manes, stamping with delicate hooves. His beasts were always smiling, always long-toothed, always defiant. Their eyes were just like Ma's, full of mischief and mystery.

In Cassie's memories, sunshine poured down through the shed's four windows; one on each wall and set high enough to prevent curious eyes from seeing their designs prematurely. Happy rays had flooded the space with promises of endless prosperity. Ma liked to sit where the beams were brightest; she would use more colours than Cassie could imagine, painting the horses after Pa had sanded them smooth. She'd adorned their bridles with orange flowers, dappled their vibrant hides with blue and white constellations, striped the posts upon which they hung the black and purple of crushed berries. Her palette had been endless, but the way Cassie remembered it, everything her Ma painted had been burnished gold.

The mallet made a satisfying thunk when Cassie hurled it at the closing door. The sound of a padlock being rattled into place on the other side taunted her, cackled that she was no match for her Pa.

Should've known you'd turn out just like her, he'd said. *Whores, the both of you.*

Cassie had pressed herself against the door, her mouth twisted, her teeth bared. *I ain't never gonna talk to you again, you hear?* Her neck muscles strained around the truth in her words. *Never.*

You'll be begging for me by nightfall. Pa's footsteps had crunched across the grass as he retreated mumbling, *Mark my words.*

Everything in the shed had faded. Even dawn couldn't break the gloom: everywhere she looked, the room had turned dishwater grey. She had to get out.

Cassie's cussing added a streak of colour that workshop hadn't seen in half a decade. If Pa'd noticed her yowling, he showed no sign. She took a breath, paused; heard crows cawing in the fields, cicadas buzzing a late summer rhythm, the creak of the weathervane spinning, spinning. Screeching was useless. Next closest farm was the Petersens' nine acres south; no chance they'd hear her from there. And Isaac was miles away, bunked down after a night's loving, sleeping through the hours 'til he'd see his girl again. Cassie's stomach had turned somersaults while she imagined the look on his face if she didn't meet him by the carnival gates at dusk.

She had started to cry then, sniffles that soon exploded into ugly sobs; howled louder and harder than she had after Ma had walked out, leaving her alone with Pa. Leaving her, without a word.

♪

The moths had kept still as they watched the girl cry. Day and night, they coated the shed's peaked ceiling—millers and road-side skippers, cloudy and sooty wings, sulphurs, duns and hoary-backs—all the cousins, big and small, lined the windowsills, the rafters, the carcasses of rotting carousel steeds. They'd shared a fondness for perching on Pa's tools, until he'd removed them that morning; next best were the desiccated carnations Ma had dotted around the place long before she'd left them all behind. A constant susurrus pervaded the room, the noise of wings and legs and antennae shifting, of tiny mouths snacking, of gradual disintegration. Thousands of compound eyes looked down, or up, or across at Cassie. All these glittering black orbs had reflected the same thing.

It would be hard to care for this one.

They'd felt sorry for her, even after her tears had slowed. She'd been in the shed for hours and Pa hadn't returned. They'd spent the morning darting around stiff-bristled paint brushes, splinters of wood, sheets of sandpaper—whatever Cassie had found to fling when a fit of temper seized her. Now the smaller cousins were frightened into flight whenever she raised an arm, so the bigger ones joined forces, used their wings to camouflage moveable objects until their guest settled down.

It didn't take long. The late night and the morning's excitement conspired to drain her energy: soon Cassie had slumped to the floor, her brown eyes unfocused. The room was too hot; its air pressed upon her, heavier than a feather blanket. She was asleep before the sun had reached its zenith, and only woke in time to see it sliding down day's slippery backside. Echoes of calliope music faded as she shook her head, clearing it of feverish dreams.

The bigger cousins heard her talking under her breath then, reprimanding herself for wasting so much time. Night would fall any minute as far as Cassie could tell, leaving Isaac waiting. The moths had known better, but didn't bother interrupting her. Instead, they'd settled on sun-warmed surfaces to watch her fuss. Their antennae had twitched contentedly.

How quickly she'd worked! Quickly, quickly: life is short. The moths could respect her urgency. Seven carousel horses, in various stages of completion, cluttered the shed; they'd waited five long years to be put to use. Cassie wended around them, hopped over piles of lathe-turned posts, ducked under a bridge of two-by-fours her Pa'd once intended for a merry-go-round's canopy. Her frame was slight, but determination had infused her with strength: she'd dragged the largest of the herd—a stallion almost twice her height, with refined head and forelegs rearing on roughly hewn hindquarters—leaving long scrape marks in the sawdust-covered floor. Breathing hard, she'd manoeuvred the unsteady thing over to the lowest window, climbed carefully up to see how great a stretch it would be to get out.

Little windowsill cousins had grazed her fingertips as Cassie reached. She'd squealed, recoiled, crouched down to avoid the flurry of moths she'd disturbed. The movement set her makeshift ladder rocking with an awful creak. Knees and arms shaking, she'd straightened up when the moths alighted once more; stretched her hand up and over them, and pushed at the dirty pane of glass with all the force she could muster. A smeared handprint was the only evidence of her efforts. The window refused to budge.

Cassie'd hopped off the horse, loosing chunks of worm-eaten timber as she did so, and hunted around for the rubber mallet. Earlier, a cluster of moths had congregated on the tool, burying it beneath their plump bodies, while the girl still had a mind for throwing things. After a few minutes' searching, upsetting chairs and shifting stacks of dried wood, she'd spied the metallic handle glinting out of a pile of rags. Shooing the moths, she'd snatched the tool and returned to scale the stallion's rickety back. Her footing was unsure, the soles of her boots slippery on the curved wood— but her jaw was set.

With two deft taps, she'd smashed the bottom pane of glass. A cool breeze rushed in through the hole, tickling the sweaty curls on the back of Cassie's neck, carrying with it the sound of approaching boot steps. Gingerly clasping the window ledge, she'd shifted her weight, twisted her head to look at the shed door to see if Pa was coming in. Such a practiced, simple gesture. And yet so disastrous.

The horse shuddered, then emitted an ear-splitting crack. Its unfinished legs, riddled with rot, tipped precariously to the right. Cassie's arms flailed, her feet sought purchase, found none. She scrabbled at the windowsill as the horse's base snapped and slid from beneath her. Her left hand was sliced to the bone on shards of glass; she'd pulled back as though burnt, spraying a fine arc of blood across her dress as she toppled. Momentum had sent her earthwards—but Pa's spindle lathe, hulking on the floor behind her, obstructed her fall.

Families of big cousins had scattered like leaves when Cassie's head made contact with the lathe. A great chunk of her scalp gouged on the corner of the instrument's table; when she hit the floor, her body had looked wrong. Awkward. Broken. Within seconds, a red halo seeped around her head. The pain was intense, but brief.

You'll pay if you wrecked anything, her Pa shouted, thumping the shed wall for emphasis. *Even if it takes the rest of your life.*

Cassie had kept silent, as Pa'd expected, but not as she had intended. She lay dazed, eyes both seeing and not seeing the hordes of moths circling above her prostrate form. The top of her head throbbed, but everything below her nose was numb. Shock had kept fear at bay; her mind couldn't compute what had happened. All she knew was that everything in the shed was moving—the horses swam in her vision, the lathe above her bent and swayed like a see-saw, and every flat surface was alive with wings. Everything moved except her.

The machine had not broken her fall, she realised, but it had her neck.

You hear me, girl? Pa's voice seemed quieter now, his complaints not so frightening as they had been that morning. *You'll pay!*

𝄞

The moths are nearly blinded by the light exuding from Cassie's chest and her wide, round eyes. Night has returned but they can still see her, shining brighter than noon in midsummer. Her glow blazes.

It beckons.

Larvae finish gnawing a great hole in her dress; their job done, they roll down her ribs to the floor and sleep with tiny mouths aching. Now Cassie's pale skin is exposed, beneath which the big cousins can sense her heart failing. They need to capture that radiance, to extract it—but which way is quickest? Through the eyes or the heart? The moths can never agree. Little cousins go for the nostrils, the ears: in their innocence, they believe these tunnels will provide a direct path to the girl's whimpering core. Big cousins know better, but let the juniors roam as they will. Littlies won't penetrate anywhere near fast enough: it's up to the big ones to act.

Cassie wants to shake her head, to clear her ears, to snort away busy nosefuls. The moths grieve for her even while they invade, even while they stab their sharp beaks into her flesh. Necessity urges them on. Their bites don't hurt, *can't* hurt; even so, they hope she will forgive them after they've unstitched her from the inside.

Darkness doesn't hinder them. The moths are brave and self-assured in all conditions; their senses as effective at night as in day.

Cassie, on the other hand, isn't faring as well as her guardians. Pa knows she's afraid of the dark; she's sure that's why the shed's only socket remains bulbless. Fear radiates from her pores, spreads in waves that the moths must negotiate while they work. It's exhausting, digging through inches of muscle, blood and bone, exhuming the source of Cassie's shining while fighting against her despair.

Outside, an engine roars. For a minute, Cassie's heart soars—it's Isaac, come with bags packed and a tank full of gas, making true his promise to take her away. The pickup's headlights glare through the shed's high windows, throwing Cassie and her handmaidens into stark relief. But soon the lights waver, bob up and down with the weight of Pa's bulk settling into the truck's cab; they swerve to the left as he backs out of the drive. The blackness he leaves behind is complete, heavy now with silence and Isaac's absence. Night is the loneliest time, has been these five years.

Not so for the moths.

Thrilled, they're chewing, stabbing, digging with gusto; single-mindedly fulfilling their duty. Between mouthfuls they whisper *Gather your courage*, though they know Cassie can't hear what they're saying. They spear into her flesh, desperately searching for an edge, afraid she's burning down too fast.

Raising their voices, they call to their green-glowing cousins and ask for help. Phosphorescent glimmers float through the hole in the window. The dark room blinks with ephemeral fire, fluctuating like an aurora in winter: black, green, black in irregular pulses. Not squint-making bright but dazzling enough to let Cassie know they're there.

Unshed tears well in her eyes. The moths notice the change, and nod their approval. Their girl's got a bit of the moth in her too, they reckon. Like them, she can't resist a bit of shine, a bit of light to brighten up shady patches. So they're doing their damnedest to fan the flame, to get her out before she's lost to the shadows.

Cassie sees the lightning bugs but mistakes them for fairies. Just like the ones in stories Ma told her as a girl: in the princess's darkest hour, sparkling creatures come to magic her away, to tell her it was all a dream, to unite her with her handsome love. Ma always got misty-eyed when she recited those tales; said, in her experience, fairies ignored wild girls like them. Had enough wildness their own selves, she figured. A pure-hearted soul is what fey folk need, to balance out their mischief.

Fairies dance near the ceiling then slowly descend, as though deliberating whether or not to get involved. Cassie traces their elliptical movements, urges them on. Eventually, they mingle with the beige angels floating above her head. Tiny green ladies and voluptuous red-speckled browns exchange kisses of greeting; then the fairies lower ornate lanterns to afford their cousins more light.

I ain't wild—I'm good. Ain't I, ladies?

The fairies congregate in the air above her chest. She can barely see them as they dip in and out of her ravaged ribcage, as they wink in and out of darkness.

Ain't I, Ma?

They bob up and down, searching. Directing the brown angels to go deeper, to net their catch.

Ain't I, Isaac?

The moths are coated in blood by the time they finally catch sight of the seam holding Cassie together. These threads don't glare up at them, even though their blue and white light is radiant as first prairie snows. No, her stitches aren't harsh. They're incandescent.

Dawn taps at the shed's windows.

So close to their goal, the moths are thrown into frenzy. The hum of their wings is deep, tribal; it sings back to the beginning of time. It calls to Cassie's hidden self, lures her out, implores her to escape.

She watches the carousel of angels and fairies spinning above her, their rhythmic movements lulling, reassuring. Calliope music plays just for her, sweet songs that remind her of Isaac. At last, she feels calm. Hopeful.

Then she hears the crunch of tires in the drive, the quiet click of a vehicle's door opening and closing. The nimble step of someone tiptoeing up to the shed.

Isaac!

The fire of her excitement burns brighter than any flame the moths have ever seen. They're ecstatic, bathed in her joy. Her outline is clear to them now; she's given them the extra grip they need. Pinching with beaks, legs, wings, the moths burrow one last time into Cassie's core and *pull.*

Tugging with irresistible power, they extract a gossamer copy of the immobile figure lying on the floor. The spectre slides out with a wet, sucking sound, speckling the girl's body with a fine spray of crimson. Even now, Cassie's ghostly face looks to the shed door, expectantly beautiful, waiting to see her lover. The moths manoeuvre her flexible silken limbs, twisting and turning her in the air as they vie for position on her back. Linking antennae and legs, they knit themselves together in droves, until Cassie's new self is complete.

Until she is lifted in a graceful arc toward the ceiling, wearing a set of living wings.

Quilted together, the moths spread out behind her, rippling and muscular, until Cassie's wingtips brush the beams more than a metre above her head. Cyclones of sawdust spin up from the ground when she flexes her back. She giggles as the breeze she creates tickles her arms and legs, as it lifts her hair like wild vines, as it knocks over paint tins and horses. She ascends slowly, luxuriating in the sensation of flight.

Her gaze never leaves the door.

She is rapt as the padlock clunks—*You came for me*—drops away—*Isaac, I'm here!*—and lands with a dull thump on the ground.

Her translucent face freezes as morning spills across the shed's threshold, bringing with it a rumpled, bloodshot-eyed Pa. His tired feet shuffle, his clothes reek from a night's worth of bourbon. Their expressions are mirrors of horror and disbelief.

Looking down, both father and daughter see the last thing either of them wanted.

𝄞 𝄞 𝄞

Down the Hollow

Down the Hollow

Reverend told Tommo and Billy to keep digging 'til they shifted enough snow to reach dirt. They've been at it nigh on an hour now, but the going could be slower. The paddocks is slick with ice—never mind that the calendar's just turned June—and the hollow's filled right up to the brink. Most folk wouldn't know there's a hell-deep gully here, if they didn't grow up 'round these parts. Dísah used to dare me to climb into it all the time when we was kids. She swore up'n down that the roots poking out of its craggy sides was really fingers and petrified tongues; that the ground at its base weren't covered with grass but human bones. Piles and piles of skulls and spines and ribs, and God-knows what else. She said it were haunted, on account of them skeletons, and I can't say I didn't believe her. None of us kids kept our shit together long enough to make it past the first ledge, so there weren't none of us fit to call her a liar.

Dísah made it to the bottom, though. More times'n I can count. She'd scramble down them rough walls, easy as a possum, 'til she were well out of sight. One time, she were gone so long I knew she must've slipped and died; but just as I were set to run back home and fetch our Pa, she wriggled her skinny arse up over the ridge and flashed me a filthy smile. "Buck up, Jesse," she said. "Ain't no ghost going to get me." In her hand, a smooth grey stone, no longer'n her middle finger. What she promised were a bone from someone's big toe.

Now Jed's working the pick-axe, forcing his way to where none of us ain't never been. His hat's pushed high on his forehead, face red and dripping, scarf rimmed with a crust of frozen sweat and breath. He and the boys is got a ways to go before they reach bottom; their tools ain't been used much for this type of work—shouldn't really be used now. Regular spades ain't built for this wrong season, regular ploughs won't do neither, and regular seeds ain't fit for sowing. Not yet.

Only sure-fire way to fight summer snows is from the inside, so Reverend says. We gots to plant something deep in the earth's belly; something so pure it'll shame them white fields into melting. That's why we're here, me and my cousins, freezing our balls off when we should be sweltering, praying for cool rains to break the heat, to draw our crops up and keep the dust down. Instead, the three of them is chipping their way through twelve solid feet of last week's blizzard. And I can't do nothing more'n watch, standing on the lip of the crater they're making, heart and knees buckling under the weight of my burden. Clenching my jaw. Struggling to keep the truth from spilling.

Reverend's plucking his steel guitar, picking nothing but minor chords. It's a brittle music, too fragile to keep time with the ins and outs of the boys' shovels, the heated rhythm of their grunting and cussing. His is hangman's songs if ever I heard them. Notes twang, dangle in the air for no more'n a second. Then gravity pulls them down, snaps their necks, and drops them dead into the hollow. Ain't no trees or cliffs for miles 'round for the sound to bounce off of—between each note there's nothing but hush, smothered under a blanket of falling snow.

Soon Reverend starts to sing. His voice is thinner than the cotton nightie my sister's wearing, and bare as her arms. Whatever hymn it is, it ain't one we sing at church. Half the time his pitch is so low I can't make out the words, but I can tell by the look on his face that he probably never sang nothing more serious. What I do catch is all about gifts and rebirth and new life, and other stuff you hear of in fireside yarns. Fat white flakes land on his eyelashes as he looks skywards; he blinks away the melt until a steady trickle runs down his cheeks. It almost looks like he's crying.

Real tears is burning the back of my throat. I swallow and cough in an effort to keep them in. Readjust the hold I got on Dísah, hoping if I keep my hands busy my mind won't notice how fast things is happening. I lean back a bit, so as to take more of her weight against my chest, then shimmy my arms into a better position beneath the crook of her knees, and under her shoulders and back. Gently cradle her face against my collarbone. Rest my chin on the crown of her golden head. Try to stretch her flimsy skirt so it'll cover more'n just her thighs. Shift her again; free one hand so I can brush away the snow that's collecting on her shins and bare feet.

"Ain't going to get no deeper now, Rev," Billy says. "Ground's froze solid."

It can't be time. My heart jackrabbits and my legs ache to do likewise. I look to Reverend, pray he'll tell them to keep going, at least long enough so I can figure a way out of here; but he's fixed on finishing his song and is ignoring the lot of us. The boys crawl out of the hole they dug, toss their tools down, stretch and flex their cramping hands. Tommo slips a flask of cheap whiskey out from inside his wool vest, takes a long swig then passes it on to Jed and Billy. They each of them warm the mouth of the tin flask with their breaths first, to keep their lips from sticking, then take turns sucking heat from the bottle. I don't begrudge them the chance to rest before they gots to fill that hole back in again—but while their faces is growing rosy, my Dísah's cold, cold skin's turning fish-belly blue.

I'm shivering so much I can't tell if she's moving at all no more. And though I rub her arms and legs as well as I can without dropping her, it don't seem to help none.

A freight train howls across the horizon, drowning out the final verse of Reverend's song. When we was growing up, Dísah teased him for looking like a prairie wolf, on account of his long pointed nose, mongrel hair, and deep yellow eyes. And for a second, with his head tilted back like it is just now, and the wail of the train cutting through the quiet, I reckon she were right. Our Rev's baying for God's help. If I could, I'd scream right along with him, bellow 'til I'm as empty and breathless as my sister.

But I know that won't achieve nothing. So alls I do is sweep Dísah's hair away from her eyes, kiss her 'til my tears leak out, and keep my mouth shut like I promised her.

"I ain't one to tread on ceremony, Rev," Tommo says. "But if we gots to do this, can we get it done before you wind up needing to bury five souls in this here hollow instead of just one?"

My eyes flick between Reverend, the boys, and Dísah. None of them meet my gaze. I back a pace or two away from them all, but soon forget how to move, how to breathe.

I'm really going to lose her.

"Right then, Jesse." Reverend's lost his coyote look. His head's bowed as he walks towards me, taking one slow step after another as if he were coming down the aisle of his church. He's slung his guitar over his back and is pulling a pair of thick mittens on as he approaches. Still not meeting my eyes.

"I know you don't want to be here, son. But Dísah picked you as her shepherd, and you got to live up to that. This is a proud moment for you and your kin, Jess; and you can rest assured every soul in town will know how you've carried yourself today. So come on now." He pauses for a minute to give me time to control my blubbering. The seconds tick by, but I can't stop. I'm choking on my tears, snorting them in, coughing them out. And they just keep coming. Harder and thicker until I think my body's going to burst. Only thing keeping me together is holding Dísah close. Squeezing her so tight I'm surprised she don't snap in two.

Maybe if she does, they won't think she were so perfect no more. They'll see how I broke her, see the truth. Maybe then I can keep her.

"Come on now, boy. Get ahold of yourself. We all know Dísah's special—hell, that's why she's here! You don't think I wouldn't have brought fat Chelsea or that stupid cow Jeanette if I couldn't have? Or one of Abe Pedlar's cross-eyed daughters, or even that retarded little girl living near Miller's Point? What's her name? Jayla?" He shakes his head.

"But that's just it, son; I *couldn't* choose any of them. Those girls get used more than the shitter at Pete's Roadhouse. And, unless I'm wrong, I've just listed every young chickadee in town what's got her bloods, apart from Dísah here. Now am I wrong?"

All three of my traitor cousins shake their heads, lower their eyes. As if, between them, they ain't left more than one load in each of them so-called shitters.

"Everyone's counting on us to do our part, Jess—oh, for Christ's sake, don't give me that look!" Reverend's jaw snaps shut. Fog blows out his nostrils in bursts; he waits for it to clear before continuing. When he does, his words is strained.

"She knows what she's got herself into, you hear? This ain't no sacrifice. This here is a *gift*—she came of her own fucking volition. And, far as I can tell, so did you. You could've said no when she picked you, but you didn't. You could've stayed back at the barn with your Pa, *but you didn't.* So unless you're keen to lose your cock to frostbite out here, I'd suggest we finish this. *Now.*"

Only reason I came, I want to shout at him, *is to change her goddamn mind.*

I turn away. Use my body as a shield between Reverend and Dísah, as if that'll make him forget she's here. Lift her up 'til my beard bristles against her temple, her body no heavier than our secret. Press my mouth to the frozen shell of her ear.

"Let me tell them," I whisper. "Please, babe. You shouldn't be here."

The only answer she can muster is a rush of air, a wheezing out of her chest, then a rattling inhalation. Dísah never could cope with winter, owing to the rotten lungs her Ma birthed her with. I ain't never seen her fight for breath as she is now, and I know if I don't get her inside quick she won't find no relief this side of life. She's making such a racket I'm worried she hasn't heard me, so again I say, "Please, Dísah. Please—"

"Shhhhhhhhhh," she whispers. "Buck up, babe."

She might've just winked at me, but it's hard to tell. Her eyes is glazed and her movements all sluggish, in part from the cold, in part from the pills we swiped this morning for her comfort. Our Pa's been hanging onto them ever since my Ma died two years back; said we'd never know when we might need them sort of drugs again. I ain't so sure he had this particular use in mind.

"I'll say I forced you." Dísah starts wriggling in my grasp. I hold her tighter, compel her to listen. "Just tell them you didn't want to do it, that I made you. They can't blame you for that, can they?"

"Do you need me to take her, son? You're looking a mite unsteady." Reverend rests his hand on my shoulder and I flinch like it were a punch. In my distraction I let Dísah slide half to the ground; she's pressed between my forearms, her tits and shoulder blades only things stopping her from fully slipping from my embrace. Her nightie snags on my coat sleeve and hikes up 'round her ribcage. I feel blood rushing hot to my face at the sight of her nakedness, and it just makes me cry harder.

"Let me go," she says. Her voice is calm, like she couldn't care less about our cousins gawking at her private bits, but her breath is coming short and shallow. I know I'm crushing her lungs from the wheeze and gurgle they're producing, but I can't do nothing about it. I feel like I'm paralysed.

"Jesse," she says, her tone near-stopping my heart. "Let me go."

"I can't," I say, even as my arms release her. I bend to pick her up again, but she pushes me away.

"Let me go."

The last time I see her alive, Dísah's not much more'n a smudge. No matter how quick I wipe my eyes, everything in sight is blurred. She's so fucking stiff she can't hardly bend her arms and legs, but somehow she crawls away from me, gouging knee-trails down into the hollow. All on her own steam, just like Reverend wants.

He takes up his guitar again, plucks a few strings, stops when he sees the boys ain't started shovelling. "Go on," he barks and, slowly, they does.

"Please, don't," I say, running to the edge of that god-cursed hole, right as Billy tosses the first spadeful onto Dísah's belly. "Please, Dísah—can't I please just tell them? It ain't too late, babe. *Please*."

Her eyes lock on mine and hold steady as the snow heaps on top of her. Tears and snot is running freely down my face, but she keeps looking up at me. Shaking her head, sad but firm.

"Please," I repeat, but Dísah just raises a warning finger to her blue lips, presses them closed. And then she's gone.

"Smell that boys?" Reverend takes a deep breath, pulls his mittens off, and starts to unbutton his coat. "I'll be damned if that ain't spring in the air already, God bless that little girl's soul."

As Jed and Tommo tamp the snow down on Dísah's grave, and Billy marks the spot with a flagpole, it hits me.

Only reason she chose me is to make sure I didn't spill 'til after she were gone.

No matter how hard I begged, my sister weren't never going to let me save her.

♭

Dísah's Ma's got some nerve, draping her stoop with black fabric like she's in mourning. Hiding inside her cabin as though, for sadness, she can't bear to show her face. Shayanne's peeking 'round her plaid curtains, drawing on a cigarette. Taking a good look at what's going on outside them grimy windows of hers, like she's just waiting for people to start filing up her drive bringing rhubarb and apple pie condolences. She's leaning so close to the glass, I can see the makeup she's globbed on for the occasion. Her black spider eyes widen, just for a second, when she notices me and Rev and the boys dragging our frozen arses back into town. Then she looks at all of us, hard, through a cloud of her smoke. Not spying to see if we's brought Dísah home with us; checking to make sure she's good and gone.

"Stupid bitch," I say, turning to Dísah out of habit, waiting for her to roll her eyes and agree with me.

"What?" Tommo asks over his shoulder. He don't look at me—his eyes is locked on the smokestack of Pete's Roadhouse, poking up like a steeple on the other side of the lumber yard.

"Nothing." Cold wind whistles through the empty air to my left, then cuts right through me. "See you at Pete's."

Tommo nods. He fumbles in his pocket, finds his keys. Gestures like he's tipping his hat as he passes Shayanne's place to reach his pickup. She dips her head, accepting his greeting more than returning it. Turns my stomach, seeing her act so high and mighty.

Pa once told us Dísah's Ma were the biggest mistake he ever did, and every day he gets on his knees and thanks the Lord my Ma took him back after he'd strayed. Even now Ma's gone, Pa still prays. He don't make no secret of it—just like he don't hide how much he loves our Dísah, no matter what act brung her into this world.

Shayanne never could stand it, the way Pa and Dísah get along. While everyone else sees my sister for the beauty she is, knowing full well she's Pa's pride, when Shayanne looks at her daughter all she sees is Pa. Both of them with their same cornstraw hair, their same green eyes, their same smile; both of them choosing my Ma over her for the long haul. Every time Shayanne bawled Dísah out for being lazy (which she weren't) or stupid (which she weren't neither) or a whore everyone knew who she were *really* talking to. Everyone, I reckon, except Dísah.

The curses I spit across the street, across the space where my sister should be standing, get drowned out in the roar of Tommo's engine turning over.

𝄞

I ain't been this drunk since Dísah got hold of that bottle of bourbon for my eighteenth two months back. She said Shayanne were giving her the shits as usual, so we'd have to guzzle it in the barn, if that were all right with me. Sure as hell was.

It were good shit Dísah got me, not like the piss Pete's serving tonight. I never asked her where it came from; must've cost her at least twenty bucks, it were that high quality. She ain't never had a job outside working Pa's stall at the markets, and harvests being what they is, ain't been much for her to sell this past year—but my girl's a clever one, ain't she? With her sweet face and quick tongue, she can talk most folk into finding her what she needs. Reckon that's what bagged me the best birthday I ever had, me and Dísah pissed out of our gourds together.

"Another," I say, shoving a wad of crumpled bills at Reverend. He looks at me for a minute, not saying nothing, then grabs the cash and heads to the bar. Dusk is falling, but Pete always holds off switching on the overheads 'til it's damn-near dark as the devil's arse in here. A couple old lanterns swing from the rafters, casting a whiskey glow on the handful of regulars sitting at the table across from ours. Pete's got Nitty Gritty Dirt Band playing on the juke, replays of last season's ball games on the tube, and a layer of fresh straw on the floor. I put my head in my hands, close my eyes to block it all out, breathe deep.

Smells just like my birthday; bourbon, hay, sweat from a hard day's work, and a hint of sadness. Only things missing is the sound of Dísah's squeeze-box breath, gasping softly in and out. The scent of her warm, clean skin. The taste of her tongue in my mouth.

I open my eyes. No girl will ever love me the way Dísah does. The way she did.

"This too shall pass," says Reverend, clunking a pint of beer and a whiskey chaser down on the table's worn surface in front of me, pocketing the change.

"Thanks," I mumble, and gulp down a third of the beer, trying to drown the lump in my throat.

"You been over to see Shayanne yet? Paid your respects?"

"No," I grunted. "And I ain't going to neither."

"You really should, Jesse. It's only right—"

"I ain't."

Booze adds growl to my voice, what Dísah says sounds sexy, but what Reverend seems to take as a threat. He shuts up about Shayanne, goes back to his side of the table, sits down beside Jed. He doesn't join in the conversation—Jed and Billy's wondering how quick the snows'll melt now that Dísah's been planted; wondering how soon it'll be before Jeanette starts wearing them t-shirts of hers, the ones that stretch so tight across her tits, so thin that anyone with a mind to look can see her nipples.

The whiskey burns a trail down my throat, sends fumes up my nose. It clears my head, instead of dulling it enough to forget what we done today like it should. There's a three-legged seat on my right; Dísah's sitting there, nursing a tumbler of gin. Pete always serves her when the crowds are light, even though she's only sixteen. She repays him by clearing up every now and again, or by running the bingo once a month on a Sunday.

"Get me another," I say. Dísah shakes her head; Billy reaches over and grabs two-fifty from my wallet, starts asking if anyone else wants one. Jed nods, says Reverend's going to need one too when he gets back from the can. Tommo drains his glass, slams it upside down on the table with a grin. So Billy takes ten more bucks out of my wallet while I keep talking to Dísah's empty chair.

"Doesn't matter what Shayanne thinks, you know."

The chair remains silent.

"Telling folk she were so proud of you for being chosen—like you had any real say in the matter." Dísah smiles, sips her drink. Tips her head all coy-like, getting ready to say something cutting. She's sharp, my sister; so I plough ahead before she can interrupt.

"Telling you it were the first time you ain't let her down." The thought makes me laugh 'til I drool. "Ain't that what you call irony, Rev? Like you taught us? Irony?"

"Sure, Jesse." Reverend returns to our table, wiping his hands on his pant legs. His laugh, when it comes, ain't as loud as mine.

"Making you think she loved you for what you was doing—what a fucking bitch. What a fucking, fucking bitch." I turn to see how Dísah's reacting to these revelations, afraid I'll hurt her with too much truth too fast. She's quiet, though, so I finish my beer and keep talking.

"When is Shayanne ever been proud of you? This weren't about you saving us, about you being important. It were about her getting rid of you—c'mon, now. Don't shake your head like that."

The chair wobbles, then spins, and now I'm looking up at it from below, my shoulder throbbing. Pete's got the lights on too bright; they're shining straight into my eyes, making my head hurt.

"What we done together—" I bite my tongue 'til I taste blood, then swallow a few times to keep from puking. "She wouldn't have hated you any more than she already does, babe. If you'd have told her instead of dying just to make her happy."

I sit up, then scramble to my knees so me and Dísah is looking at each other eye-to-eye. The words is shaking out of my lips, and I can't stop them. I harden my voice, my heart, make it strong enough to say, "She ain't proud of you—but you bought her act. You bought it, hear me? You bought it!"

"Jesus Christ, Jess—settle down. What did you think I were doing, you drunk fuck?" Billy doles out the drinks, then lifts me back into my seat, puts the change in my left hand and a shot of bourbon in my right. He waits a minute to make sure I ain't going to tip over, then sits on Dísah's chair.

"Shots of Southern Comfort's a buck each 'til eight. You up for another one?"

I look at the full glass in my hand, drain it off, blink without clearing the blur. "I love you, but still you bought it. And now you're gone."

Billy doesn't say nothing. Just goes and gets us another round.

♪

Haven't been able to keep anything solid down for three days, my guts is been that rotten. Pa reckons I poisoned myself with drink; so he gave me a double-shot of brandy this morning to keep the jitters at bay, then made me promise I'd call past Doc's after me and the boys get back from the hollow this afternoon. He could've told me to go first—probably wanted to—but we both know I couldn't have listened. Unfinished business comes before a bellyful of sour piss every time, far as Reverend's concerned.

"Way I see it," Jed says, hocking a cheekful of tobacco juice into the snow bank, shielding his face from the splashback, "we shoulda seen a change by now. I mean, didn't take Jesus no longer'n three days to work his miracle—"

Reverend cuts him off with a cuff to the back of his head. Wind catches Jed's wool cap, sends it skittering a foot or two over the frozen fields. "Jesus ain't got nothing to do with this, boy. There's a fuckload of worldly doings ain't in that fella's jurisdiction, and this here's one of them."

Jed's face reddens. He traps his hat beneath his boot, sinks down 'til he's knee-deep in the drift. "But last time—"

"Just shut it," Tommo says, scowling. "Save your steam for the dig, hey?"

Jed shoots his brother a look I seen a million times before: his jaw's clenched and he's squinting like a dog who's just been muzzled—but it never lasts more'n a second. Face blank, he pulls himself up, brushes off, jams his hat on his head. The rest of us is walking fast, but he gains on us quick by following in our foot holes instead of ploughing a new track through the snow.

Tommo don't never talk about last time. I try to catch Jed's eye, let him know I get him; but he keeps his gaze forward now, plotting the easiest route to the gully. Billy lights a cigarette—oblivious, or pretending to be. Reverend tells us we're nigh on there, says he can see the marker we left on Dísah's grave, a smear of dark on a ground of white. None of us need say nothing else. We know it were different all them years ago, when it were their sister got planted instead of mine.

Prairies that'd been flooded for weeks was bone dry a few hours after Raelene were gifted to the hollow, as though she gave the earth one hell of a thirst; one that meant it didn't stop drinking 'til its tab were good and spent. Following day, my uncle and auntie were out tilling, the soil moist and pliable, with love and thanks for their little girl mixed in each handful of seed. The day after that, Dísah left her Ma, came over to our place for good. Seemed the sun wouldn't never stop shining down on us then.

But now clouds is thick overhead, hanging low on the horizon, just about ready to drop. The wind bites my cheeks, the air slices my lungs with every breath. Ice sticks my eyelashes together each time I blink. My nose hairs is stiff with frost. Inside my coat, I'm sweating; my shirt feels clammy with it, and the smell of stale liquor and nerves wriggles up my neck, through the gap between my scarf and collar.

Whatever we done the other day, I keep thinking, *it weren't right.*

I ain't got enough booze left in me to see Dísah's face purple and twisted from suffocation, her arms and legs scalded with frostbite, her roundness flattened under the weight of all that snow. Her lips frozen shut, dead on account of our silence.

I ain't ready to think of her as just a body.

♪

We see her long before we get to the hollow.

She's sitting with one leg crossed over the other, her feet dangling down a girl-sized wormhole in the snow. I can't fucking believe it.

"She's still alive," I say, half-whisper, half-chuckle. The sour in my belly dries right up, and I get a rush that starts in my chest, powers down through my legs and out the soles of my feet. I drop my shovel, half-stumble and half-run towards her, shouting, "Dísah!"

Three days and nights we left her out here, half-naked and alone, buried so deep even gophers couldn't reach her, and she's fucking survived.

She waves like she's just been crowned queen of the Holloway county fair, looking prettier than ever. Her hair's mussed but shiny clean, her lips is wet and red, her eyes is got a sexy shadow to them, and her skin's got a sheen to it like she's spent the day out in the sun. She smiles at me, teeth straight and white. Roses bloom in her cheeks, just like they did that night in the barn.

"The bones, Jesse! Down there, nothing but bones, bones, bones," she says, laughing. Her voice is clear—and so is her lungs. Her chest is rising and falling silently; there's no strain in her expression. I ain't never seen her look so healthy.

"How'd you—" I bite the question in half, the words pushing out of me as I fall headlong into the snow. Reverend dislodges his foot from round my ankles, pins me down with his knee, then grabs hold of my arms to keep me from getting up.

"Stay back now, son," he says. "Don't go near that thing."

"Get off," I growl. I flail in Reverend's grip, using the advantage hauling crops gives me over a man who's spent thirty-odd years sitting around looking at books. Digging my knees in the drift for leverage, I arch my back and *push*, muscles tense and straining, 'til Reverend's either got to let go or find himself arse-up in the snow.

He lets me up, but stays close.

Dísah claps her hands. "Don't stop on my account. You know I like a bit of rough and tumble—don't you, Jess?"

"Don't listen to her, boy. That ain't your sister," Reverend says.

My face goes so hot, I reckon it must be redder'n my hair. "Enough of that talk, babe. Sounds like the cold's gone and addled your brains."

I try to laugh, but even as I'm saying she's crazy, in my head it's my birthday all over again. I can feel the straw poking into my bare knees; the strength of Dísah's legs wrapped around me; the weight of her on top of me; the thrust of her beneath me.

Dísah acts like she ain't heard a thing I said.

"I'll always be a one-tumble girl now, won't I?" She shakes her head, looks at Reverend, giggles at the shocked looks he and the boys is wearing. Then she turns back to me. "Ain't no point keeping quiet about it. Like you said: ain't going to change a thing."

"Hush, now," I say, but I'm nodding even though I don't remember saying no such thing. "We'll tell everyone after you come home—let's just get you home, okay?"

Dísah looks at Reverend, then back at me, like she's measuring our worth with her gypsy eyes. Slowly, she gets to her feet. As she stands, a pile of bones tumbles out of her skirt and scatters on the ground. She looks at them and smiles. "Told you it was bones down there."

I can't help it: I start to laugh, and it builds until the sound is deep and long. "I'm so glad you ain't gone," I say and take her hand. Through my gloves I can feel the icy cold of her palm.

"Bones, bones, bones," she sings. Her grip tightens on mine 'til my fingers grind together, but I ain't going to pull away for nothing.

"Guess the gods didn't need her, hey Reverend? She weren't the answer after all."

"No, Jesse." Reverend's knuckles crack as he collects the shovel he dropped before our tussle. He hefts it in his right hand, says, "They took her all right—they just ain't given nothing in return."

He, Tommo and Billy make their way over to me and Dísah, stepping careful so's they don't fall into her burrow, never taking their eyes off her. Jed hangs back, though; shifts his weight from foot to foot without going nowheres.

"I knew this weren't like last time," he says. "Something you done didn't work, Rev. We done all this again, and you fucked it."

Reverend's voice is heavy; he don't look at me as he says, "I think it's fair to say it weren't me doing the fucking here, boy."

Silence.

Loose snow squeaks in the treads of Tommo's boots as he comes up behind me. A raven circles overhead, lets out a single shrill caw. Taking that as some sort of divine cue, Reverend nods.

"Watch out for them bones on the way down," Dísah says, right before Reverend takes her head off with the edge of his shovel. Right before Billy kicks her body back into the hollow. Right before I hear Tommo grunt, hear the whoosh of his spade speeding through the air, hear the twang of its steel on my skull.

Right before this damned white world goes black.

♪

My head's thick from too much bourbon, but the straw's comfortable beneath my back; it's nestled so tight around my body I almost feel like I'm floating. The barn's air is stuffy and close, warm with the heat of my breath. I ain't shivering no more even though my pants is still down round my ankles. My belly's roiling.

"Dísah?" I say—or try to. Snow fills my mouth, muffles all sound. It's so dark, I ain't even sure she's there 'til I feel her arm snaking around my middle, feel the press of her body against mine. She lies on top of me like a shroud of ice.

"Meet you at the bottom," she says, then kisses me 'til my lungs freeze. I look down and see a field of bones below, and then Dísah's gone.

I close my eyes, feel the sun on my face, and hear the musical drip of melting snow.

𝄞 𝄞 𝄞

Them Little Shinin Things

Them Little Shinin Things

"Keep them legs open, Seelya. Like this." I grab at her slick-sweat knees, pry 'em apart as best I can, prop a couple pillows underneath. "What gotcha into this bind's goin'ta getcha back out, now ain't it? Knees open then, knees open now. And *push*."

I'm speakin the truth, sure as. I don't jest deliver them bebbys: I had a poke or two in my time with Atli, a fine trader man I thought as loved me. But his lovin didn't give me no swollen belly, even though we practised enough when Seelya weren't around. While she were off learnin to be m'Lady—on accounta her Ma and sisters droppin off with the plains sickness and all—I were doin what most maids does out in the cowshed every now and again: a little skirt-liftin. A little wriggle and plunge.

"That's it, take deep breaths now. Fresh air'll clean out yer belly—I'll even open my big window up for you. How's that? Nice gusty breeze'll blow that bebby right out."

Gods, look at her. Now she's coverin her nose at the smells comin through them screens: horse shit and fresh hay and a whiff o' winter. Good smells them, and honest. But she wouldn't know honest if it bit her on the arse.

I pull the curtains wide and peek through to see if them twiggy creatures is out there yet. Nope. Can't see nothin 'round them talismans I scattered on the grass afore the sun set: corn cobs and cedar branches, sumac dust and wooden bowls full up with oils I charmed meself.

"Them's lucky smells on that wind, m'Lady," I says. "You breathe them in deep."

I never had much luck meself. Seems it all flied away when me and Atli's pokin stopped right afore his weddin. Which were right after Seelya's—*m'Lady's*—Pa figgered out I gots the know-how to be a bringer o' bebbys. That I can twist branches for fortune, make invisible scratchins for fine health, and other tricks that ain't quite so shiny. Messr Geir tells me it were a gift, what I gots; a magic none too many come by. He tells me I ain't gotta be wastin my time drudgin no more, that there's more'n enough I can be doin 'roun here for m'Lady instead. But while he were talkin I were thinkin about Atli. Thinkin that if I ain't gotta milk them cows and feed them chickens then when am I goin'ta see him? My kind only mixes with them rich trader folk when they gots a hankerin for a secret poke, for a bit o' warmth and a easy deal in the barn.

So I says to Messr Geir: *I never knowed how I got that magic,* I says. *It were jest there all the time—musta drunk it in at Mama's tit.* My mama always were one for spellin and charmin and makin all manner o' things as suited her own Messr's wants. *I ain't gotta think about it much to make it happen,* I tells him. *Jest come natural, same way's I gots Mama's blue blue eyes.*

But it were no use. Messr Geir says it don't matter how I got it, jest so long as I use it for good purpose. He shoulda said for *his* purpose. Sometimes I catch him lookin 'roun his homestead like I already filled it with bodies, brung him more hands to work them fields, magicked so many childs into his girl she'd be clean wore out with birthin. Well, I ain't really gotta help him with that last bit, do I? Clever Messr Geir gone and bought a husband for Seelya, one who's fit and ready to take all care o' *that* type o' magic.

And I were a weddin present for them two. Made no difference to no one that me and Seelya's been livin on this 'stead together since we was both young'uns. I were bought straight out—papers was signed at the Mayor's and everythin—all 'cause Messr Geir had the coins and a wantin to keep me on his land. If Messr had his way, he wouldn't spare a seed for a chickadee; so it shocked me all to hell when he tells me I should feel right proud to be m'Lady's helper, and he gives me a feather bed in my own little cabin and even puts me in new clothes for the job. No way from Tunesday I could say no to that, could I?

But proud?

No. I ain't got no proudful feelins, not now Seelya's cryin birthtears that should be mine; bleedin all over *my* mattress; squeezin away pain *I* should be feelin in her place. Sure as.

Another spasm dances a two-step up'n down Seelya's round belly. Her pretty-girl's face is gone all wrinkly and red; her nice teeth showin bright white but snarly. Us two stinks to the high heavens from this work—'specially Seelya, who's gone and squeezed out more stenchy wind these past few hours than even them cows paddock-side does in a busy week. We's both hot enough to boil eggs—our blonde hairs is lookin dark brown with wet—and we's filthier than Messr Geir's hogs out back. To top it off, I traced mud charms all over m'Lady's skin soon as the pain started, and got the magics all over meself at the same time. Seelya don't know I were scrawlin them symbols for my own luck rather'n hers, but never mind. Long as it works, she'll have her hands too full to care which luck is whose, and that's truer than Messr's pennies.

She gives another grunt. There's a sound o' skin tearin and the tangy smell o' blood, and I think it sure ain't gonna be long now afore it's all said and done. Seelya's knees knock me upside the head as I crouch down to take a glance at her slit. I gots to see if the fur down there's more'n jest her own thatch; if it's them bebby's head or ain't it.

"Knees open, girl! I'll tie them legs to the bedposts if I gotta—you jest try me."

On the way down, I catch a peek o' my fierce scowl reflectin in the window glass and almost scare meself at the sight. It's a moon-sliver night: not much light comin in from outers, but there's a shinin-bright fire for boilin water, and enough candles burnin to let me see how Seelya's rollin her brown cow-eyes at me jest like she used to when we was kids. Only this time she weren't tryin to bust me up with laughin. This time she were bein rude.

"I'm so tired, Hesteh. Let me rest, won't you? Give me a potion." She scrunches up her fists 'til the mud on her knuckles cracks. She grits her teeth, her words all strangly, and says, "Put me to sleep—make me numb—take the fight out of this child! Please! Do something to end this torture." Then she slumps back in a cryin fit, all sobbin and feelin sorry for her situation.

Seelya's jest so dramatic. Squawkin like she's the first and last lady ever's been split open with bebbys. Comes from bein youngest in her family: she always were tryin to get every kinda attention, however she could. And now it's all hers, ain't it? Lady o' the whole goddamn house, livin easy with her Pa runnin the show. Married to the finest man I ever laid eyes on—the kindest, most generous— yeah, the *finest* man. A man what's made Messr Geir a grandpa. He planted a strong child in Seelya's belly, one what's got the fight to get hisself birthed this night. But even with all that love and attention, Seelya's actin like she don't want half a bar o' it.

Selfish sow she is, sometimes, m'Lady is.

I stand all the way up so's I can glare at her better. I stare over the big white hill o' her nightgowned self on the bed. She looks back at me good and long, 'til I start runnin my fingers up'n down the handle o' my belt knife. I always wear it over my fancy apron, hangin on the leather sash Messr Geir gave me as part o' my new kit.

"How 'bout I cut you right up the middle then?" I says to Seelya. "I could magic yer voice all quiet with one o' them bowls o' water over there—*still water for still tongues* my Mama always did say. How 'bout I quick-slice you on the sly, pop that bebby right out yer belly and no-one 'roun to see it? Put us all outta yer misery that way." I snort at the *hell-no* look she gives me then. I ain't seen nothin so funny since them little twiggy creatures left a great big turd in Messr Geir's soup last Tuneday. The kinda look Seelya throws me now is jest like what her Pa threw back then—like she swallowed a mouthful o' shit.

Makes me laugh full out, thinkin on the pranks them twiggy folk pull, and imaginin how scary I must look to Seelya now. Standin atween her chubby knees; sleeves rolled up and dirt written to the elbows; apron smeared with blood and pulled tight across hips wide and strong enough to carry two bebbys at once; cornsilk amulets twisted through my long hair, stickin up like a crown and woven 'roun my neck atween the herb-knots and strings o' milk teeth I always dangle there; my shadow loomin ahind me, creepin across the wall like a soul-suckin ghost who's achin for a good feed. *Hoo-ee*, don't my looks jest make me cackle like a hen!

I pull out my knife. Ain't no law says I gotta to be nice to Seelya, jest 'cause I gots to bring her bebby into this world. She shrieks so loud I won't be half surprised if she's waked up deaf Jacob next farm over. I lean in, movin the blade closer and closer—but I ain't really goin'ta slice her up the middle, mind. Any cuttins I do'll come later.

O' course, Atli don't know that. Too late I were wishin I'd coated my tongue with sweet 'stead a sour jest then. Or that I'd held the knife low-like, so none but me and Seelya coulda saw it.

"What the hell, Hesteh?"

There he is, standin in the doorway, no more'n two feet ahind me. I ain't heard him come up. I ain't used to the musics in this place yet, this tiny cabin built wood-side, far from the field-side buildins I worked in since I were six. My little shack ain't got the same creakins the big house attic gots, up there where I used to sleep. It ain't got no rickety ol' staircase complainin whenever a soul steps foot on't. No Cook's butcher knife choppin, takin heads off chickens and hares (now she gives me them guts an gizzards for my magics—Messr's orders—and I pass 'em on to Twigs). No sheep-dogs' feets scratchin at the screen door, beggin for scraps afore heading back out to the paddocks.

No pebbles ticklin my window.

No-one callin me down to the shed for a tumble.

Jest Atli's voice, deep and rumbly, soundin like a prince outta Cook's yarns. "What the hell are you doing?"

He's angry, sure; but hearin him speak, no matter what he's sayin, always gets a shudder startin in me that shoots straight from my heart and winds up hittin me right atween the legs.

"Course I weren't doin nothin to yer missus here, Atli," I says, quick-like. "Course not."

I shake my head—it ain't his place to tell me what I can and can't be doin. Not in my own cabin, with my own magics 'roun! 'This ain't men's business—go and take yer worryin self outta here afore you mess everythin up."

I can tell Atli don't wanta go, but he's gotta. He's lookin at Seelya like I ain't even here no more. Now he's holdin her hand, callin her things like *love* and *my dear heart;* kissin her forehead, sweat and mud and all. I ain't never seen a bloke so caught up in his wife's pushins. No, never.

Seein' it makes me want to howl my guts out.

I near bawled meself hollow on them's weddin day last year. Out ahind the horse stalls where me and Atli use'ta go to share *our* lovin; howlin and howlin til there were no sound left. Jest a feelin o' bein oh-so heavy, filled with barrow-loads o' tiredness. So I laid meself down right there in the slops, not mindin the floor planks were wet and chilly with the comin o' autumn. Muck and cold weren't botherin me one speck; I balled my bran-new apron up and used it like a rich person's pillow. Closed my eyes and says to meself, *Go to sleep now, Hesteh. And never wake up ever again.*

But them twiggy creatures weren't havin it. *No*, they says to me. They was lookin hard at me with their sparkly eyes—none too friendly, but not mean neither—and they kept pokin their heads in and outta my sight. One minute 'bout four or five o' them was there, and next they was all disappeared. It's like they was testin me, seein if I could see them proper.

Well, I ain't stupid. I seen stuff other folk don't notice, I pay attention. Sure, it *were* hard to tell what were boys and what girls; but one o' them done all the talkin, and I *knowed* she were a she.

This ain't yer time, she says without ever openin her mouth. Sayin straight into my mind, usin plain words an honest. Not talkin all fancy like Seelya does now she's rulin the roost. Nor sayin one thing but actin jest the opposite, pokin here but marryin there. No, this here critter were truthful.

Don't go outta yer head, my girl, she says to me. *You ain't lost nothin yet.*

Maybe I shouldn'ta listened to that twig-wife, but I done so anyway. Maybe her'n the rest a them little critters—and they is little, no bigger than bebby sheeps and skinny as Granny Geir gets after fastin for holy Vinesdays—maybe they knowed my Mama while she were alive. Seems to me they coulda. Hell, it were easy as workin Mama's magic, was talkin to that twig-wife. And ever since that first meetin it's jest got easier and easier, our talkins.

Me'n her, we gots plans in common.

The bebby's head's full circle atween Seelya's legs now. It's rotten hot in here and it only stands to get worse afore it gets better. "Go on, Atli," I says. "Get outta here. I gots work don't need yer interference." He hardly looks at me, so I raise my voice like I would to any old farm dog. "Get!"

He stares me straight on then, his looks makin me so wobbly I gotta turn away and whisper a few quick words to help screw my head back on proper.

"I think I'll stay if it's all the same to you, midwife." He stands up, tall as a Grainspole, never lettin go o' Seelya's hand. "It's not every day a man witnesses the birth of his first son." Seelya tries on a smile but it twists upside her face. She's lookin at me with beggin in her eyes, and there ain't much more I can do. The bebby's comin.

"Stay outta my way, then." I point to a shady spot near the door, ahind me and lookin right up Seelya's nightskirts. If he gots to be here he may as well get an eyeful. Nothin like the sight o' his wife's tore apart nethers to get Atli back in my knickers where he belongs.

♪

"Out you hop if you're hungry, Twigs. I ain't got more'n a few minutes."

Atli were right: bebby's a boy. He's bundled tight under my arm, and we's huddled together on the outers o' my cabin, crouched down in the dark. There's a slanty bit a firelight shinin out my big window, but I steer clear o' it and wait in the shadows, my finger stuffed atween the bebby's slimy gums. Can't take no chance he'll start screechin. We ain't got no time for tangles.

"Come and get it," I says, my voice shakin with jitters, and none too loud in case Seelya hears me from inside. I keep shiftin my gaze from the forest to the bebby in my arms, wonderin which one's goin'ta wake first. Both, for now, is quiet.

Bebby's sleepin, praise all them gods. Seems he blowed all his steam blazin a path from the last world into this one: his wails was shrill enough to bleed yer ears. I'd had enough o' that mouth after a handful a seconds—but I ain't never seen Atli lookin so pleased with hisself as when he heard the racket his child were makin.

"What spirit!" Atli says, laughin and smilin like a goon. "The strength of wolves is in that bellow." So the two a them calls the boy Connell after them wolf-warriors so famous for battlin in Vinesday songs. It were Seelya's idea. I reckon she brung it up jest to remind Atli she gots schoolin in her, the show-off.

Still, I knows it were a good name. Loud and strong and worth braggin over. And I says as much to Atli afore I shoo'd him off to fetch Messr Geir, sayin he should share him the happy news. Then soon as he's out the door I wraps Connell in a nursin blanket and says to Seelya, "If yer child's goin'ta stick in this world, m'Lady, I gotta clean him up and oath him to the moonlight."

Stupid cow. Seelya's that spent, I coulda told her the truth and she wouldn't o' stopped me. She jest flicks her hand as like to say, *Do what you gotta do, girl. I ain't goin nowheres.* So I leg it fast as can be, near slammin the door off its hinges ahind me as I go outers, while she snuggles her sweaty face into my pillows.

There's a rustlin in the bushes off to my right. Them twiggy folk's seen us now, sure as. I put Connell down on the dirt, unwrap him so's his pale skin glows under them bright stars, then I start tuggin at what's left o' his birthin cord. The noise comin from the undergrowth gets rowdy as I takes out my belt knife and cut the cord into small pieces; I can see them greedy eyes twinklin afore I even tosses the sausage chunks o' it out to the trees.

"Get yerself over here, Twigs. Soup's on." I stab my knife point-down into the grass so's they'll know there ain't no more comin 'til they shows.

Twiggy hands scramble and grab at the meat I throwed—then them mouthfuls was all gobbled, faster'n blinkin. None o' them touched the cornbread, the ashes or them yellow coneflowers I charmed and scattered 'roun the cabin afore the birthin begun. All stick-folks wants new flesh; none o' them wants my magics. Either way, they gots to wait 'til that twig-wife gets her share first. So they stay hidden in the scrub, fidgeting the time away.

"I swear, Twigs. You get yerself out here for this snack I brung you, else I'm goin'ta—"

She steps so dainty outta them bushes it were like she thought she were some fancy lady 'stead've a shrivelled up old critter. Tip-toein in total silence, movin toward me and the bebby, she holds her head high while her dry straw hair is wavin in the breeze. Walkin calm, tryin to fool me into thinkin she ain't as hungry as I knows she is.

Don't get yer knickers all in a twist, she says. Looks like she's about to say somethin else but changes her mind when she gets close enough to whiff Connell, his skin sticky with afterbirths and still smellin like the insides o' his mama's legs. Now she's lickin her dried lips, smackin them together so's they makes a crunchin-leaf sound. She ain't gots many teeth, but the ones she's showin now look sharper'n my knife.

"I knows you got the hunger, Twigs. Been years since you lot done a swap like this one, ain't it? And don't I know it's yer turn." That twig-wife, she's inchin closer to Connell the whole time I'm talkin, sneaky bitch.

"Take one step more, Twigs, and I'm snappin that bebby up and leavin you here to starve. I ain't goin'ta get screwed, you hear? Not one nibble o' this here feast is goin'ta hit yer belly 'til you done what you promised."

I weren't really goin to abandon our plan, mind. I ain't like Atli: I finishes what I starts. That there's a lesson he'll be learnin soon enough. "Give me a new one as he'll be horrorfied with. Make it look jest like this'n but fill him with blackness and filth and years o' foul spirit. Do it now, Twigs. Do it fast."

She nods at me once.

My skin's near tinglin with excitements and I gots the biggest smile ever—I can't help it. Soon Atli's bebby'll be linin that twig-wife's belly and I'll be givin him one that's goin'ta make his head spin. Few weeks from now, he'll be wore out with this demon child and he'll be needin someplace to escape, someone to give him some comfort. Someone as ain't spawned that dark bebby.

Twigs plucks a couple hairs from Connell's head, winds them 'roun a thistle she pulled outta her back. She looks at me as if to say, *You sure 'bout this?* and I says, "Hurry! I gots to get back inside." And hurry she does.

She pops that thistle into her mouth, swishes it 'roun once or twice, then spews up a splashin pile o' nastiness smells like it's been in her guts for years. Crouchin down, she starts smushin dirt 'roun her upchuck, always checkin that the thistle's tucked well and good inside. Two arms start formin, then two legs; chubby face and dimpled potbelly; seashell ears and the sweetest lips and nose I ever seen. Looks jest like Connell by the time she were through. 'Cept, o' course, that dirt bebby were all brown, and not movin unless Twigs made him to.

This one needs sparkin to get goin, she says to me—and afore I knows it, her hand's in my belly, rummagin 'roun straight through my clothes and all, causin me no end o' pain. She's tore a stack o' twigs from her scalp and is stuffin them into me with the other hand, while the rest o' her fingers is diggin, diggin out somethin glowin I can't quite see. I don't know what plan she gots cookin, but it hurts real bad; feels like I gots to shit blood, like I gots to spew up nails, like a thousand tiny teeth's eatin away at my innards. Everythin goes black and afore I knows it I'm lyin on the ground.

Can't be more'n a minute later, I gots my focus back. The pain's leavin me, but I lie here for a while longer jest to be sure. Lyin here, watchin that twig-wife slip a handful a white lights into her open gob.

Where did she get them little shinin things? My belly's achin, but already it ain't so bad as it were afore. She's crunchin away at them sparklers like they was the maple candies Atli sometimes brung from up north. And my belly's achin. Twigs is gettin brighter, smoother, less twiggy-lookin, and my belly's achin. She eats 'em all up, all my little shinin things, 'round the last one. That one she puts in the dirt bebby's middle—the flicker gone straight from my guts to his.

"What you doin, Twigs?" I'm sittin up now, feelin 'roun my belly for holes. There ain't none there; nothin apart from streaks o' muck from where I felled over. Don't matter what my hands tells me: I knows that faery thief gone and stole all the makins for bebbys outta me, stuffed me full o' brush instead. My guts is twistin with it and I ain't stupid.

I open my mouth to yell at her, but she cuts me off.

A deal's a deal, she says, gettin fleshier by the minute. *I done what you wants; Atli ain't got no reason to stick 'roun no more. Seelya ain't got his child: you does. So jest give that dark bebby a kiss, and he's all yers.*

Well, didn't that hit me jest like Pa used to? Smack, right in the head. *This new bebby weren't no changelin.* He were made with my fixins. All my makins tore outta me, and he's all that's left o' them. I lean over and look at the little manikin that twig-wife's left for me. Looks jest like Connell, but he gots *my* shinin things in him and nothin a Seelya's. *Mine.* That's right: this boy's mine, ain't he?

Me and Atli made him.

Me and my cleverness.

I kiss his muddy cheek. There's a deep blue cornflower dug into it, high up near his left eye. I kiss it right on the bud. Afore I can blink, it goes and changes into a dimple in the creamiest skin I ever seen. Spreads across his squeaky-clean face, down his wrinkly neck, 'cross his twiggy belly-button, all the way to his wrigglin toes. Yeah, he looks jest like Connell—'round more gorgeous 'cause he's *mine*.

My heart's all fluttery with feelins I ain't never had afore.

"Gods love ya, Twigs. He's a stunner." I ain't seen nothin so beautiful that I ain't had to give right back. Seein me happy, Twigs knows our deal's really done. She's lookin so healthy now, I can almost see the girl she used to be. There's patches o' bark still clingin to her, on her face and arms mostly, but I figure Connell's juices'll fix that up for her soon's she swallows.

He's no more'n you deserve, she says. Her smile's gots a edge o' wrongness to it, but I don't care. This bebby's a keeper, and I *does* deserve him. Ain't no way Seelya's gettin her hands on another o' my men.

"Go on, then," I says, and afore the words is left my mouth, Twigs is snappin the first Connell's neck and draggin his body off to the woods. Reckon I won't recognise her next time I sees her, when she'll be wearin her proper skin and all. Don't matter, really. I'm through with her tricks for good, and right now I gots to get movin.

I bundle my bebby up in my apron—he don't want nothin to do with Connell's dirty blanket—and he snuggles in right close. Jest like that: he knows who his mama is. I stand up real slow and take a peek through the window. Seelya's lyin on the bed with her eyes shut, dumber'n a bucket o' slops. If she ain't asleep she's darn close. Not even thinkin on her bebby, is she?

Good. Gives me time to hightail it outta here, get through them woods and to the road on th'other side. I'll set me up a little cottage, somethin nice for me and my boy, then come back here to fetch Atli. He'll be so glad to leave his wife once he sees how unresponsible she is—first night o' his life an already her bebby's gone missin! Lord, it makes me laugh. Ain't no way to prove it were me what took him: all I gotta say is I brung Connell back inside and tucked him in bed aside his mama.

In the mornin when they see he's gone, everyone'll know it were Seelya got rid o' her bebby. They'll think she's crazier'n a headless goose.

And I won't accuse her o' nothin. No, I'll play her friend on accounta our long years together. Atli'll be so impressed with my kind actin, he'll be itchin to get back with me. Easy as that. Jest like Twigs says: without them's bebby, ain't nothin keepin Atli with Seelya. Nothin at all.

"C'mon," I whispers to my dark-haired boy with his beautiful, sleepy brown eyes. "Let's get you to beddy-byes."

"A splendid idea."

My heart near jumps outta my chest and I squeal like a sacrifice pig at the sound o' Messr Geir's voice.

"Calm yourself, Hesteh. You'll wake my grandson carrying on like that." I shut my mouth, but my breathin's hard. "I've had a bed in the attic made up for you—why don't you give me the boy and take yourself off for a well-earned night's rest?"

Afore I can stop it, "No!" bursts outta me at top soundin.

Messr Geir looks at me sorta funny, then gets ahold a hisself. "Oh, dear," he says, chucklin warmly. "You're right. Seelya will need you to help the boy suckle. Lead on then, my girl. A mother's arms shouldn't stay empty for too long. It's bad luck."

Ain't nothin I can do but let Messr Geir nudge me back inside, holdin my bebby close, takin all that bad luck in with us.

♪

I'm stuck.

Seelya, that thievin trollop, is nursin my bebby, forcing me to wait. I suppose a child's gotta eat, don't he? But Messr Geir's smilin like a Cheshire, stokin the fire and makin it too toasty in here. Now I'm sweatin worse than afore, fidgetin like I got the crabs, jest waitin for a opportunity. Still plenty o' night left. If only Messr Geir'd *skedaddle*! I'll take back what's mine and scat afore Seelya even knowed we was gone.

"He's gorgeous, sweetheart."

"Isn't he?"

Seelya's high voice is cracklin with proudfulness and—oh, for the love o' all them gods—is that tears in Messr Geir's eyes? He's rubbin his rough hand up'n down his beardy face, snufflin and snortin the way our horses do in winter. Yep. He's cryin. Pullin a chair up close to the bed, settlin in for a long spell o' watchin. He ain't goin nowhere fast.

"Ain't you got nothin to tend to, Messr? Harvest comin in soon and all?"

"It's two o'clock in the morning, Hesteh. Where else would you want me to be, except here with my grandson?"

I feels my face steamin red up to the roots o' my hairs. I think, *Go on, shake yer head at me all you want, you rat bastard. I can send you places worse'n here if I gots a mind for it.* Out loud, I says, "Course, Messr. If you's intendin to stay, should I getcha somethin warm to drink? A nice cuppa somethin?"

"Yes, please do. Make it three: Atli will be joining us any moment now."

"Yes, Messr." I gets three cups and my kettle, still boiled from the birthin, and sprinkle in some tea leafs. In two o' them cups I drop a handful o' seeds my Mama magicked afore she died. Three times I whisper the words she taught me, ones what will make folk sleep like they's dead. Last thing I needs is a drop o' blood and Seelya and her Pa will be out 'til mornin, both o' them, afore Atli even sips on his plain tea.

But my knife ain't on my belt where it's s'posed to be. It ain't on the table neither, nor near the bed. Then I remember where I left it, and start hustlin towards the door *quick as.* "I'll be back in half a tick, Messr. Jest need to get some mint for m'Lady's tea—" but afore I can finish the thought, my knife's right there.

In Atli's hand.

It looks a real mess. Covered in Connell's blood and stuck with dirt. Atli sees my bebby—what he thinks is them's bebby—in Seelya's arms, so he don't say a word. He looks at the streaks on my apron, the stains on my hands, and keeps his mouth pressed in a firm line. He gots a look on his face tells me clear as mornin he knows somethin ain't right. No way I'd be lovin a stupid man: my Atli knows how to make two plus two. Won't be long 'til he figures it out. 'Til my bebby shows it weren't his.

"Who knew bringing a baby to life was such *filthy* business," he says, handin me my knife, blade first, followin it up with Connell's ruined blanket. 'Neath his other arm he gots the bluest silk shawl

I ever seen, fit for wrappin a queen in. So lovely, it hurts my eyes lookin on it, on that birthin present for Seelya.

And I know, sure as I know I ain't fit for such fine material, he ain't never goin'ta leave her.

"Atli, I—"

He don't care what I gotta say. Seein that hurt look in his eyes, that disappointment I knows I put in there, my belly starts achin afresh. Painin and painin, with all them brushwoods Twigs shoved in me stretchin and pushin up my innards 'til it feels like I'm about to burst. My skin gets smaller, stiffer, my fingers'n toes stretch while the rest o' me's shrinkin. Them branches change me total, suckin the wet right outta me. I'm shrivellin but the hurt in me keeps growin. Soon it's the only thing leavin me standin, givin me the giddup to walk my twiggy legs outers, trailin my long leafy hairs ahind me.

Oh, Atli, I says to his back. My voice don't make no sound; it's all in my head now. But he wouldn'ta stopped, even could he hear me. He's walkin toward the bed, movin closer to his family. Movin far as he can away from me.

I know feelins change. They change as easy as a girl turns twiggy, quick as a bebby gets stolen from his ma. But paths don't jest go one way: what you lost gotta come back to you some day, sure as spring follows winter. That's what my twiggy folk says: they tells me a twig-wife's gotta be patient. That she'll never know when her chance'll come to turn things 'roun. They says I gots to be vigilant. And I am. Oh, I am. My teeths is sharp, my diggin fingers is ready, my eyes is always lookin. Watchin Seelya raise my bebby, waitin for my luck to change. Jest waitin to take back what's mine.

♪ ♪ ♪

Fur and Feathers

Fur and Feathers

"Where's Reynard got himself to, Rori? I ain't seen him for days."

There's a waver in Ida-Belle's voice as her question travels up the henhouse stairs, a straining to be casual. Her feet scuffle in the dust, sandals shifting back and forth with toes pointed in. Clouds of dirt lift, cling to her ankles, then settle like sighs on the ground.

"Answer to that will cost you." Aurora's response comes from within the whitewashed structure; it sails out the multi-paned windows on a wave of chicken giggles and clucks. A minute later the woman appears, apron-covered legs framed in the lower half of the screen door, head and torso indistinct in the shadows cast by the coop's overhanging eaves. One stride short of emerging, she looks down the five wooden steps to where Ida-Belle waits.

"I got coin," the girl says, fumbling for the cotton purse she wears slung over her shoulder. She's just gone twenty-one but long hours in the woolshed have wizened an extra decade into her face. Her hands—one now lifted to shade her eyes from the glare reflecting off the tin roof, the other pressed flat against her belly—are pink and soft. Years of gathering, combing, and carding lanolin-rich fleece has left even the creases around her knuckles smooth.

"Bet you do." Arms wrapped around a pail of feed, Aurora uses a hip to push open the door. Springs squeal as the hinges stretch wide to let her out; they recoil with a clatter of wood against wood.

"Call me batty," she continues, clomping down the steps, "but I reckon you ain't drove half way across Napanee to talk about Rey."

"No," says Ida-Belle, eyes cast down. "I reckon not."

Aurora shifts her grip on the pail, cradles its weight in her left arm. "Well, out with it then."

"Jimmy'll kill me if he finds out I came." The girl's voice trails off as she looks up, takes in the henhouse. The place is bigger than her cottage and twice as old. Foundations raised four feet off the ground, the weatherboard building tilts to the right. Its porch sprouts support pillars like dozens of running legs caught beneath its bulk in mid-stride. A brace of hares, necks slit and draining red, dangles over the railing just high enough to be out of predators' reach. Garlands of bones and feathers, poppy heads and rosehips hang in rollercoaster loops from the eaves. To the left, a ramp sticks like a laddered tongue out a rooster-sized hole in the wall. Though a scrub brush and pail wait below the rainwater tank's faucet, every horizontal surface remains speckled with bird shit.

"Ain't no one forcing you to stay, girl. Get on with it, or get moving. My lasses have had themselves an upset this week; *they* sure as hell need my help if you don't want it."

"It's just—" Ida-Belle pauses, begins again. "I can't give you much in the way of payment, but I was hoping?" Her eyebrows and shoulders lift as she speaks, then slump as she sees the older woman's stern expression. "I was hoping."

Aurora sighs and puts down the pail. Straightening up, she wipes her hands on the back of her pants, then adjusts the fox's tail tucked under the ribbon of her hat band. With a flick of the wrist, she sets its length drooping over the brim, its fur a striking contrast to the faded grey of her braids.

"Me and hope ain't exactly seeing eye to eye these days." She directs Ida-Belle to the Shaker-style rocking chair at the foot of the stairs. The girl perches on the edge of the seat, clutching her purse in her lap, close-lipped while Aurora continues. "That vixen blinds fools with promises then snatches them away just for kicks. Makes a person think she's doing the right thing for her relationship when, in fact, she ain't."

"Oh." Ida-Belle slouches under the weight of her disappointment. When she goes to stand, Aurora places a grimy hand on her shoulder to keep her seated.

"Quit your fluttering, Ida. If I had a mind to be rid of you, you'd already be gone." From the way her client's hands keep straying to her midriff, Aurora can see what it is the girl wants, why she's here—but the words have to be said if the magic's to work. "Get your thoughts in order, once and for all, then talk loud enough for my lasses to hear you. Nice and clear, mind; none of this faffing about hope."

Ida-Belle takes a deep breath, exhales as she settles back into the chair. "Me and Jimmy's been married nigh on six months now."

Aurora keeps quiet as she waits for the girl to go on. The silence lengthens, broken only by the chickens' chattering and cooing, and the steady creak of cicadas conversing in the cornfields. Aurora searches through her apron pockets for a pipe and some leaf. Finding both, she presses a thumb's worth of tobacco into the bowl, clenches the stem between her teeth as she rummages around for a match.

"My friend Loretta said you helped her out once—" Ida-Belle's face reddens. "She said you could see the future." Aurora lifts an eyebrow, puffs her pipe to life, neither confirming nor denying the girl's implicit question.

"I know it sounds crazy," Ida-Belle says, "but ever since she came here Loretta ain't had to face a single one of her mother-in-law's visits. Even the ones what weren't planned ahead! And when I asked how she got so lucky, always being out when Gerdie comes 'round to piss her off or tell her how to run her own household, Loretta showed me the little calendar you gave her—the one what's got a bunch of dates and times written on it, starting from the day she came here and running well into the next five years."

For the first time, Ida-Belle looks Aurora straight in the eye. "She wouldn't tell me how you done it, Rori. Only that you done it."

Aurora doesn't smile, even though she's glad to hear her previous clients continue to remain discreet in advertising her wares. Wouldn't do no-one good to have the whole town flocking to her for answers whenever they got too lazy to do things the hard way. Ain't time for that, far as she's concerned.

Head wreathed in blue smoke, she leans against the elevated porch and gives Ida-Belle no more encouragement than a simple, "Uh-huh. And?"

Visibly steeling herself, the girl says, "I need to get knocked up, quick."

Aurora nods, head bobbing to a familiar tune.

"Six months we've been married, Rori. *Six months* and so much fucking my nethers is rubbed raw—and still. Nothing." She leans her head back, watches a sparrow flit from the henhouse roof to the chimney of Aurora's cabin on the opposite side of the yard. Her lower lids well with tears. "Jimmy's been eyeing that skank from the Buy 'n' Save all winter. I reckon if I don't give him some reason to stick around, he'll be gone before shearing time."

Aurora takes the pipe from her mouth, flips it and taps it on the edge of the porch. Soft clumps of ash drop to the ground as she asks, "So which do you want to know? If you'll be pumping out wee ones soon, or if you're going to lose Jimmy? We can only cover one thing at a time."

Tears spill onto Ida-Belle's pale cheeks. "Babies," she whispers, while twisting the ring with its tiny zirconium stone, spinning it around and around her wedding finger. Aurora looks down at her own left hand; still surprised, even after a week, to see the bright white space where her own band of gold used to be. She clears her throat.

"You do realise there's only so much we can do?"

Ida-Belle smiles through her tears, thoughts of Loretta's success making her deaf to the older woman's caveats. "Anything's better than nothing."

"Fine." Aurora pockets her pipe and heads for the stairs. "Stay here. A few minutes and we'll have you an answer."

𝄞

Aurora's chickens would never be satisfied with a standard coop.

Stacks of cramped aluminium boxes, barely large enough to accommodate a hatchling much less a brooding hen, definitely wouldn't suit them; nor would short plywood walls, so low they'd force their keeper to slouch while visiting her charges; nor wire mesh ceilings or floor-level apertures of the sort typically knocked together to aerate, and confine, egg-laying chooks.

Aurora's lasses wouldn't have a bar of that. They perch on overstuffed cushions; each nestled securely on mahogany bookshelves stretching well over forty feet to the rafters of the house's double-peaked roof. They are hand-fed three times daily, given heaters when the seasons turn cold, and special treats on their birthdays. Unlike ordinary hens, Aurora's tiny oracles smile, snack and lay their fortunes in comfort.

When she enters the henhouse, the gabble of voices crescendoes in fear; the racket ebbs once the chickens recognise Aurora's shape silhouetted against the screen. Hanging on the wall next to the door, an enormous blackboard gives the names and shelf numbers for every bird in the coop: fourteen hundred and seventy six clairvoyant biddies—one for all but two of Napanee's townsfolk. Enough warm light streams in to illuminate the hand-written list, but it isn't bright enough to hurt the lasses' sensitive eyes.

Scanning the columns of names, Aurora mutters, "Ida-Belle Caplin . . . Ida-Belle . . ." and wishes, not for the first time, that she'd had the presence of mind to house the girls in alphabetical order. Sixteen rows down, she sees what's left of her own entry. Aurora Jenkins, ~~Q42.~~ She glosses over it when she notices Ida-Belle's berth is *P43*.

Damn you, Rey, she thinks. She's steered clear of Minnie's roost all week; now there's nothing she can do but try not to stare at it while she negotiates with Ida-Belle's hen. Double-checking the supply of Tic Tacs she keeps in her top apron pocket, and hooking a pouchful of dry-roasted seed to her belt, Aurora weaves her way between bookshelves to reach the far side of the room.

The oracles generally pay her comings and goings little mind, unless she's got riddles for them to solve. But this week they're bursting with questions, most concerning Reynard. Every third step or so she's forced to stop, kiss their baby-smooth cheeks, stroke the bridges of their button noses, and reassure them that he won't be back any time soon. Although her caresses calm them, her words sound hollow. She knows it'll only be a matter of minutes before they forget and get anxious again.

Their far-seeing skills are flawless—except when the future involves that trickster she's called husband for twenty-five years.

"Excuse me, Miss Rori?" A tiny voice chirps at her as she passes aisle G. She stops and looks up to the top shelf, into the pale green eyes of an ancient Plymouth Rock lass. The oracle's plumage is patterned like black and white tweed, each feather neatly groomed despite the bird's age; her face a perfect replica of old widow McGeary's, the crone who'd just celebrated her eighty-fifth winter.

"What can I do for you, Valma?" The hen tut-tuts at being addressed so informally—she prefers to be called Madam. She wrinkles her coffee-coloured face into a grimace; her wide lips shrivel into a frown. A red pillbox hat slips down her forehead until her arched eyebrows are hidden beneath its decorative veil. She leans over to scold Aurora.

"Rape!" The word shrills out of the hen's throat, then is clipped short in a panicked *bu-gock*. "Those gold demons you let loose in this place keep making *advances*, trying to have their filthy way with me while I'm asleep. I feel them pecking at me—peck, peck, pecking all night! I just know they're aching to get beneath my frillies."

"Oh, Valma," Aurora says, her tone exhausted. "I thought we dealt with this already. The roosters can't reach you all the way up there, hun. That's why we moved you, remember?"

"I ain't so sure about that, Miss Rori. I see them eyeing me all day, just waiting for me to nod off. No matter how high I fly above their heads to show they can't have me, they keeping coming back. The perverts."

Aurora sighs. None of her sibyls can fly—in that way they're no different from bird-faced chooks. And the roosters are just that: roosters. It's their nature to be curious; they don't know any better. A pair of twin Brahma hens to Valma's right, one girl and one boy, start giggling at the oracle's rant. Their near-identical faces, accentuated by tufts of herringbone feathers, are both at least half a century away from her kind of senility. To the aged hen's left, a New Hampshire brown studiously avoids Aurora's gaze. She gently shifts her bulk to hide a long, sharp piece of straw sitting next to her pillow.

"Stop crowding me!" Valma squawks. The twins' laughter redoubles.

"Be quiet, the lot of you." Aurora reaches up, snatches the straw, lifts the heavy brown lass back onto her cushion. "You been using this to torment Val while she's sleeping, Jolene?"

"She snores like the devil," the oracle announces, head tilted at a haughty angle. "It's the only way to shut her up." The twins nod their agreement, clucking, "It's true, it's true!"

"You're a pain in my backside, that's what you kids are." Aurora turns back to Valma and says, "Open wide," then tucks a mint beneath the old woman's tongue—both to still her complaints and to reward her for putting up with the other chooks' crap. Ignoring the jealous looks Jolene and the twins shoot her way, Valma hums with satisfaction.

"I ain't got time for this now," Aurora says. "But I will deal with you—mark my words."

It's enough to have Rey stirring shit in here, she thinks as she walks away. *Without the seers getting in on the pranks as well.*

𝄞

H, I, J, K—there's a gap in the rows, a small crossroads separating the double-digits on the left from the triple on the right, bookshelves and chooks on all four sides lit by a series of crazed skylights above—*L, M, N, O* . . . Aurora's pace slows. She passes through mote-filled beams of light, reluctantly moving into the shadows beyond.

The space where Minnie used to sit is still littered with ragged feathers. A lavender-scented blanket lies twisted like a snarl across the cushion. Red is splashed on both where the other lasses had drawn blood defending their shelfmate. Even now the air stinks of fear, smeared straw, and gore.

"Calm down, ladies, gents," Aurora says, barely audible above the oracles' shouts.

"It ain't fair, Rori—"

"—where's my goddamn bird? What's my future?"

"Hush now," Aurora urges. The hens keep yelling, their scratchy voices repeating the argument she and Reynard had had in front of them last week.

"I can't take it no more, this bird telling you secrets—"

"—shitting out eggs filled with god-knows-what each week—"

"—unnatural stuff what keeps you looking like you was twenty-five—"

"That's enough," Aurora says.

"Stay away from her, Rey—"

"—put her down!"

Minnie's neighbours lunge at her vacant pillow, as if Reynard were still trying to throttle her. Meanwhile, the lasses on higher and lower shelves mimic the trickster's pleas, his accusations.

"—you said you'd stopped using!"

"—and I ain't got no magic yolk to keep me fresh—"

"Enough," Aurora repeats.

"—I share my magics with you all the time, but things ain't even between us—"

"—ain't my fault I'm different from you—"

"—Am I even in that future she shows you?"

"Shut up!" Aurora's chest heaves, her pulse races. That's twice now she's lost her temper in this very spot; twice her words have brought the bickering to a halt. *Life ain't even*, she'd hollered a week earlier, walloping her husband's pointed ear. The blow had saved Minnie, but not before the prophet's little face had turned blue, neck purple from the crush of Reynard's frustration.

It took a sedative tablet to keep the oracle from flapping herself into an early grave; a lavender-scented blanket draped over her shivering body had helped soothe her into a doze. Such measures wouldn't cut it now. Faced with several dozen anxious birds, Aurora's patience is stretched. "I don't want to hear any more of that talk, you got me? Either look *forward* like you're meant to, or shut the fuck up."

Apart from a few sniffles, a couple squeaks of dismay, the hens do as they're told. Hands shaking, Aurora reaches up to wipe tears away from P43's blue eyes. The chick's nose is red from crying, its tip curved exactly like Ida-Belle's.

"It's all right." She pushes damp feathers away from the white Delaware's freckled cheek, adjusts the red coronet so that it sits straight on her head. "Everything's okay." She offers two Tic Tacs; the chook gobbles them up. Holding a third just out of the hen's reach she asks, "What's your name, hun?"

"Ellie."

Aurora pops the mint into Ellie's mouth. "Good girl," she says, tracing the grey barring on the ends of the bird's hackles, wings and tail with a finger. Smoothing the feathers down; settling the hen's nerves along with her own. "Did you hear what Ida-Belle needs?"

Ellie says, "I think so," but her expression is uncertain. Aurora takes another mint, places it in the flat of her palm.

"The girl wants babies. Will she have them?"

The oracle licks her lips, looks up like she's consulting the heavens, though her gaze has turned inward. A moment passes, then with a confident, single nod she says, "Yes. Sure will."

As if on cue, the instant Ellie's prediction is voiced the other oracles begin gossiping about her technique; critiquing her accuracy; commenting on how much better *they* would have done in her place. Aurora rewards the young lass with another sweet; waits until she has stopped crunching it before asking, "Any chance you can give her something to speed it along?"

Big smile. "I reckon."

Ellie inches her hindquarters over the back of her green pillow, which is heavily speckled with white. Throat vibrating with the force of her clucks, face crimson, pearl teeth making semi-circular dents in her full lower lip, the oracle pushes.

Grunts.

Pushes.

A throat-tearing squawk. A sound like a marble rolling across a wooden table. Sweat beads Ellie's forehead. Her colouring returns to normal and her breathing steadies. She grins sheepishly as Aurora reaches beneath tail feathers to poke around through the straw and moult. Pride gilds her features as she sees what Aurora digs up.

A bright red egg, displaying Ida-Belle's name in silver cursive, sits large and shiny in the cradle of Aurora's hands. Congratulations roar out from all sides, deafening, as the oracles in rows P and Q compliment Ellie on her first delivery.

♪

"You're in luck." Aurora places the egg, still warm, onto Ida-Belle's lap. "She was feeling talkative."

Confusion creases the girl's brow. She picks up the egg, turns it over. "What am I supposed to do with this?"

The older woman lights her pipe, takes a long pull. Sweet smoke fills her mouth and drifts out her nose, temporarily replacing the lingering scent of fowl. She lifts her hat to wipe the sweat and feathers clinging to her forehead and says, "What do you think? Crack it."

"D'you got a bowl or something I can drop the yolk into?"

Aurora shakes her head. "Just crack it as is, Ida. On your knee."

Ida-Belle is only half-successful at keeping the sneer from her lips. She looks down at the egg, then at the clean culottes she put on special for her visit to Aurora's. Such a clever design—she'd stitched them herself. Grey cotton patterned with orange and red pansies, they look like smart pants when she's sitting, and a skirt when she's standing. But they won't look nowhere near as stylish with yolk dribbled all over.

Hesitant at first, then more forceful when she sees how tough the shell is, Ida-Belle strikes the egg against her kneecap. With a crunch, fractures appear across its red surface, spreading out from a circular indent. She digs her thumbs in, waits for the white to ooze out. Her hands remain dry. Small fragments break off as she splits the shell in two; it separates with a sound of twigs snapping, and releases its furry contents onto her lap without mess.

Three miniature bunnies, perfectly proportioned, each one no bigger than a lamb's eye. All white with beige patches, velvet ears, and pink noses twitching, they roll across Ida-Belle's thighs and snuggle into the warm space where her legs press together. Blinking, they look up at her; sprigs of parsley, chives and garlic tied like bows around their necks.

"Good work, Ellie." Aurora's voice startles Ida-Belle from her inspection of the rabbits. "You got three chances to get it right, thanks to your generous lass. Now, tell me. How does Jimmy like his stew? Beef? Lamb? What's his favourite?"

"Lamb's cheapest," Ida-Belle says, slowly.

"Of course," Aurora says. "You got some ready for cooking back home?"

Ida-Belle nods.

"Good. Seems clear what you're meant to do." Aurora picks up one of the bunnies, raises it to the level of her eyes, tries not to think of it in a roasting pan. It stares back at her blankly. "You gots to pop one of these here baby-makers in with your dinner tonight—Jimmy like chives and 'taters with his meat?"

Again, Ida-Belle nods.

"All right then, use this one first." Aurora reunites the chive-necked bunny with its brothers, places a hand on Ida-Belle's shoulder. "Chop him up good and small so's Jimmy won't notice it. That's real important: it's got to be kept secret, you hear? This ain't nobody's business but yours."

"Yeah, all right—"

"And don't go spilling to Loretta, neither." Aurora gives Ida-Belle a hard look, gestures for her to stand up. She collects the eggshells for compost, and helps the girl tuck the rabbits into her purse. As Aurora walks her client to her truck, she gives final instructions. "Some magics is quieter than others, and this here's one of them. Understand? You keep them creatures out of sight until it's time they get ate. Like I said, you gots three chances— your lassie said you've got babies coming, and this here's how you're going to get them. All right?"

"So we just gots to eat them? That's it?" Ida-Belle turns to unlock the car door, keeping her back to Aurora to hide the hope shining in her eyes.

"That's it."

"Thanks, Rori." The girl spins on her heel, flings her arms around Aurora's shoulders, then quickly steps back for fear of crushing the bunnies. Her face is flushed. "How much do I owe you?"

With a sniff, Aurora considers the collection of boxes stacked in the tray of Ida-Belle's pickup while the girl digs into her purse for some money. "How's business going with that lot?"

Ida-Belle looks up, sees what's caught Aurora's attention. "Buy 'n' Save's just ordered another two crates—they say ladies drive all the way from Overton to get our creams. Can you believe it?" She burrows beneath the trio of rabbits, snags another two-dollar coin.

"Do they really work?" Aurora wonders if lanolin by-products will smooth her face as well as the pure stuff does Ida-Belle's hands; if they'll be even half as effective as Minnie's fortunes.

"Well, I ain't going to shit you, Rori. Not after today." Ida-Belle reaches into the cab, opens a box and pulls out a jar of homemade moisturiser. "You gots to use a fuckload of it to see results—but, yeah. I ain't heard no complaints."

Ida-Belle offers a handful of change, all she can muster from the bottom of her handbag.

"Keep your money," Aurora says. "Give me a couple jars of that night cream you got there, and maybe some of that SPF stuff too. However many you think's fair for a bellyful of wee ones."

Buy 'n' Save's order is one carton lighter when Ida-Belle's truck backs down the gravel driveway. Aurora rests the box on the ground, straightens to wave goodbye. Halfway up, she comes eye-to-eye with a fox poking his scruffy head out of the long grass across the lane.

Aurora's heart leaps.

She's so glad to see he's back again, that he's still okay, she takes an eager step forward—but is brought up short by the box at her feet. Happiness turns sour as she takes in what he's reduced her to. Using *products* to replicate the youth Minnie gave her every week; the clear skin, the deep auburn curls. She snorts. Next she'll be relying on *chemicals* to dye her hair! It just ain't natural.

Hefting the carton, Aurora spits in the fox's direction. Heart pounding, she snaps, "Bugger off!" The tail dangling from her hatband bobs in time with her retreating steps as she makes her way up the drive, trying to appear unruffled as she enters her lonely cabin.

In the brush, the fox yips after her. He waits a moment, but she doesn't give him a second glance. Reluctantly, he slinks out of sight, convinced that progress had been made.

Yesterday she wouldn't even talk to him.

♪

"C'mere, Rori," Reynard had called from the kitchen. "I got a surprise for you."

"Just a minute," she'd replied, rinsing the rest of the soapsuds out of her thick red hair, scowling to find strands of grey. The water scalded, filled the bathroom with steam. She'd stood under the shower until she could hardly bear the heat any longer. She'd hoped it would wash away the guilt that had clung to her since she'd lashed out at Reynard that afternoon, guilt that even a three-hour walk into town and back hadn't alleviated. Hoped he'd forget about their fight, and what caused it. Hoped they'd be okay. Her skin reddened.

Faucets squeaked into the off position. Aurora had grabbed her plaid housecoat, wrapped it around herself, tied it. Her feet left wet prints on the scrubbed wood floor as she collected the pile of clothes she'd shed on the bathmat. She'd looked at the closed bathroom door, hesitated.

"I'll just be a second, hun," she'd said, crouching down to open the cabinet beneath the sink. Shifting spare rolls of toilet paper, boxes of tampons and half-empty bottles of mouthwash and shampoo, Aurora had reached all the way to the back to grab a quilted makeup bag—one Reynard thought was filled with cotton balls. Sitting back on her haunches, she'd unzipped it; released a breath she hadn't known she'd been holding until the tension in her lungs eased.

A deep blue egg, her name inscribed bronze in its thick shell, sat perfect and whole at the bottom of the case. She'd saved it for two days.

Despite what Reynard thinks, Aurora thought, *I have been trying to cut back on taking Minnie's fortunes. I really have.*

But today had been too much to cope with; the new shoots of grey in her hair were proof enough of that. Muffling the sound with a washcloth, she'd gently tapped the egg against the basin, spinning it deftly between her fingers.

Tricksters like him have their own ways of dealing with things. Aurora shook her head. Not that it mattered. So far, the fates simply hadn't laid a Reynard-faced chook in her coop. There was nothing she could do about that.

A piece of shell flaked off, landed silently in the sink. Aurora snapped away shard after shard, until only the base of the egg remained. Perched in its curve was a three-tiered fountain, decorated with peacocks, ferns, and doves. At the very top, a nymph balanced on the tip of a finial, her arms stretched to the sky. From each of her fingertips, a jet of water arced into the air then collected in a pool at the bottom of the shell.

Aurora had leaned into the spray, dousing her face with its rejuvenating waters. She'd felt the skin tightening around her eyes, the laugh-lines smoothing from her cheeks, the shrivel of her lips puckering, the sag of her chin straightening. Wiping steam from the mirror, Aurora looked at her youthful features. Satisfied, she raised the fountain in silent salute to Minnie, then tilted her head back and drank it dry. By the time she'd towelled her hair, the troublesome greys had disappeared.

"Close your eyes," Reynard had said, when she'd stepped out of the bathroom. Actions following words, he'd swept her into his arms, used his furry hands as a blindfold, then danced her in the dark across the kitchen.

She'd smelled the feast long before she'd seen it. Aromas of roasted onion and garlic, fresh bread and warm butter, gravy and boiled potatoes; the scent of wine mulling with spices; an apple pie cooling on the counter—all combined to make her heart lift, and to curve her mouth into a smile.

"Ta-da!" Reynard unveiled his surprise, arms flung wide. Tears had sprung to Aurora's eyes as she'd taken in the spread laid out before her. Reynard had set the table with their finest crockery—most of the plates and bowls actually matched. Her grandmother's silver cutlery lined the place settings, arranged just the way Aurora liked it. Casserole dishes heaped with food covered the table, so many it was hard to see the fine linen cloth beneath. Occupying the place of honour, in the centre, was a roasting pan covered with aluminium foil. Aurora's smile had widened.

Reynard only wooed her with treats like this when he wanted to apologise.

"Thanks," she'd whispered, sliding her arm around her husband's waist. Unlike her, he'd dressed up for the occasion: a sport-coat over his denim shirt, ears tucked beneath slicked-back hair, and sideburns plastered down with so much pomade he almost looked tame. Only his tail hung free, swinging out beneath the rough hem of his jacket.

She'd kissed him, scratched her nails up and down his back until he purred. Giggling, she'd said, "Why don't you shift into something more comfortable?"

Reynard chuckled and licked her cheek. Soon his nose lengthened, as did his ears. Rusty fur spread from the top of his head across every inch of his skin. His limbs retracted, leaving a puddle of clothes around his black paws. Lifting his head to look up at Aurora, he leapt onto one of the kitchen chairs and yipped in delight. Instantly, night replaced day. "Take a seat," he'd instructed, humming the moon into the sky, frosting the room with its blue light.

"For you," he'd said, and pulled the aluminium foil off the roast with his teeth. "Carve it up, love."

"With pleasure," Aurora had replied, reaching for the carving knife.

Her hand froze in midair. Looking up at her, amid a bed of garnish, was her own face in miniature. *Minnie's face*; body plucked and stuffed, basted and glazed with spiced butter.

Aurora had sat, paralysed, staring at her oracle while Reynard stood, muscles tense, staring at his wife.

Outside, a rooster hopped onto the sill of the kitchen window, pecked at his reflection in the glass. The sound fractured the silence, the shock that had held Aurora in thrall. Springing to action, she'd snatched the knife and, so quick as to have been done without thinking, brought it whistling down on the tabletop.

Separating Reynard from his tail.

There was barking then, and shouting. Neither had run as long as the thin ribbon of blood that followed the fox out the front door. Neither had hurt as much as the wedding ring being torn from Aurora's finger. Neither would be harder to forget than the corpse of her future lying cold on their Wedgwood platter.

♪

The telephone jangles Aurora awake.

It takes her a minute to get her bearings. Images of Reynard's betrayal slip like a veil from her mind. *It's morning*, she tells herself, *and bright.* The disgusting smell of roasted chicken fades, replaced by the scent of clean sheets. Echoes of her husband's nightly howling—his skulking below their bedroom window, snuffling and whimpering for forgiveness—are drowned out by the phone's insistent ringing.

The tightness in her chest gets sharper as she reaches for the cordless receiver, rolling over the pillows stuffed in Reynard's side of the bed. Poor imitations of his absent form. Pillows don't throw their arms around her at night, don't wake her with a hot tail pressed against her backside. They don't make her feel safe.

Her throat constricts. They also don't murder innocent lasses for jealousy.

"Rori?"

"Yeah."

"Rori, it's Ida-Belle. You gotta help me." Her voice is pitched so high it could scrape paint off the ceiling.

"Just chop that rabbit up nice and small. Jimmy won't notice a thing."

"Don't you think I know that? I done it already—and now I'm a fucking blimp! Ain't no way even a fool like Jim won't notice *this*.

What am I supposed to do? He's going to think I cheated on him, ain't he? No way this thing in my guts is a one-day-old kid. I look like I'm ready to pop!"

"Hang on a sec, Ida." Aurora sits up in bed, swings her legs over the side. "When did you eat that stew?"

"Jimmy takes supper at five."

Aurora looks at the clock. Seven in the morning. Either Ellie's got some powerful magics in her eggs, or else Ida-Belle is skimping on the truth. "Any way you might've ate more than your share of that rabbit? Did Jim get any at all?"

Silence.

"Out with it, girl."

"Well," Ida-Belle begins, "I really wanted to make sure it'd work, right?"

"Uh-huh . . ."

"So I started chopping up that first little bunny, and it were so much easier than I thought, so I said to myself, "If one's good, don't you reckon all three'll be even better?" And—"

"And you put all of your chances into the stew. At once."

Ida-Belle sniffles, her voice thick with tears. "Am I going to die?"

Aurora shoulders the receiver, pulls on a pair of jeans, tucks in the shirt she slept in. "No," she says, taking her apron from the hook on the back of the bedroom door. She slips it around her neck. "You ain't going to die."

"But what am I going to do?"

"Quit your blubbering, for one thing." Aurora gives the girl a chance to control herself. Grabs her fox-tail hat, plunges it onto her head. "I'll have a word with the chooks, see what they've got to say about this *situation*. But if I was to have a guess, I'd say you should make way for triplets."

"Oh God . . ." Ida-Belle's tears pour out thick and fast.

"Hush now." Aurora's tone slips down an octave. Quiet and soothing; the same sing-song she's used in the henhouse every day this week. "Come see me this afternoon, all right? And, this time, bring Jimmy."

Ida-Belle can't reply for crying.

"Hush," Aurora repeats as she walks to the front door, propping it open with her foot. "We'll sort something out, all right? All right?" She can sense, rather than hear, Ida-Belle's nod. "That's a girl. It'll be fine, Ida. The lasses won't let you down."

$$\oint$$

Reynard would think this was a hoot, if he were here.

Ellie knew the girl would eat all three rabbits at once, and she didn't say nothing about it. Probably reckoned she were doing Ida-Belle a favour. The whole thing makes Aurora feel tired, and she wishes her husband would put his fox-gloves on and work some trickery to lighten her mood.

But he ain't here, she thinks. Right before she sees him.

He's lying at the base of the oak tree they planted outside their bedroom window the year they got married. Morning sun is still low enough to hit him full on; the tree doesn't provide much shade until late afternoon. His fur is mangy, streaked with red gashes, like he's been on the wrong end of a fight. The stump of his tail is crusty with dirt and blood. More than a few flies buzz around him, alight on his eyes, in his ears, around the mess of his arse. Aurora's heart races.

Oh, God. Don't be dead.

She runs toward him, stops two feet away. Without going any closer she can see his face muscles twitch, like he's winking at her in his sleep. With an effort, she turns back, crosses the packed-dirt yard and walks up the henhouse steps.

"Morning, chooks," she says, and smiles to hear a chorus of greetings clucked from all sides, from both girl- and boy-faced lasses. Some, still not fully awake, stare vacantly at the moths fluttering up near the rafters. Others flap their wings for attention, *bock-bocking* demands for mints. Jolene and the twins avoid meeting her eyes as Valma looks on, disgusted; while yet others perform a waddling turn, point tails out, and doze off to pass the hours until feeding time.

Ellie, she notices upon reaching the aisle between rows P and Q, is one of the latter. Worn out from the effort of yesterday's prediction, the Delaware hen is sleeping deeply.

"The mess, O-Rori," chides a masculine-featured Cornish hen. From his berth in Q41, he stretches his head out to block Aurora's path. His royal blue neck feathers, knotted beneath his bearded chin like an ascot, give him a regal air that suits the disdain in his voice. "Isn't it high time you cleaned up this filth?" He peers over the top of his gold-framed spectacles, shudders at the mess still littering Minnie's satin pillow.

"Honestly," he says, now directing his gaze at his keeper, "preserving the scene of the crime in this fashion is downright *macabre*." He sniffs. "And the fleas are becoming unbearable."

Aurora looks across at Ellie, at Minnie's soiled roost, then back at the sleeping oracle. *I reckon letting her rest a few more minutes won't hurt.*

Adrenaline surges through her as her subconscious whispers, *I reckon it's time to move on.*

She fetches a hand-broom and dustpan, fills a bucket with water, drops some soap and a couple old rags into her apron pockets. The pail clunks on the floor in front of Q42. Aurora hunches slightly to get a better view of the damage. Feathers, muck, and blood. A lump forms in the back of her throat. Straightening up, she tries to melt it by sucking on a Tic Tac—then has to dole out doses of the oval sweets to every open-mouthed bird from Q22 to Q57.

With most of the bay satiated, if not quiet, and the air sharp with the scent of mint, Aurora begins the task of sweeping away all trace of Minnie's death. First, she removes the blanket; cleans off the pillow, sets it aside; then launches in with the broom. Bristles rasp across the bookshelf's surface as she tackles the worst of the mess, moving as quickly as possible. Dirt, straw and down swirl into the dustpan's waiting tray. While she works, Aurora's eyes don't stop watering.

"You've missed some," the Cornish hen bosses. "Reach all the way to the back."

"I know what I'm doing," Aurora snaps. The insult she'd been about to unleash comes out as a strangled gasp as her broom snags on a clot of feathers. Dragging it to the shelf's edge, she catches a glimpse of royal blue peeking out of the mass of red and white.

She picks up the egg with trembling fingers, brushes it off. It's smaller than any of Minnie's other fortunes, but still big enough for her to read the dedication clearly:

Aurora and Reynard Jenkins

Although the henhouse is as noisy as usual, to Aurora it seems the whole world has gone mute.

Why is Reynard's name on *her* egg? Minnie couldn't have laid it on the fox's last visit—sluggish with sedatives, she would have barely had time to struggle, to scream, before he'd slit her throat. Aurora places the egg on the shelf, leans it carefully against the Cornish's cushioned roost. Staring at the bearded lass without really seeing him, Aurora realises that Minnie must've laid it while Reynard had been throttling her.

While the two of them were too busy fighting to notice it.

"Get that flea-bitten thing away from me." The hen's foot connects with the egg, sends it over the shelf's edge. As if in slow motion, Aurora watches the treasure sail earthwards, her hands clumsy and slow, swiping at empty air seconds too late.

A dark blue fault line splits the egg from top to tail as it cracks against the bucket's rim, then bounces in with a splash. With a shriek.

Surrounded by shards of bobbing blue shell, a fox-faced hatchling cries as he fights to keep his head above water.

Oh, Minnie. Aurora's eyes flood as she watches his baby wings weaken, his thrashing grow more frantic, his screams more shrill. Without moving, she waits to see if the newborn far-seer will resurface. *Fair's fair, ain't it?* The fox-hen gasps for breath, goes under again. And again.

Even is even.

Outside, Reynard whimpers, calls out for his wife. Just as he's done every morning upon waking, finding himself tailless and trapped in animal form, bitten by flies and regret. Tailless and alone.

Life ain't even, Aurora thinks. She knocks the pail over and its contents drown the henhouse floor. Leaning over, she rescues the sputtering lass. Uses a rag to pat his wings dry, then dabs at his cheeks with her fingertips. "I'm sorry," she whispers.

The chick sneezes. Opens his golden, Reynard-shaped eyes, and winks.

Aurora snorts. She pulls the fox-tail from her hatband, wraps the sodden oracle in its russet length. Holding the bundle close to her heart, she takes a deep breath. Gathers her nerve. Plans what she's going to say to her husband, then slowly walks outside.

♭ ♭ ♭

From the Teeth of
Strange Children

From the Teeth of Strange Children

What do ghosts look like?

The whisper cracks my voice, but I know he's heard me. He takes a hesitant step forward and drops his rucksack inside the entrance. Dust lifts off the bag, settles onto the scuffed floorboards. Then he stands there, half in the daylight, half in the dark of our lampless, curtained sitting room. He clears his throat and fingers the house key like he's amazed it still works. As though Ma was the one who'd left, not him, and changed the locks on her way. I couldn't have been more than nine when his pack last disappeared, leaving nothing but a few scratches in the doorframe to show where he'd dragged it out behind him. Eight years later, he's got a truck to carry most of his things, more white in his hair, and an expression so downcast I can't yet tell whose father he is. Mine or Harley's.

"Ada," he says, nothing more. No questioning lilt to the way he pronounces my name—he recognises me even though I look nothing like the little girl he once protected. And hearing the rumble of his coffee-and-cigarette voice, I know him in return. In a familiar, unconscious gesture, Banjo runs his hand over his stubbly beard. Harley's dad always was a fidgety one, never could sit still for more than a minute. A need to see the world beyond our farm, to do things the way city folk might, set his muscles twitching and kept his feet planted on the trail. I reckon he's much like his twin in that sense; Ma once said neither he nor Jez, my father, ever had it in them to stay put for long. And as long as they didn't mind other men keeping the chill from her bed, she didn't begrudge them their freedom.

Again, Banjo coughs. Too many excuses, too many overdue answers fight their way up his throat. A lifetime of words glue his mouth shut.

I don't get up from the couch, so I have to crane my neck to the right to see him. "That's what Harley asked me," I explain, motioning Banjo to come all the way in and close the door. The summer months have scrubbed the sunlight thin over the fields but it's still too bright for Ma. She's curled up on the cushions beside me, skin clammy with sweat though she's stripped to her petticoat, mouth clamped on wads of cotton and gore. I pull the afghan up to cover her shoulders, wipe the blood from her cheek. "The first time we saw Mister Pérouse at one of Ma's parties, Harl asked—almost hissing, so Ma wouldn't catch us sneaking—he asked, "What do ghosts look like? Ain't that one?" Peering through the slats in the pantry door where we were hiding, Harl's eyes stretched wide enough to swallow the night. His hand shook, clutching mine, but a smile tickled his lips as we stared. A mix of dread and awe— but that's just like our Harl, isn't it? Always mistaking fear for excitement. Then again, seeing that man, so pale he was more blue than white, so skinny he seemed to float while the rest of us clung heavy to our footsteps, for once I knew how Harl felt."

My gaze drifts to Ma's face as I speak. Anxiety lines her forehead, even in sleep. Each breath she takes is shallow; her exhalations are thick wheezes of air.

"I've thought about this a lot," I say. "Spent years doing little but."

Banjo's fingers worry at his chin, *scritch-scritching* over his bristles.

"I can't stop hearing his voice," I continue. "Even now I'm back here." 'Cause, far as I can tell, that was it: the parties, those outfits, that ghost of a man. His dreams. His high notions of what made proper living. Everything that changed us; right there, dancing on the other side of the pantry door.

"Of course, how could we know that then? Harl always was young for his age—you said so yourself, remember? And Ma thought I was too sweet for fourteen, too innocent to wear such a grown-up face." I feel the colour rising in my cheeks. Outside, Banjo's truck cools, settles with a series of metallic pings. There's no wind to shake the trees ringing our twenty acre lot, no harvest for revving tractors to tend. Crickets hum pure white noise, thrumming beyond register in the heat. Silence plods into the room, sits like a boulder between me and Banjo.

I can see he wants to ask more about Harl.

Instead, he shifts from foot to foot, still hanging back. "Where are the girls?"

"With their brother." I swallow hard; there's no time for tears. "It's rude to linger in doorways, you know."

Harl's dad squints and takes a good look at me, but doesn't show any sign of moving.

"I'm fine," I say, sighing. Baring my teeth, I run my tongue across their blunt edges. "See? Harmless as Ma."

He releases a pent-up breath and finally lets the door swing shut. My eyes take a minute to adjust to the returned gloom. Outdoor scents waft from him as he sits in the worn recliner across from me: maple and pine and a rich hint of hot earth. He brushes invisible dirt from his jeans. Smooths out the lifelines they've collected over the years; exhausted white wrinkles like the ones on the backs of his hands.

"I'd offer you a drink." I look down at Ma, then back at Banjo. "I don't know if she's got any. And after this morning . . . She couldn't even tell me if she'd change for the phone box. I hunted for her purse and she kept crying the whole time; crying and pulling at my arms, telling me not to go. When I found it I had to lock her in the cellar—don't look at me like that! It's the only way I knew, to keep her from chasing me to the truck stop . . .

"She's only just dozed off. She might not even remember telling me to call you." I hesitate before admitting, "You and Jez."

Banjo nods once. Doesn't ask who I called first—he's never been much of a talker. I think that's why Ma got together with him in the first place, why she kept taking him back though she kept the door closed on his brother. After a while, my father's opinions were just too vocal, too hard for her to handle. *You call this living?* Jez'd said, on more than one occasion. *Scouring dirt for scraps what ain't fit for eating, guzzling potato wine, pumping out babies what ain't got no hope of leaving this heap?* Even when she made an effort, took a job in town, it wasn't enough for my dad. The costume shop embarrassed him—as did the parties Ma threw. Our closest neighbours happily travelled the five miles between their places and here, just to come dressed in Ma's wares. The stitching on her pieces proved so fine, she started getting mail orders from all over the country—her boss even gave her a raise! All that only seemed to make things worse with Jez.

Ain't no old-fashion time we's living in, Wendy, he'd say, looking at her fine silks and brocades like they were sewn from pig-hide and dung. *This here's the future, fer fuck's sakes—even them radio jockeys says so. Why don't y'all give them a listen, since you clearly ain't gots the sense to hear me?*

Guilt trips didn't work so well on Ma. Day after day, she frocked up in skirts with bustles, whalebone corsets and elaborate jackets. Jez hollered like a good thing when she stopped taking us to the church ladies' bazaars to buy our clothes, and started making everything but the hard leather boots she selected from Roebuck catalogues. He split her lip when she cancelled the electricity, opting to use candles and a woodstove. An old icebox and the house's root cellar kept our goats' milk fresh and veggies from our garden cool. And when she sold the car for thirteen bales of cotton, Jez grabbed a bag from the linen cupboard. Shouldered it and said he needed to check out a breach in our property's fence.

We loved Ma for all of it; more so after Jez left. Even Harley, who kicked up a stink fighting for costumes much plainer than us girls'—even he never said our way of living was odd. Chopping and carrying wood to heat the house, drawing water from a pump out back, shitting in a flea-bitten outhouse. Anyone who came 'round our place played their part in Ma's old-style life, right up until it was time for them to go home.

Ain't it just a lark, Ada? they'd ask, buttoning themselves back into overalls and faded work shirts, putting on their regular life suits. *Ain't it grand playing the regal lady like yer Ma?*

And I'd smile, knowing how lucky we were to have her, how special. Knowing it wasn't just play. *Ain't goin'ta deny it,* I'd reply—that's how I spoke then, all *ain'ts* and *y'alls* and *none of yer never minds,* uttered without the slightest shame—*Bring them fiddles and guitars with y'all next time, and we'll have ourselves a regular honky-tonk!*

Their music burned like fireweed down the hall to our bedroom at night; in the morning, fast jigs and slow reels echoed through our daydreams. While Ma worked her shifts in town, Harley and I stayed home and explored our land's twenty acres, learned the ins and outs of its crazed wheat fields and dry river gullies. Sometimes we spent hours, days, searching the flat land for Panagonquin treasure. Empty-handed we ran as far from the highway as our short legs could take us; took shelter in copses of birch and sycamore; made bracelets from wisps of white bark. Around us Chinook winds whistled through parched branches, told us our fortunes in the language of dried autumn leaves.

As the oldest, it was only right that I'd watch the kids, keep them from climbing too high or falling off edges. Feed them when they were hungry, bandage their skinned knees. I didn't mind. Most of the time, it was no more trouble than caring for puppies.

On burning summer days, when the sky stretched along with the hours and scalded air leached clouds from the endless blue, we'd stay inside. Harl hated being cooped up—his skin was baked brown as clay from all his time outdoors—but even he'd settle down if it meant Ma would tell us tales of our seafaring ancestors, folk whose ships had led them astray, stranding us in this landlocked county. He loved those ones most, Banjo's son. Stories of heroes and betrayals. Of men thriving against all odds.

The way I remember it, Banjo mostly observed all this without comment. He wasn't fussed about what we wore, or that we didn't go to school—said he reckoned a lady with Ma's talents was well-suited for teaching her own children. With Banjo, Ma never had to worry about being contradicted or criticised. Not so she could hear it, anyway. He was easy to smile when the mood struck, open with his affections—even with me, his brother's daughter. Even with Bethany, who was born a year after he and Ma split the first time. And so too with Miah, who followed her sister into this world ten months after Banjo's boots found their way back to our porch. Yes, even Miah got her share of his love, though her black hair and tawny colouring screamed she wasn't of his stock. Dandling the brown babe on his knee, Banjo never said a word: the grins she and Ma wore all his doing.

Sometimes, that was enough.

When it wasn't, his opinions were no louder than the front door hinges squeaking open. Quiet as footfalls receding down the gravel path to the highway.

"Wendy's dress fits you pretty nice," he says now, trying small talk.

It doesn't. The collar is too high for my neck. I have to wear it open, ruining the aesthetic of having a long line of buttons up the front. The bodice and sleeves hang loose, emphasising the swell of my belly, the sag in my bust, the scrawniness of my arms. And I'm swimming in heavy red drapery, skirts swinging too low around my distended waist. With her curves and her deep brown hair, Ma could pull this dress off. But after so long with Mister Pérouse, I know I'll never again wear her creations comfortably.

"She seemed so upset . . . I thought it might help her relax." As if, after three years, I could've zipped back into her life like nothing had happened between costume changes. I look down and shrug. "And you don't notice her blood as much on this fabric."

He raises his eyebrows. I tell him Ma wore this dress when she revealed what it was to be a woman in our family. Fabric red as the moon bloods she told me to tuck away where no-one could touch them. *Don't tell a soul where you hid them,* she'd said, handing me rags for the task. *Out here, blood is power. It ain't just a bond. Ain't just what gave you my eyes and Harl that great cleft in his chin.* Leaning so close I could smell her lavender soap, she took my hand, pressed until I felt the throb of her pulse. *There's folk out to take advantage of that red tide, baby. Wrong folk and cold. Keep them rags safe, like you do yer kin. Yer blood carries our secrets, our stories. Our future. Believe you me; it's gonna hold our memories long after my body is dust.*

"Well," Banjo says, shifting in his seat. His eyes trace the mess of Ma's mouth. His hands clench to keep from wringing the blood-soaked cotton stuffed between her gums, to keep from wiping and wiping until her face is clean. "I s'pose I should take her. Keep her from turning to dust too soon, hey?"

He doesn't smile though his tone is friendly. I hold his gaze, lock onto it.

"Not yet," I say, getting my thoughts in order, my voice under control. "I need to tell you this. My tongue—my lips need to shape these words, need to push them out. I can't send it in a letter. Paper is too flimsy to carry the weight of Ma's head in my lap, the history in my belly." I tear open the useless buttons on my bodice, lift my camisole to reveal scars dotting my swollen abdomen. Dozens of puncture wounds scabbed over, raised in tiny red welts. Anyone can see the nape of my neck is unblemished, smooth as a pearl. My stomach tells a different story.

One shaped by the teeth of strange children.

"For three years I've told you what's happened. You, Ma and Jez. In my head I've rehearsed, imagined how I'd explain where I've been, what I've done. What's been done to me." I wish I had that drink now. My mouth is so dry, my voice already breaking. "And now you're here. Bethany and Miah—and Harl, poor stupid Harl—they may never get a chance like this. So you'll wait, and maybe you'll judge."

Again, I take in the sight of Ma nestled against my pregnant belly and I almost can't say, "But no matter what, you won't end up like us."

He opens his mouth and I cut him off.

"Stop. Before you take or lay blame, sit here a spell and listen."

Listen.

They came for us at night.

Mister Pérouse shook me from a dream. The light from his candle obscured my vision. My head was bleary with sleep, so what I saw after I'd rubbed my eyes didn't make much sense. Strangers, two men and an old woman, were leaning over the children's beds. They were pressing their faces too close to Harl's; to Bethany's; to Miah's. Each adult paired with one child, as though whispering secrets into their ears, or nuzzling their necks so they'd laugh. But there was no laughter, no talking. More like a snuffling, a smacking, accompanied by the kids' night-time sighs.

"How are you feeling, *chérie*?" Mister Pérouse's voice ruffled like pages in a book. His breath smelled of roast lamb.

"What?"

"Are you well?" He brushed my forehead with his fingertips. I flinched from the cold of his hand, not from his touch. It felt like months and months had passed since Harl and I'd first seen him from our hidey-hole in the pantry; in that time he'd become Ma's favourite evening visitor. With his wan colouring and milkweed hair, he was a hit at her parties—he had no need for makeup or wigs. He wasn't stingy with the grog either, though he rarely drank. And while he always left in the wee hours of night, more than one morning greeted us with a gold-toothed smile when we found the coins he'd left behind for our trouble.

"Leave it to an out-of-towner to show us locals how to treat a host," Ma had said, the only time she commented on Mister Pérouse's contributions. "Ain't no hick 'round these parts would spare a crust for a starving man unless he were kin."

That didn't stop her from inviting these hicks to her shindigs, of course. But from then on she kept the newest and best apparel aside for Mister Pérouse: a square-cut velvet waistcoat belted with a fringed sash, tied in a drooping bow; ribbed leggings tucked into high boots; a lacy cravat spilling from his collar; a floor length, hoodless mantle worn open on the shoulders. All of which, apart from the blue-black cloak, were the fine grey of sodden ash.

Mister Pérouse fired questions at me. "Does your head hurt? *Mal au ventre?* Can you sit up?" He stroked my cheeks with the back of his hand, then took hold of my chin and forced me to look directly at him. His irises were pink in the candlelight, his lashes long and white. Over his costume he wore the rancher's coat Ma had made for him when she learned he dealt in livestock.

"Ma?" The strangers were lifting my brother and sisters from their beds, carrying them like sacks of spuds over their shoulders. I tried to turn my head to see where they were being taken, but Mister Pérouse's fingers were bands of iron around my jaw.

"*Elle est malade, chérie*—she has come down very sick," he said. And then I heard her groans through the wall between our rooms. Her head knocking against the plaster. The bedsprings squeaking as she thrashed. Her cries, muffled, turning to whimpers. A man's rumbling voice, deep and close, strained as though struggling to speak. "*Attends,*" I think he said, I think he growled. "Hold still and take it," he said, and other things I couldn't quite understand.

My confusion must have been obvious. "I've summoned a doctor to inspect her," Mister Pérouse said. "He'll see to her, *ne t'inquiète pas.*"

The words didn't sound right, but he was so earnest I couldn't *not* believe him.

"It's a miracle you haven't fallen ill, Ada." He released my chin, pulled back the covers. Immediately I started shivering. "The children are all afflicted, though nowhere near as badly as your mother." I straightened my thin cotton shift while he smiled down at me. His gaze lingered as I searched for my slippers. "There's hope for them yet, but I'll need your help."

"I gots to piss," I said, though it wasn't strictly true. My bloods were coming; I could feel their arrival as a pain in my lower back, a warm ache in my belly. I wanted to check they hadn't started yet.

"No time," he replied. "Come along, quickly."

I followed him past Ma's room—dead quiet now—to the lounge. Weird light streamed through the windows and the open front door, casting odd shadows across the room, tricking my eyes into seeing headstones instead of dining chairs, coffins instead of empty couches. Most times I'd find at least one or two of the neighbours snoring there come morning, sleeping off the bourbon and gin I could still smell in the air. But maybe they'd had less to drink, or they'd been called home early; either way, the only ones left that evening were Mister Pérouse and his gang.

"I'm gonna fetch my coat," I said. Mister Pérouse shook his head. "Take nothing with you, *ma chère*. We don't know what's contaminated." He pulled me behind him, offering reassurances that things would be better tomorrow. Outside, the high-beams of his black four-wheel drive, his companions' sedans and pickup trucks, illuminated the house in a way I hadn't seen before. My home looked so small, so forlorn in that artificial glare. Crouched in the spotlight, it cowered from menacing night.

If only Harl was awake, I thought, watching as he was buckled into the vehicle's back seat. *He always talks about riding in cars.*

"Get in the front," Mister Pérouse said, opening the door for me. The seats were leather, so cold they felt slimy, and the interior smelled of smoke and plastic. The odour was suffocating. I wanted to open a window but couldn't figure out how to work the controls. Mister Pérouse walked around to the driver's side while giving his friends orders, strobing the headlights with his movements.

"He's not a ghost," I said to Harl, who couldn't care less, wrapped as he was in the ignorance of sleep. Directly behind me,

Nellie and Ike Porter were huddled beneath a blanket, their rosy-cheeked faces now blank with illness. Like Harl, the flax farmer's kids were unconscious, their necks smeared with red.

Mister Pérouse slid into the cab beside me and closed the door. "Ain't no-one healthy no more?" I asked. He ignored the question, rolled down his window with ease, and spoke to the tall splotchy-faced man waiting in the driveway.

"Jacques, drop by the farmstead two kilometres north. See who's there then meet Théo at —" He turned to me, "What is the name of that couple, Ada? The ones who dip the *chandelles* for your mother?"

"Allambee."

"*Ah, oui.*" He directed his attention back out the window and pointed at the squat, bald man who still cradled Bethany in his arms. "Join Théo at the Allambee farm. I'll see you back at the Haven before dawn."

Without a word, they accepted his directions and got into their cars. "Arianne," Mister Pérouse continued, "go inside and collect the doctor. He's done all he can for tonight."

The old woman nodded. As her head bobbed up and down, the light played across her features: one moment she was wrinkled, the next smooth. A half-smirking, half-frowning Janus face that gave me chills as it glared first at me, then at Miah in the sedan's passenger seat.

"Can't we say goodbye 'fore we go? Ma'll flip her top if she don't know where we gone."

"*Non.*" Mister Pérouse rolled up his window, cutting off the fresh breeze that was helping to clear my head. Reaching over, he patted my knee. My stomach cramped, and I felt a dampness, a slickness in my knickers. "It's best if we leave her alone. But tomorrow." He stopped, sniffed the air, stared at my legs, my hands fidgeting in my lap. "Tomorrow," he repeated, "things will be different."

Tears welled in my eyes as the pain in my belly increased. I looked down and two salty drops plinked onto my nightie. I hoped I hadn't stained the seat with my blood—how could I hide leather upholstery? I hoped it hadn't spread beyond my shift, beyond my skin. Ma would be so disappointed.

"I'm sorry," I mumbled.

Again, Mister Pérouse patted my knee. Patted and patted, the motion fervent and hypnotic. He licked his lips, and tore his gaze away with visible effort.

♪

Things changed the next morning, but not for the better.

The sun was inching over the horizon by the time we arrived at Mister Pérouse's compound. There were no houses around, no farmsteads. The land here was untilled, untenable: skeletons of crops long gone to seed stretched as far as I could see, dotted here and there with sentinel trees and shacks even hobos would disdain. Anyone with a mind for survival long ago followed the highway, arrow-straight and pointing the only way out of here. A wall rose ten metres high and ran a jagged loop around the property, too long for me to judge its distance at this early hour. Layers of grime outlined its rough sandstone surface, the lower half shadowed further with soot. The gatehouse, smooth white plaster cornered with chunky yellow bricks, was dingy with dirt. Rows of barred and blackened windows perforated the walls, bracketing a tall set of arched double doors.

I knuckled my eyes as Mister Pérouse hefted Harley over his shoulder, leaving the Porter kids in the backseat for the moment. Grit and sleep blurred my sight as I followed him into the dark gatehouse, then beyond into a courtyard that smelled dank with an undertone of manure. Inside, peak-roofed walkways connected a series of wooden buildings, all bleached pale grey and pocked with patches of silver-green lichen. I could see the bottom half of an old barn, empty of horses, slumping close on our left; three large pens to our right, in which dozens of hogs lolled, grunting as they slept; five or six little shacks a few hundred metres away, their windows dark and chimneys cold. Pigeons cooed from the rafters overhead, dropping feathers and dead spiders as we passed beneath. I kept my head low, and prayed we wouldn't emerge covered in droppings. At the far end of the promenade down which Mister Pérouse led us, the first storey of the largest mansion—or warehouse? I couldn't tell which—I had ever seen blocked my view of anything else.

I stepped off the path and into the yard as dawn licked red streaks across the building. Caught a glimpse of three or four more hulking storeys; rectangular windows boarded up; a crooked weathervane squeaking a slow circle above a gable—then Mister Pérouse hauled me back into the shadows.

"I weren't dallying," I said, but he silenced me with a glance. Behind us, the gatehouse door opened and I could hear that Arianne-woman as she spoke to the doctor; her voice grating across my soul. I was almost overwhelmed by an urge to hide behind Mister Pérouse's thick cloak. Instead, I patted Harley's back to reassure him everything was fine; straightened my shoulders as the great door clanged shut. The sound of iron bolts shunting into place rang across the courtyard.

I swallowed tears and dust. My neck was stiff from sleeping upright, my heart stiffer at the thought of Ma sick and alone at home.

"It's rude to linger in doorways," Mister Pérouse said, striding past. "Come."

Eventually I got used to the command in his tone, but right then it came as a surprise. As long as I'd known him he'd always been, if not jolly, at least pleasant. Friendly in that way adults are with children who aren't their own: familiar and a little bit fake. His presence used to set us at ease—we knew he'd make Ma happy.

But this Mister Pérouse was different. This version showed an interest that demanded attention. He made my stomach roil.

Inside the hallway stretched from left to right, describing the Haven's perimeter instead of plunging straight into its heart. We crossed it in no more than ten steps, the sound of our footfalls petering out before reaching its ends. Mister Pérouse took me by the hand. Led me into a room resounding with the whisperings of children.

Large enough to house at least three barns end to end, it nevertheless felt claustrophobic as soon as Mister Pérouse closed the doors behind us. Columns ran in arches around its border, dividing the space into cloisters. Single beds with woollen blankets and plain pillows were tucked behind these pillars, placed in orderly lines against the chocolate brown walls, leaving the larger, central part of the room free. All around us snippets of sound murmured up to the ceiling, four storeys above our heads. Shuttered galleries climbed the walls, gazed blindly down on two long refectory tables running lengthwise down the centre of a hardwood floor. Skylights

perforating the ceiling would have brightened the place enormously
had they not been covered in cardboard. Instead, dim light issued
from oil lamps dangling from chains and dotting the tabletops.

At the back, three groups of school desks, a dozen at least, were
arranged in rough circles. A stern-looking man slipped into the
room, and with a nod from Mister Pérouse locked the door. He
crossed to consult a young girl who'd obviously been supervising
the students in his absence; his tweed jacket, matching pants,
and bowler hat could've easily been rented at Ma's shop. One
by one, the kids sitting or standing there noticed our entrance.
Conversations hushed. Pencils and books hung forgotten in hands
that had stopped tidying up. Pink irises shone as they all openly
stared.

"Good morning, children." Mister Pérouse waited until he had
everyone's attention. "How go the lessons? Diction? Vocabulary?
Memory-drills? I trust you've all had a productive night."

A babble of replies, all positive, filled our ears. At the sound of
so many voices, Harley lifted his head, and looked blearily at our
surroundings.

"Ma?" he croaked.

I reached up and absentmindedly patted my brother's cheek
while trying not to goggle at the other kids. Bright eyes ringed with
dark circles were worn all around; hair slicked colourless with
grease; skin the hue of old lard. To someone accustomed to unique
outfits, bright fabrics, elaborate headwear, the *sameness* of their
features, the sloppiness of their clothes, was breathtaking. Here
it was dull tartan dresses for the girls, short pants and collared
shirts for the boys. On the far wall, boxy jackets hung neglected
on hooks, dust lying thick across their shoulders. No jewellery to
speak of. No hats.

"Good," Mister Pérouse continued, his breath fogging in the
chill air. "We've been blessed with six new souls today—and if
all goes well Jacques and Théo should return with more. For now,
Dr Jeffries, I'll trust you to amend your lessons to accommodate
five extra pupils. Initiate them quickly: these children have been
unschooled for far too long."

"I know what I'm doing, Anton."

Mister Pérouse conceded the point with a tilt of his head, but
still proceeded with his instructions. "No field trips until they are

made familiar with the curriculum, *d'accord*? *Bon*. Now, as for the rest of you, allow me to introduce Harold *et* Adelaide."

My heart stopped at the names. I was sure he knew us better than that.

"Excuse me, sir," I said, shivering with more than cold. Ma taught me always to be polite, especially when correcting someone's mistake. "That's *Harley* and I'm *Ada*."

Mister Pérouse's only reaction was to adjust his hold on Harl, and place a heavy hand on my shoulder. "The sun is well up, children. Help get Harold ready for bed. The Haven is his home now: make him welcome. Adelaide, this way."

My feet were rooted to the floor as Harl was passed from Mister Pérouse to a boy a year or two older than me. Everything about him was lanky: limbs, earlobes, unkempt fringe. He carried my brother in arms that looked like bone sheathed in tissue, too weak even for such a light burden. But when he smiled his teeth were overly long. Sharp and white. The cleanest things in the room.

A panel stood open in the far wall, not so much a door as a breach in the room's symmetry. Mister Pérouse drew me through it, then I was led down a narrow hallway. Small electric lights nestled in wall sconces, illuminating little but a series of old photographs—all depicting my guide standing proudly beside class after class of the Haven's students. His steps were assured even in the darkness between lamps; I knew he could run these corridors blindfolded, if necessary. I stumbled in the black, and was pathetically grateful for the bulbs' small haloes. I needed their comfort.

It's weird how, in moments of panic, our minds focus on absurdities. Though my pulse raced and my throat cramped from holding back tears, I found myself wondering why they'd used plastic lights shaped like candlesticks; why they'd topped them with glass flames. Why not use real candles? And if they could see fine without them, why turn the things on? Except to allow black-and-white children, their faces so like the ones I'd just met they could have been one and the same, to follow me with their eyes as we sped past. They watched, expressionless, organised and catalogued in their wooden frames, as my feet were dragged along grooves their soles had worn in the floor.

Mister Pérouse's apartments were at the far end of the manse. Up three flights of stairs, along the hall, and back down so many steps we might have ended up in the basement. My legs were shaking by the time we arrived; blood dripped down my thighs. A receiving room, a study, a chamber maid's cupboard, and a master bedroom with modern en suite were all barricaded behind a thick oak door, secured with a brass deadbolt. The costumes he'd worn to Ma's parties spilled from a wardrobe, littered his bed. Their fine fabric chafed my skin when he threw me upon them. When he showed me, in no uncertain terms, what my role was to be in this household.

I flailed and kicked. My screams, half-formed and breathless; wrists trapped in the vice of his hands. I butted my head against his until my skull ached, but he simply leaned back, waited for me to tire. He used the advantage years of practice had given him, pinning me down with his torso. Hungry saliva dripped on my cheek, trickled down my neck.

"Mama, Mama, Mama," I cried, as he shoved my nightie up, pulled my drawers down, revealed the mess of blood between my legs. He wriggled more firmly on top of me, pressed my arcing back flat with his weight, then slid down my body until his face was in line with my crotch.

"Your mother is dead," he said, matter-of-factly. His tongue, rough as a cat's, began to rasp along my inner thighs.

No. The fight, the life went out of me. *She can't be.* I'd squeezed my eyes shut, but now they flew open. My mind was blank, my mind raced. I looked up, not down. Ma's voice rang in my ears, telling Harley tales. The cinnamon smell of her breakfast oatmeal filled my nostrils—not sweat, not blood, not Mister Pérouse's lamb-carcass breath. In my mouth, raspberry cordial laced with brandy; the drink Ma gave me the first time I'd hidden my blood-soaked rags. *No, no, no.* I looked up, *stared* up. A watermark shaped like our state stained the ceiling. I tried to pinpoint the county where I grew up—a splotch of mould covered it. Covered Ma. I cried out—

Not dead.

I didn't look down; wouldn't. In my mind I saw Mister Pérouse's chin drip with my blood. Saw his teeth lengthen, glistening and red. Felt them pierce. The prod of his tongue. Sucking, drinking deep. Taking his fill.

Everything was silent.

A tornado howled through the room.

Face contorted, mouth shaped words. Expression evangelical, like Bible-bashers Ma sent from our door each Sunday. Still wearing the cowboy coat she'd made, he slithered back on top. Nicked the tip of his penis. Smeared his blood. Mixed it with mine.

Searing pain to dull throb. Breath whooshed out. In and out.

In and out.

His body preached at mine: I didn't hear a thing. I looked at the county lines overhead, traced their borders with my eyes.

No.

He grew stronger, stronger. Licked my jugular. Moaned. Didn't bite.

Numb, I watched us from the settee on the opposite side of the room. Looked at the spectacle we made on my mother's costumes. My legs like slabs of ham on the mattress. His hips twitching, plunging. My hands clenching, unclenching, clenching. Intent and inert.

Waited for him to finish. Waited for my spirit to return. Waited to feel.

Not dead.

𝄞

I didn't see Harley or the girls for days afterwards. By then I was too tired to be scared for any of us.

Mister Pérouse kept me in his bedroom until my menses stopped flowing. Nightmares plagued me all day, then came to life at dusk. For five nights he drank his fill, reopened the thin cut on his cock, climbed on top of me. Humming all the while about a child born of blood. He rubbed my belly before pulling out, for luck or to mark his territory, or both.

Though they came knocking, claiming their turns with the 'live one', Mister Pérouse wouldn't let Théo or Jacques in. "*Mais, monsieur,*" they'd protest, their voices muffled through the door. "Arianne hasn't bled for decades—"

My master wouldn't hear a word against her. "Patience, *les gars.* I won us three *filles* this time, *non*? The two youngest are yours—take them as gifts. *Pour vous remerciez.*"

The men said nothing.

"Aha," said Mister Pérouse, sighing, rolling off me. "You've opted for the weakling's fare—sucking a few hours' of youth from babes—and now you're here to challenge me? *Mais c'est drôle!* You want the Prime's share? You haven't the patience. *Mon dieu,* our houseful of little changed ones prove *you have not the patience.* A few short human years—what is that to us? a blink, no more—and Adelaide's sisters could have been yours for breeding. To start your own empires, *peut-être?* They've many years of blood in them, these girls; many chances of bearing true kin. Can't you see the benefit in that? Our numbers increased with children *born,* not simply *made?* Reinvigorating our bloodlines, *les gars.* Extending it, drawing power direct from the fountainhead. From our newborns right back to Adam's kin, *comprends?* Linked all the way back to the *source.*"

I didn't hear the men's responses. My eyelids drooped; I pulled a chenille blanket up to still my shivering. If the past few evenings were any indication, Mister Pérouse would want another round with me before morning. I needed sleep more than information.

By the end of the week my master looked healthier, stronger. Ten years younger, more than fit to squash Jacques and Théo if they razzed him without the protection of three inches of oak. His back was straight, step springy, as he set me in the chamber maid's closet, and told me to get cleaned up for school.

"You must learn to speak properly, Adelaide, if you are to raise our child to prominence. I will not have my heir speaking like a *pécore* for all his mother's failings. Fine soaps will only scrub so much of the yokel from you, *chèrie.*"

I didn't want to wash, I wanted to go home. But the windows were blocked, the outer doors bolted; my freedom subject to Mister Pérouse's whim. And for the first time since my arrival he fancied I could be let out. I could see other people. So I rubbed myself raw with the soap and sponge he provided, then slipped on a uniform so misshapen a hundred other girls might've worn it before. I folded my nightie and stuffed it beneath the low pallet I'd sleep on when my master had no other use for me. The shift was soiled and smelled rotten, but it was my last tie with Ma. I didn't want to look at it, couldn't bear to throw it away.

I don't know what happened to Harley's clothes. Like me, he was now dressed in a drab copy of the other children's outfits. Unlike me, he looked content to be so.

"You okay?" His neck was swaddled with bandages, and the sun was fading from his skin. Veins were visible in his eyelids and temples and he smelled of sour milk. I brushed my hand through his hair, trying to ignore the hints of grease I found there, and pulled him close. He returned my embrace quickly then stepped away, too embarrassed to be seen hugging his sister with so many eyes watching. The other children were too occupied with their tasks to notice. Some recited poems in my master's language; some tidied the beds, then arranged folding screens to separate sleep and work areas; some clambered high up the walls, scaling the bricks from gallery to gallery under Dr Jeffries' watchful eye. No matter how hard I tried, I couldn't see any ropes. Catching my perplexed gaze, Harley shrugged and rubbed his hand along his jaw, so much like his father it hurt.

"Mister told us about Ma," he said. "Beth and Miah ain't took it so good—Miss Arianne gave them medicines so's they'd calm down. They're a lot better now, though."

"And you?" I asked.

Again, that shrug. Who was this boy? The Harl I knew got fired up if he didn't get his way; if he thought Ma spent more time with us girls than with him. And now that she's dead? A shrug. It didn't make sense.

"My gums is sore," he said, almost sheepishly.

"Give us a look." To my surprise, he peeled back his lips and opened his mouth. I couldn't trust what I saw: it wasn't bright enough where we were standing. I drew Harl over to the first long dining table, sat him close to the lamp. The results were the same.

His incisors, top and bottom, were more than twice their usual length. I explored their rough edges, hoping touch would prove their appearance a trick of the light.

Gently, I positioned my forefinger behind the tooth and pulled towards me. It had grown far too sharp, far too long. I tried again, just to be sure it was real, and as I did so a pearl of creamy liquid, like snake venom or dandelion milk, beaded on my fingertip.

"That hurt?" I asked, tugging, watching the drop grow fat and heavy. The syrup spilled over, soon began marbling with red. Harley's blood oozed down the length of my finger and pooled, ghosted with white fluid, in my palm.

"Nuh." He shook his head, unintentionally snicking my digit in the process.

"Watch it," I said, snatching my hand away, sucking to stem the flow—

—being leached from my neck. No; Harley's neck. Energy sapping from my body, pulsating. Teeth stinging like horseflies in the dip beside my collarbone, the crook of my elbow. Smiling faces, kissing, drinking. "He tastes like swimming," *a high voice says. That's Nellie Porter, maybe. Or Ike. No: Ike's at my feet, draining the webbing between my toes. They like me, I think—* Harl thinks: *and,* They need me. *I'm warm, so warm the room is fuzzy. I'm sleepy, so sleepy. I can hardly feel the table beneath my back. My plate is broken; rare beef from dinner squelches under my hip.* "He tastes like sunshine," *says Alistair. I giggle. My friend is giving me a hickey, and now there's a fire in my belly. A hunger. I sit up, nip him on the shoulder. Barely break the skin.* "That's enough." *Dr Jeffries claps, whistles till the tingling stops.* "End of lesson." *The small mouths pull away, melt into the room's dim corners. The doctor keeps Ike and Alistair back.* "What have I told you? Stun with the jus; drink only enough to make you feel strong; bite hard to inject your charge. Don't be greedy: no killings within the Haven." *My head is woozy, I can't lift it to see where they've gone. Too heavy.* "No killings in the family—"

"When did this happen?"

Harley looked at me like I'd gone crazy. "What?"

"This —" I licked the last trace of Harley's venom-laced blood from my finger. "*This.*" I yawned, felt a prickling in my lips. "The biting, them other kids—"

"Oh, that." Harl crossed his arms, flicked a lock of hair from his eyes. "Ain't nothing. You know, it happens."

I wasn't convinced by his cool demeanour. Again, I tasted the blood and milk from Harl's tooth, and it hit me like a kick to the ribs. The scent of cedar and hot dirt. Bullfrogs at the bottom of gullies on our land like croaking men clearing their throats. Ma's chamomile shampoo. Her soft singing lifted on bathroom steam. Pure, unrefined memories of home. The other children had tasted these moments. Ingested them. And Harl hadn't stopped them.

"I can't believe you'd let them do that to you," I hissed, emphasising the word *let.* "You ain't even tried to stop them—not even a little bit!"

Harl sighed, and for the third time his shoulders rose and fell noncommittally. He looked empty. Emptier. "I can't always fight, Ada. Not always."

Beth kicked me in the shins when I took her face in my hands, drew her mouth to mine, and sucked blood and venom from her teeth. Where Harl's fangs had grown close together, adding a rat's angular profile to his already narrow features, Beth's had sprouted from her canines. Blunt but strong. When the hanging lights reflected in her dark eyes, she was no longer a seven-year-old girl but a feral cat.

I dragged her behind a folding screen, checked that no-one could see us, and sat her down on the foot of a cot.

"This ain't—*isn't*—my bed, Ada. I mean, Adelaide. Mine's over there—"

"Quiet," I hissed, grabbing her face again and drinking. I stopped the instant the flavour of her memories shifted from ash to honey, when the liquid was more red than clear. My mouth was numb from her poison; it itched down my throat, made me woozy. Beth bit my lip as I pulled away—then immediately asked what had happened, why was there blood on my chin? Exhaling, I swallowed visions of her and Miah smothered in a swarm of grabbing hands; suckling at Arianne's shrivelled neck and breasts. Something was missing, and it wasn't just my sister's memory of the past thirty seconds.

There was no essence of fear. Not in Beth, not in Harl. Tinges of sorrow seasoned the cloudy blood I drank, yet it wasn't overwhelming. It wasn't purely their own. They felt Ma's loss, I could taste it. But not acutely, not like I did. That sadness was buried in them, beneath dozens of other, foreign sadnesses. Those they'd adopted from their new playmates.

For a few moments Beth was bright and happy, the way she'd always been at home, and I knew it was because of me. When she sat on my lap, wrapping her scrawny arms around my waist, the hug she gave was genuine. Threading her fingers through my hair, she seemed content. Harley loitered by the closest pillar and watched us for a while, not joining in but not discouraging. I wanted to ask him to come sit with us, to hide beneath the blankets, to help keep the ghosts at bay.

But at that moment Arianne strode past a gap between the screens concealing us from the common room, leading by the hand the boy who'd carried Harley the day we'd arrived. His eyes were glazed, a silly smile plastered on his face. His feet scuffled along the floor as though too heavy to lift.

Four steps later, the clunking of Arianne's heels stopped. Four more steps brought her back, her glare so sharp I winced. She released her companion's hand, then pushed the screen away, sending it clattering to the floor.

"*Va t'en!*" she growled at Beth, her gaze never leaving mine.

She wrenched Beth from my lap, slapped her bottom. "Go!"

Harley shrank from Arianne's wrath, inched away to avoid drawing her attention. As it was, he could have tap-danced and she wouldn't have noticed: her crimson-eyed stare was reserved for me.

"Stay away, you *espèce de salope*! You'll have your own soon enough—these are not for you."

I rose clumsily. "Arianne—"

She held up her hand to silence me. "*Non*—not a word, *petite bête*. The classroom, you can enter. Do not come behind here again."

As though on cue, Dr Jeffries called us to our lessons. Diction and composition first; then while the other children climbed, learned techniques of stealth, and practiced bleeding each other on the table, I was isolated from the group. Taught to pore over books tracing the history of Mister Pérouse's people. By the time the tutorials were over, I was shaken—and Beth's posture had stiffened. When I crossed to her circle of desks, she looked at me as she would a stranger. Her mouth twitched, barely suppressing a hiss.

Harl had drifted away to join Alistair and the other boys. His footsteps already more like floating than walking.

♪

For the next two years I did what I could for Harley and the girls. I'd milk them whenever they let me; whenever Arianne was away; whenever Mister Pérouse released me from our rooms. I dreaded the coming of my bloods, not because it meant I'd have to endure my master's attentions—these moon-time visits were exercises in stamina on his part, and I'd become expert at *being* and *not being* there while they lasted—but because it meant I was kept away from the kids.

Twice it seemed Mister Pérouse's work had paid off: my periods stopped, the second time for twelve weeks. My master, already confident in his role as Prime, now strutted like a peacock as he gave Théo and Jacques their instructions; directing them to tackle Tapekwa County next, to find themselves suitable mates in Napanee. To steal farmers' young, the more isolated the better, to become pupils of Mister Pérouse's *school*. Fatherhood, it seemed, made him benevolent.

He let me wander wherever I wanted, the child in my womb almost as good as a skeleton key. Whispers followed me as I roamed the hallways, or dropped in on Dr Jeffries' classes. "Breeder," the children would say, perhaps at Arianne's bidding. Perhaps not: often the jealousy in their words rang too true to be second-hand. "Breeding *enculeuse*." They taunted me for doing what they couldn't yet do—their metabolisms so slow now fifty years would pass before they hit puberty. Sometimes I think Harley joined in, just to be one of the crowd. But with Mister Pérouse's spawn in my belly, none of them could do more than jeer. Even Arianne was compelled to leave me alone. And when her back was turned, I'd inevitably make my way to one of two places: the front doors, to test the locks; or the dormitory behind the screens, to draw poison from my sisters' mouths.

In these quiet moments, the girls would become themselves again; all smiles, crass jokes, and innocence. Hearing them giggle, anxiety would seep from my body and I'd weep with relief.

At the Haven, joys like these were always short-lived.

Soon it became clear that my understanding of the girls' happiness didn't quite match their reality. Though he wouldn't admit it, Harley could remember our other life: Ma and her friends, the itch of newly-sewn garments, the brush of wind on our sunburnt faces. But Miah? She was three when we came here. Now five, she'd spent nearly half her life in this place. *This* was what she knew, *this* was her home. No doubt she'd be as fond of the fields and the sun as she would a stake through her heart. She thought it a game when I drew sap from her baby teeth, a romp like the ones she enjoyed with the other kids. She didn't know any different: she'd snap at my cheeks, then wait for my reaction, just as she would when seeking her classmates' approval. None of the children looked more than a week or two older than when we first arrived, while I continued to grow up as well as out. Beth and Mia laughed at the changes in my height and figure—and when they did, I'd pluck at their fangs until my fingers were thick with scratches. Always, I came away from these meetings coughing up dust.

I didn't realise I could give something back, return parts of their memories, until I miscarried the second time. Arianne had sniffed the truth of my loss before I was aware of it myself—her knowing laugh was triumphant and bitter. Her teeth were so sharp; her hunger was sharper. The scent of my baby's death beguiled her. She followed me so close, waiting for the blood to flow, that Mister Pérouse sequestered me in his rooms three days early.

The pain of expelling the foetus kept me bedridden that whole time.

My master's old mattress had long ago conformed to my shape. I aligned my back with the contour earlier versions of me had made, and tried to ignore the sound of his jaw cracking as he devoured the remnants of our failure. I imagined it was all the same to him; he benefitted whether the child stayed in my belly or was digested in his. I convinced myself he wouldn't be angry for something beyond my control. And for a moment, I almost believed it.

Sucking the blood off his fingers, Mister Pérouse's face was pure joy, almost handsome. He actually smiled as he leaned back. I didn't know how to react. Then he exhaled, and disappeared.

Disappeared.

Two years ago, I'd have leapt from the bed right then. Tried my hand at the door, tried anything to get free. Now I was smarter—I knew this wasn't the right time. He'd never done this before, never just dropped out of sight, but he wouldn't have left me this way. I froze while my gaze darted like a frightened goldfish. *That's it.*

Body tense, I sat up, suddenly gasping. *He's not gone.*

I can still hear him breathing.

I felt his weight on the mattress before I saw his shadow reappear, growing from pale grey to charcoal across the floor, his youthful features brightening back into view.

"*Merveilleux,*" he whispered, actually grinning. "See what we can do, Adelaide? The two of us together?"

I tried to smile, I honestly did. But if devouring the hint of a child meant he could vanish at will, what would happen when I carried one to term . . .

My master's expression darkened at my silence. He fingered the puckered wounds his teeth had left; two deep blots of red, oozing far below my navel. In that instant, he looked so much like Arianne I gasped.

"Stay away from those children," he said, remnants of my milkings rancid on his breath.

"I wi—" He crushed the lie from my mouth, his kiss a punishment not a reward. Out of habit, I ran my tongue up and down sharp fangs, sucked. He gouged at the insides of my lip, pierced the soft palate, scraped until blood from my shredded gums mingled with that from my womb. Blended with the potent serum stretching like cobwebs from the tips of his teeth.

Oh, what a feast of visions.

In his mouth I tasted incoherent feathers of our unborn baby's thoughts. I sampled my agony, distilled in his venom. But there was more, much more: Miah's giggles as Ma tickled her feet; Beth's disappointment when the birthday cake she'd baked for me sank in the middle, a cool draught from the chimney flue ruining her hard work; and Harley, confident as only ten-year-old boys can be, leaping from high rocks into the black waters of a quarry on the edge of our property. Their joy, their recollections, trapped in Mister Pérouse's bloodstream.

He's bitten them, I thought, and in the same instant, *I've tasted these moments in their teeth.*

Which did he get from their necks? Which from the depths of my belly?

My head spun with the power of his sedative, but I lapped at his fangs until my jaw ached. I swallowed all the memories he'd stolen. Kept drinking until their tone changed, deepened. Aged with Mister Pérouse's years. I gulped his love for Arianne, as a mother or wife I couldn't tell; slurped the certainty that Théo—his own cousin!—was kept close for enmity more than friendship; savoured all the small vipers in Dr Jeffries' schoolroom, now knowing they were offspring he had *made* not *fathered*. Just like Harley, me and the girls, they all came from poor families, single mothers—humans my master deigned unworthy of raising children. I drank it all in, this and more, until I was too drowsy to move. Until all I could feel was a weight like lead in my guts.

I did as my master bid for several weeks, though I would've rebelled given the chance. If Mister Pérouse could leach the children's blood and *jus* from my stomach, I realised, they could do the same. I could rescue their memories, I knew it.

I could return them. *Re-turn them.*

So I kissed Mister Pérouse, devoured him whenever he came close enough to bite. Let him take my interest as affection, as enthusiasm, as a gesture of reconciliation; let him think I was grateful for being his brood mare. I didn't care, so long as his mouth was on mine and my family's history trickling down my throat.

In those moments, I closed my eyes and imagined the sensation of Beth and Miah's tiny bites as they drank down forgotten stories. But no matter how hard I tried, I couldn't picture Harley joining in.

♪

That image of my sisters sustained me for five months. I tried reading to pass the time but the books cluttering Mister Pérouse's apartments were failed distractions; their plots like snowflakes melting in my fevered mind. I hardly remembered a word. Always I thought of the girls as the days turned to weeks, refined my plan until the flutter of kicks in my womb drove me to act. I needed fresh air if this third baby was to survive; I needed to move. More than anything, I needed to see if I was right.

When Théo delivered my food tray, as he had morning after morning, I stopped him before he went to bed.

Lifting my hand from his sleeve as though it were infected, he sneered at my belly. "You think to keep this one, *non?*"

"She'll survive," I agreed, positive my child was a girl. I straightened into every inch of my height, a head taller than Théo. Looking down, I met his gaze and held it. A shadow fell across his face. He tilted his bald head, stared up at me with magpie eyes. If I'd flinched then, the moment would've been broken, my opportunity lost. But though I spoke quickly, my voice was steady. "I can barely breathe in here —" Carefully-timed pause. "You don't know what it's like to be trapped, Théo."

He didn't blink. A slight frown furrowed his forehead. Of course he knew what it was to be held unwillingly. He'd been here three times longer than I'd lived. Was that enough to poison his mind? Enough to convince him to let me out? Maybe not, but I was willing to risk it. Even those whose hearts have stopped beating must *feel*, sometimes. Loneliness isn't governed by the warmth in our veins.

"I just need to see my family," I said. "I'll come right back—I just want to kiss them goodnight."

Théo snorted. "*Sensiblerie.* Stupid girl, what do I care for family?"

Silently, I wrapped my arms around myself and hunched. Tried to make myself look small and vulnerable. Again, Théo blew air from his lips; half laugh, half derision. I didn't respond, but sank to the edge of Mister Pérouse's bed as his cousin left the room. The door closed with a hollow clunk.

Floorboards creaked as he paused on the other side. The key slid in, scraped out.

There was no sound of bolts shifting home.

I waited a heartbeat, two; then sprang to my feet, crept to the door. Pressing my ear to the wood, I could hear the diminishing scuff of Théo's boots as he moved down the corridor. Away from me.

My pulse was so loud in my ears I couldn't tell if he'd actually gone or if it was a trick. Taking deep breaths, I steadied myself— or tried to. Of its own volition, my shaking hand moved to the doorknob, turned. Spots whirled in front of my eyes; the excitement was almost too much. Exhaling, I flung open the door.

I sped toward my sisters as though I were being chased.

They showed no delight in seeing me, not until I guided them away from Harley and the boys to the private corner where Beth's bed resided. Harl watched us pass but pretended not to: his back was too stiff, his laugh too loud to be natural. The girls didn't spare him a second look. Frantically, I pulled the screens to; quickly, so quickly. When I thought we were out of his sight, I raised my pinafore and urged my sisters to drink. Then, finally, they were all smiles. Voracious and thirsty.

Stretched out on Beth's quilt, I closed my eyes. Mister Pérouse rarely lifted my skirts higher than necessary; so unless they marred my neck or cleft, he wouldn't see any marks they made. I bit my tongue when their fangs perforated my belly. Again and again, their heads bobbed as they sought the sweetest blood I had to offer. I directed them around the places I thought my daughter lay curled—soon a double band of dripping holes was scratched beneath my ribcage. Time slowed. I floated on their quiet slurping, the musk of unwashed skin and blankets. I didn't have to force them off me; satiated, they stopped on their own. Looking at the mess of red pooled beneath me, soaked into mattress and clothes, I hoped they'd guzzled enough to remember.

For a moment, none of us spoke. Miah sniffed, went back for seconds. My heart sank. I couldn't bear to look at her, or at Beth. Couldn't see the forgetful glimmer in their eyes, the dew on their lips.

I'd done it for nothing. Risked everything for nothing.

"I've got to go." I swallowed the lump in my throat, and gently pushed to dislodge Miah. Tried to muster sufficient energy to stand. "Dawn's breaking: time for night creatures to go to sleep."

Warm tears spilled over my cheeks as Beth wriggled up beside me until her head was parallel with mine. Flinging an arm across my chest, she squeezed and said, "Tell us a story before you go. The one Ma always told. You know, with the crazy bird in the gumdrop tree? The one who cried and cried instead of laughed and laughed?"

"Okay," I said, though I could hardly speak for crying, hardly breathe for hugging. Beth's eyes had gone from pink to blue. Focused. Clearer than I'd seen them in two and a half years. A giggle burst from my throat, and its echo came from Beth's. Neither of us had heard that story since Miah was smaller than the baby inside me. My laughter died off as I looked at my youngest sister. When I began the tale, the pressure of her mouth at my waist increased. Nothing more.

"Once upon a time—"

"*Qu'est ce que tu fais?*"

Mister Pérouse's voice whipped me upright. In a blur he was upon me. His fingernails pierced the soft flesh in my upper arm; yanking me from the bed, he knocked the girls to the floor like ragdolls. Neither of them cried out: already the memories were fading from Beth's eyes. "It isn't enough!" My face hot with tears. "I need more time." But there was none to be had.

A fist slammed into my cheek. I stumbled, skinned my knees. He pulled me up, tearing my hair, my dress. Théo shook his head, pretended not to hear the commotion as he skittered up the far wall, taking refuge in a fourth-floor balcony. Arianne nodded at my master; with a lift of her eyebrow, beckoned him to visit her chamber after punishments had been meted. Few of Mister Pérouse's young flunkies paid any attention, no matter how hard I sobbed, nor how loudly I begged as he dragged me down the hallway. Except, that is, for Harley. Shuffling from foot to foot, he loitered just outside the *grande salle*. Like a puppy waiting to be let in after he'd done his business.

Like a messenger just returned from an errand.

Harl averted his eyes as we screamed past. Back to Mister Pérouse's apartments; back to thick musty draperies; back to stagnant air. I cried out and clawed at the wallpaper, at the doorframes, until my nails were split and bleeding. Harley followed, staring at his toes. My stomach churned with lava. Rage, not fear, filled my mouth. I spat at my brother, a big shining gob of hate.

The least I could do, the most I could do, was ruin the traitor's boots.

𝄞

Rats crawled all over me.

Claws scritching, scratching; jaws squeaking like door hinges. Skittering across the storage room's cold concrete floor, they spoke with my brother's voice.

"Get up," they said. Thump, thump; a herd of them landed on my shoulder. Jump, jump; they urged me awake.

"Get up," they repeated. I didn't want to. My head was heavy, my lashes stuck together with the glue of dried tears. The bites on my stomach itched, already healing; the bruises Mister Pérouse had left on my face, thighs and buttocks throbbed. My ears rang with the sound of his blows, the echo of his words.

"You think I've hidden you for my sake?" Whack. *"Imbécile."* Whack. *"Idiot."* Pause. *"I've done this for you,"* whack, *"not*

me." Whack, whack. "*For the baby.*" Whack. Whack. Whack. "*He'll not be born for years if you're turned.*" Whack. Pause. "*We don't need another Arianne!*"

My cheeks grew hot with shame. They stung like someone was slapping me. I rolled over, but the feeling persisted.

Someone was slapping me.

"I'm sorry," I said to the baby.

"Get up, hurry! It's almost dusk—he'll be awake soon."

I peeled my eyelids apart; it hardly made a difference. Harley's silhouette blocked most of the light sneaking in from the corridor. Eyes open or closed, the space was dark, and so small it hardly deserved to be called a room. It was barely a cupboard, just outside my master's quarters; no more than a few metres deep, half again as wide. Bare shelves lined the walls and a rusted bed frame was crammed in at the back. Three of its legs were twisted. One was snapped off at the base.

I sat up, my back and joints aching. The baby turned and kicked, as unhappy to sleep on the floor as her mother. Harley put down the pail and broom he carried, then pulled at my hand, "Come on. You don't have much time and this—" he gestured at the cleaning supplies "—won't fool anyone for long."

It took me a second to realise what his presence meant. "You have a key?"

The question was redundant: I could see it clutched in his fist. I stared at him, mouth agape. My hand rose to my belly, and Harl read the gesture for what it was: *Why haven't you used it before now?*

"I don't want any trouble. Just go. You're ruining everything, Adelaide." Adelaide, not Ada. "It was all fine—everything is *fine*. We're happy here. I'm happy. We're *happy*." He dragged me to my feet. The door was open, yet I couldn't go through it.

"Harl—"

He shook his head. "See? That's what I mean. My name is Harold—get used to it." His voice went up an octave, and for a second he was the little boy I chased snakes with. The boy who leaped from quarry ridges, a coconut oil sheen on his skin. "But you can't, can you?"

I thought I'd wept myself dry on the storage room floor, but my sight blurred as I looked at this young man who'd taken over my little brother's body.

"No," I said. "No."

Emotions streamed across Harley's face; I couldn't catch all of them. Confusion? Maybe. Disappointment? Certainly. And resolution. Yes, that most of all.

I looked for love, for remorse.

Kept looking.

"Go," he said, firm as the key he pressed into my palm. "Go home. Now."

"Oh, Harl." My voice cracked as I squeezed his hand. "I'll get Bethany, you get Miah—"

He pulled away. "No, Ada. Just you."

I stopped halfway out the door. Miah might be lost, but there was still hope for Beth. "It won't take long, I'll just—"

"No." Every line in Harley's face read, *Don't make me regret this.* "Just nothing. Leave."

Ma would be so upset if I left them alone. *There's so many dangerous critters in this land,* she'd reminded me, almost every day, before she went to work. Then she'd tickle me until I squirmed, adding a witch's cackle to her voice. *And ain't they all got a hankering for children's sweet meat!*

Irrational, unbidden thoughts. I stamped them out. "Who'll look after you?"

"Go," he repeated. No reassuring smile, no farewell embrace. "We're fine. We've been doing just fine."

"I can't," I begin to say, but my daughter kicked me into action. *You can,* she assured me with a jab to the ribs. *You will.*

"You sure he's asleep?"

Harley shrugged.

Without another word I slipped from the room, the key warm and slippery with sweat. *I can't thank you,* I wanted to finish, but didn't. Such thanks would be too much for what Harl hadn't done. Too little for what he had.

♪

That evening, I watched the sun set.

Its vibrant colours reduced my eyes to slits. The ochres and golds mirrored the late summer fields; the highway's black line the only sign of what was ground, what sky. I ran towards the road, towards the light. Tried to shake away the darkness. Tried to stop looking over my shoulder, to stop imagining Mister Pérouse appearing, disappearing, appearing. Tried to erase images of Harley luring Jacques away from the front door, and Arianne to his bed. His manipulation, their hunger: a whiff of his lukewarm skin all the bait he needed to secure my escape.

Headlights in the distance spurred me on. I moved as fast as I could, forced to stop and catch my breath too frequently. Even I knew the highway belonged to truckers at night: if I missed this one, another would be along sooner or later. I couldn't afford it to be later.

Dry air scraped in and out of my lungs as I ran. Every tuft of chickweed, every patch of wild wheat seemed to hide my master. I didn't stop at the freeway's edge—lifting a thumb was too subtle for my needs. I staggered onto the road, waited on the painted division between lanes. Solid white double lines: *no passing*. A good omen, I hoped.

The hiss of hydraulic brakes accompanied by blinding headlights. I scurried to the driver's side, knelt like a supplicant. Wasn't refused.

"Where you headed, darlin'?" The trucker nodded as I mentioned the crossroads between our acreage and Kaintuck town. "I know it," he said, lending me a hand getting into the cab, squeezing my fingers as though making sure I was solid. "Buckle up."

He turned the radio on, whistled through tobacco stained teeth along with four hours of country and western tunes. Once, he offered me water and half an egg salad sandwich, both of which I gratefully accepted. Otherwise, the bulge of my belly, the dried blood on my dress, or the anxious scowl on my face kept his eyes on the road, hands firmly on the wheel. When we reached my stop, I had no payment to give him but a smile. He took it kindly then returned it twofold.

"Take care now," he said. "And good luck."

"Thanks." The croak of my voice was lost in the drone of bullfrogs and crickets; the chorus of my childhood. The adrenaline that had sustained me all night left my body in a rush, and exhaustion flooded in. As the truck's taillights winked out over the horizon, I stumbled into a ditch by the roadside, immersed in familiar, foreign sounds. Five kilometres separated me from my family's doorstep, but it might as well have been a million. Every part of me cried out for rest.

I slumped to the ground. With both feet plunged in murky water pooling in the dip of the trench, my face and arms scratched to bits by thistles and long grass, and my back twisted on hard soil, I slept.

I woke hot and thirsty. The sun was a half a hand's width above the hills; the dried grass waving above me scant protection from its harsh rays. I was too exposed: the top of my head felt like it was on fire. Already the water at my feet had dwindled to muck—I scooped up as much as I could, coated my face and hair in it. More mud than liquid, it wasn't fit for drinking. So with a sandpaper tongue and black slop dripping down my back, I started the final leg of my journey home, wishing I had one of Ma's bonnets.

My thoughts wandered as I walked. Would raccoons have infested the house? What if it had burned down? Would there be anything left for me to return to? Would Mister Pérouse have beaten me there? Most of all, would my blood-rags, hidden in jars all these years, still be safe? The urge to destroy them quickened my pace.

In and out, I thought. *Break all blood-ties. Don't let master sniff them out . . .*

I knew I couldn't stay. But it was important I see the place, see that something had remained. That all wasn't lost.

The baby was restless. My stomach didn't stop churning until I got to the familiar wooden fence. Until I followed it to the open gate, rusted but still intact. Until I saw the birches and cedars unscathed by axe or fire. Until I reached the yard and the house. Both worse for years of neglect, but both whole. Both there.

I released a pent-up breath.

Home.

The front lock held, which surprised me. I rattled at the doorknob, but the noise only inspired a scurrying inside. A stir of scrabbling feet.

Raccoons, I thought, relieved. *Or squirrels.* I could handle vermin and I could handle a barred door. These were the least of all evils I'd envisaged. At the back of the house, my bedroom window was slightly ajar. I had no praise for useless gods, just gratitude to the carpenter who'd constructed frames prone to contracting in the heat. After jimmying it with a stick, the glass slid easily in its tracks. The casement was low—any higher and I don't think I could've managed it. My entrance wasn't graceful, but it did the job.

Inside, the air was close and rich with decay. Fluorescent orange splotches of possum piss dotted the sheets and area rugs; brown pellets covered every flat surface and led like a breadcrumb trail out of the room. Slumbering and still, the house wrapped me in its embrace. I walked down the hall carefully, quietly, lest I wake it. The living room was darker than whiskey dregs. My feet crunched across the floorboards, snapping and popping on unseen twigs. At the far side, I stubbed my toe on the corner of the woodstove—it never felt so good letting loose a blue streak of curses.

Heavy woollen curtains, three layers deep, were draped in front of the windows. These were . . . new? I fumbled at the unexpected fabric, trying to recognise it, trying to situate it in my memory of this room. *Light streamed in through the windows the night they came.* I searched for the split between panels. *Light streamed in through the windows the night Ma died.* In the end, I felt my way to the edge: the material was fastened to the wall with staples or pins. Furious, I dug through the layers, through the metal. *How dare they?* I thought, tearing to unveil Ma's picture window. *How dare they.*

"The light! Close it, close it!"

Her voice was a hot poker up my spine. I jumped and spun to see Ma cowering on the couch. She crab-walked into the shadows, looking at me between strands of lank hair. Her figure was wizened beyond recognition. Bones protruded from her chest and shoulders, visible through her threadbare gown. The curve of her stomach was the inverse of mine, despite the litter of rabbit and cat bones on the floor. She continued to plead that I cover the windows—I responded by standing and staring. Her mouth, double-fanged like a panther's, stretched wide; it unleashed a wail of illness and starvation that sent me scaling a rickety chair. Hooking darkness and silence back into place.

Despite my efforts thin shafts of light oozed in, sluggish with dust. Ma's eyes were glassy as she moaned, "Stop haunting me." Knees pulled to her chest, she rocked back and forth mumbling, "Oh Ada, oh my Ada. Jesus Christ, stop haunting me."

Ice water ran through my veins. "I'm here, Ma." She continued her mantra, her rocking. "Ma, I'm here." I hurried to her, arms outstretched. "I'm home. Look: I'm home. I'm home."

"Liar!" The force of her anger was enough to give me whiplash. "That's what you always say—and it just ain't true, Ada. It ain't true . . ."

My knees buckled and I dropped to the couch. "No, Ma." I spoke softly to keep the tremble from my voice. She looked at me sideways, sniffed and tasted the air. "*Liar.*"

"That's the hunger talking, not you." I inched closer, gently laid my hand on her shoulder. I wanted to pull her to me, to fill the gaps between her bones with my tears. But I recognised the look on her face: Mister Pérouse wore it each time my bloods drew near. "Look at me."

She turned away.

"Look at me." I cradled her chin in my hand, not pressing too hard for fear of breaking her. Forced her to see me. To accept me as real. Thinking of the jars I'd kept stacked beneath the front porch, I repeated, "I'm here, Ma. I'm here, and I'll feed you."

Her hallucinations must've never made such an offer. She blinked slowly, focusing her gaze.

"Ada," she croaked. When she frowned the tips of her teeth caught on her bottom lip, distorting her mouth in a maniac's grimace. I wondered which of her fangs would produce the milk, the blood. Which ones I should drain first. She looked down, stared at my belly—her expression frozen between joy and horror. Saliva wet on her lips.

"Oh, Ada." She got up, searched for something on the coffee table, on the armchair, the dining hutch. "Oh, Ada. My baby."

"I kept my blood-rags safe, like you said." I twisted in my seat, followed her bewildering progress from room to room. "You can have them—might not be fresh, but—they're yours. You'll feel better once you've eaten."

Dishes smashed in the kitchen, pots and pans clanging as Ma pushed them aside.

"I remember exactly where I hid them," I continued, clearing a path to the front door. "Just outside—"

"No!" Ma raced over, clasping a hammer. "Don't leave." Her eyes were wild, her breathing frantic. "I swear I ain't never gonna touch a drop from you—from neither of y'all. Them bloods ain't mine, baby. They's yers. All I ask is for you to stay. I swear to God."

And before I could stop her, she kept her promise. Twice the hammer connected with her mouth, an unholy collision of flesh and iron. "Don't leave me alone."

Her words bubbled red as she spat shards of teeth on the floor.

♪

Banjo gathers Ma's few belongings, I collect mine. There's nothing more for us to say: no apologies, no forgiveness. One's not his to give, the other's not mine to request. For now, that's enough.

We wait until nightfall to bundle Ma into Banjo's truck, swaddled in the first cloak she ever sewed: hooded black felt, fringed in elaborate lace. The iron tang of her injury follows us outside. I brush it away with the flies.

"Keep safe," Banjo says, handing me a shotgun and a pouch of ammunition. From its heft, it's filled with enough lead to last until doomsday. Messy bullets, these. The thought of testing them on Mister Pérouse makes me smile. I keep one eye on the horizon, but neither my master nor my father show by the time we say our goodbyes. I check Ma's seatbelt, kiss her forehead, and swear I'll visit soon.

Her words are muffled but I can hear the smile behind them. "That's what you always say, Ada."

No point in waiting until morning; I've grown accustomed to night. Before I leave, I take one last tour of the house. I don't take anything more than I can carry: a sleeping bag and tarp, a good coat, one of Banjo's old packs. A sackful of Ma's finer creations to sell or to cherish—at this stage, I'm not sure which.

Her boots, good as new. Comfortable on my swollen feet.

I tip the candles we lit in the sitting room, wait to make sure they catch. The carpets, curtains, couches wick the eager fire, spread it rumour-fast. Soon the whole house is ablaze. Walking out, I leave the door open.

My lungs stretch full with fresh air.

Flames gnaw at the veranda, chew away the front porch. As I hike down the driveway, I can hear jars shattering, popping. I smile. None will find them now. The heat of my past is warm on my back; before me is only darkness. Gusts of fiery wind urge me forward and I comply. It's time to move. I won't go far; just far enough to be both here and away. To stay alive and reacquaint myself with this land; its lore and its language. Maybe I'll study Ma's pieces, teach myself to sew. And when my daughter is born and can wield the right tools, maybe I'll teach her too. With each stitch she'll discover our history: Ma's and mine. Hers. A child made for darkness, she'll be my shadow as I walk across fields drenched in sun. Wherever we end up, when she's draped in suits of our making, my girl will know where she belongs.

And when it's time, be it a dozen years from now or sixty, she'll know where to bury her blood.

The Wager and
the Hourglass

The Wager and the Hourglass

Never cross a man who smokes his own soul leaf cigars.

In the litany of Daddy's warnings, this is the only one he enforces and breaks in the same breath. The very day the Mayor's eyes first weighed the roundness of my thighs and the child-bearing strength in my back, Daddy strapped a delivery satchel across my shoulder, perched me between Springwell's wings and sent me messagin' from one province to the next. *Out of sight is off the bartering table*, Daddy still says, knowing the Mayor can't hogtie me with a wedding band when I'm in some far-off corner of Alabaska or down a dark hole like Tapekwa County.

Being away don't bother me none. Over the years, I met enough friends to fill a circus, so there's always a warm bed for me on the road. And when there's not I come home, stay an evening or two, let Mamma catch me up on the Mayor's latest doings. How he burns cheroots packed with soul slivers so fine he must've collected them since he was a boy; how he goes on using all that hard-bought power to fill his coffers, in one way or another, without caring who it helps or harms. Daddy gets edgier by the minute when I'm 'round. Soon as the gossip's left Mamma's lips, he fills my pack and saddlebags with at least a week's worth of parcels; tells me to be safe, but be gone. It's not an act of open hostility on our part, this keeping me scarce, not really an obvious affront. Xavier Grace always aims for subtly in his dealings, 'specially when they involve folk like Alimunny Maldoon.

Unlike his daughter.

Back in Plantain for less than a day and already I botched Daddy's plans good and proper. Three arrows jut from my ribs, stretching like quick-movement lines from my back. They clack together and against my bones whenever Springwell lands a hoof. Clenching my teeth, I lean forward and dig my spurs into his heaving sides, praying for shock to work its numbing magic. For now, I have to ignore his frightened whinnying, just like I'm ignoring the agony soaking through my best shirt. Until we've played the Mayor's game, neither of us has time to stop for pain.

Neck straining toward the first of three county lines, muscles frothing as twilight grips the horizon, my steed gallops with an urgency that echoes the throb in my chest. Springwell would fly to save my hearts; the one pounding between my lungs and the other marking each minute, each second, leaking life into my satchel. He would fly, if he still could. But how does Daddy's saying go? *Beware the slip between mind and lip?* A couple measly words lodged in the wrong ear, a few more sent to hook the first ones back—and here we are. Bloodied and running from the saloon, Springwell's shoulders a mash of bruise and broken bone, his white wing feathers snapped and dragging through the muck. Who knows what stung the Mayor's pride more, Cord's careless boast or the one I flung, meaning to distract. You might say a quick tongue's what's left my windcharger in a state no sawbones can fix. Then again, anyone who's had dealings with Maldoon knows that when it comes to the cause and effect of things, it don't pay to go with the obvious.

Already sand streams from my bag, and we're not yet clear of town. Grunting like an old hog, I stand in the stirrups and nearly pass out as the arrowheads make nasty with my kidneys and spleen. I hike up my skirt—a hell of thing to be wearing for this type of riding, but getting ready this afternoon I'd planned on drinks, maybe dinner, not a goddamn race against the clock. One-handed, I try to catch the shimmering grains in layers of long paisley fabric. And I watch as they fall like breadcrumbs to the ground, tracing my path back to Cord.

Dust from Springwell's drumming hooves falls on Main Street, but there's few folk around to disturb it. From the corner of my eye I see Jake and Lew closing the barber shop's shutters, young Bluet barring the grocer's doors, dark-haired tanners from down

Nippissing way dropping tarps over market stalls. None paying me no mind, or so they'd like me to think, then making themselves scarce as their wares.

"Fucking cowards," I whisper, too breathless for yelling, 'specially when my heart's not really in it. I can't blame them for keeping their eyes down. Though no one's been to the polls in a dozen-odd years, election posters still hang from each light post and eave. The Mayor's wild hair, too white for his years, strains against handbill borders like it wants to reach out and trap us all in its web. Lining the roadside, black shoestrings tie his jowls in place on billboards twice the size of Connelly's barn. Rows of pennants stretch from rooftop to rooftop: each fluttering triangle bears Alimunny's thick-lipped smile, and his ever-present havana.

Twisting my fingers through Springwell's mane, I kick him a good one. Speed makes my eyes water and blurs the Mayor's papery faces, but it don't shake the image he's left in my mind. Sweat beading on his round cheeks in the smoky, half-lit saloon. Arm stretching across the blackjack table, hand reaching for Cord. Holding my gaze as his wrist twists, jerks. Holding time in his hand, leaving a fleshy shell on the table. All while puffing on his cigar, head wreathed in a grey cloud of power.

The lingering taste of his tobacco is sour as foolish words on my tongue.

"C'mon, Spring!" I lash out with the riding crop, striking my windcharger's sleek flanks. Over and over, the leather whips up and down, each stroke sending lightning pain through my body. The bag wrapped in my skirt is getting too light, too fast. "C'mon, c'mon!" I flog my horse with every ounce of self-loathing I can muster, as if it's his fault I'm an idiot.

Daddy thinks mistakes are like bulls. *You can't wrangle either with your back turned*, he says. *Look the beggars in the eye, else run the risk of being chased down and gored.*

He can't always be right, my Daddy.

Only way to fix things is to run, and fast. Across three counties before losing a life's measure in sand. Keeping my smart mouth shut, my whip thrashing. Praying Springwell's legs will hold up; that the hourglass in my bag won't stop pulsing; and that when I cross the finish line, it won't be as the wife of one Alimunny Maldoon.

The Mayor don't own much in this town. A few hundred cattle, an oil field that ain't drawn nothing but dirt for decades. Like most folk 'round here, he's got shares in the bank and interests in old Milo's stockyard. Nothing special, apart from his house. Two storeys tall, with pillars out front that serve no purpose but to show he's got the coin and the wherewithal to haul redwoods here all the way from the west coast. The great white monstrosity sneers from a hilltop, its grandeur deriding the plywood sheds the rest of us call home. This mansion, with its fresh paint and huge empty rooms overlooking Main Street, is the Mayor's only outright possession. But as he strolls down the long drive with his walking stick swinging, he tilts his head and surveys the town as though he were looking in a mirror. In every dusty corner, every swinging shop sign, every pane of smeared window glass, Maldoon sees himself reflected. Daily he patrols the late afternoon streets, shaking folks' hands, sampling their wares, offering advice where it ain't needed, asking questions only to supply his own answers. Like a jealous beau checking his girl for hints of two-timing, the Mayor inspects Plantain's every mile, marking his territory with well-chosen words and a repertoire of seigniorial glances. Then he goes to the Highway Robber for an hour or so, reassured the town remains loyally his.

That proprietary look—the half-cocked chin, the money-countin' squint—got deeper as he entered the saloon and saw me sitting at a blackjack table, sipping a mint julep while Cord tried his luck on the cards.

There was no crowd to speak of, not at that early hour. Just the bar staff, the diehard card sharps, and a boozer whose missus had lately found Jesus. Lingering by empty booths, a handful of girls wearing strategically loose sundresses kept the joint looking pretty, but left us as exposed to the Mayor's scrutiny as their pale, well-fondled tits.

"Evenin', Herramiss," Maldoon said, addressing me by my first name as though we was pals, his cane thumping in time with his confident gait. Slinking behind the croupier, he placed a hand on the small of her back and nodded for her to go take a break. Flushing, the girl snatched her purse from under the table, then got out of the way as the Mayor hung his cane on the ledge.

"Alimunny," I said, taking the same liberty he had, avoiding titles and formalities.

"Up for a bit of a game, are we?" He picked up the deck and started shuffling, gaze never leaving my face. Slowly, slowly, the cards slipped through his fingers. They snicked one by one on felt worn thin with the grease of desperate, sweaty palms. Two for Cord, two for me, two for the dealer.

"I ain't playing," I said. He flipped the first card, feigned surprise to find the ace of hearts staring up at him. His head tipped so slightly in Cord's direction you could almost think the movement was natural.

"You sure? Looks to me like you are."

Oblivious, my date examined the hand he was dealt. "Hit me."

Maldoon smirked. "Don't mind if I do."

"Alimunny—"

"Tut, tut," he clucked, pushing a card across the table, leaving it trapped beneath his fingertips when Cord tried to take it. "Such a nasty tone to use between friends." Straightening up, he pulled the card away. "It's no fun for anyone when you stay so aloof. Always out of reach ain't you, Ms Grace?"

Cord turned his big hazel eyes at me, then looked at Maldoon. "Y'all know each other?"

Now, I'm not one to waste time answering stupid questions, so me and Cord don't talk overmuch when we're together. To be fair, guys like him, them that worked ridiculous long hours in Connelly's chook shed next county over, ain't renowned for their thinking. But his brown hair curls down his neck just the way I like, long enough to grab hold of if the mood's right, and his butt simply begs to be smacked. Though it ain't always verbal, we converse well enough our own way.

My hand sought and squeezed his thick, warm fingers. "Babe, this here's the Mayor of Plantain."

"How d'ya do." Maldoon resumed his dealing, eyes and hands steady. "Y'all been together long?"

What he didn't say, but what I could read in his posture, his calculating glance, his concentrated placing of a single card in front of my date, was *Long enough for you to miss him, if'n when he's gone?*

Cord chuckled. "Herramiss brung me my pink slip a few months back. That Connelly's a whoreson, ain't he? Getting an angel to deliver the devilest news I ever got." He tapped his finger for another card, then winked at me. "I reckon she keeps callin' on me out of pity."

My laugh was forced. "Least you know I ain't after your money."

Any other man would've taken offence at that, but not Cord. He just smiled, laid his cards on the table and said, "Twenty-one."

"And dealer busts." Maldoon counted out Cord's winnings, tossed him the chips. He anteed up for another round while the Mayor drew a thick cigar from his jacket's breast pocket. Biting off the end, he called one of the saloon's cigarette girls over to light it for him—which she did with heel-clicking swiftness.

Tinged with red, the smoke smelled of cloves and burnt hair. He breathed deep, held the soul fumes in his lungs for two heartbeats, exhaled in tight-throated bursts. Most smokers' faces relax after taking those first few drags, but not Maldoon's. His inhalations were methodical: in, hold, out; in, hold out. Concentrated gearings-up for something worth burning a piece of his own soul to get.

"Keep it up and this here chickadee will be riding your wallet faster than you can say Springwell," he said.

Again Cord laughed, but this time his words came out dark. "Keep dealing hands like that last one, Mister Mayor, and 'fore you know it I'll buy that big white house on yonder hill, and kick the lonesome schmuck who owns it out on his fuckin' arse."

"Now wouldn't that be something?"

"Cord," I warned, my heart racing, but he ploughed on, not knowing or not caring who it was he was challenging.

"I reckon. So all's you got to do is keep piling them chips in front of me like you done just now, get me them few steps closer to sleeping under that shingled roof. Then this bad-news angel can ride me *and* my wallet to Hades and back, for what it's worth, until the three of us is fucked dry."

"And where does Springwell come in?"

Cord snorted and adjusted his bet. "Last I checked my girl weren't into fucking no horses, winged or otherwise."

"Oh, he's a quick one, Herramiss," Maldoon said, eyeing my date. He took the cigar from his mouth then licked his thumb, marking each card with his soul-laden spit as he snapped them down on the table. "Ain't he just?"

Maldoon turned to me for a response, but Cord got in first. "Fastest windcharger I ever seen."

God bless you for an idiot, I thought. *Not so much as a blink when a man insults you to your face*. After a swig from my drink I took the chance to divert the conversation to safer ground. "I'll wager he's faster than the chest-beatings of two shit-talking men."

As soon as the words came out, I realised my mistake.

On a dais next to the bar, a band started tuning their instruments. I strained to hear Maldoon over the jangle of off-key mandolins and the screech of bowstrings waking up for a night of old-time fiddling. His voice, when it came, was so deep it sounded black. "You'll wager, will you? Well, now. It's high time you gone and made things interesting."

He drew on the cigar until its cherry flame singed new threads of grey into his goatee. Swallowing smoke, he dropped the chewed cigar butt; it hissed to the bottom of my glass. I pushed the wasted liquor away, my throat too constricted now for drinking anyway. "Alimunny," I began, as the musicians launched into their first number. "You know that ain't what I had in mind."

"Now, now, Herramiss." Maldoon's arms seemed to grow longer—a trick of the light, surely—as he reached over and placed a wide hand on Cord's shoulder. "No reneging on a fair bet. Already your man has set the prize: he wants you *and* my house. Fair enough; I want the same." Cord's eyes widened as Maldoon's fingers kneaded, kneaded. "What's say winner gets both then. Agreed?"

"All right," Cord said, those two words so stupid I'll never forget them, no matter what other, more pleasant, things he might do with his tongue.

I stood so quick my chair clattered to the floor. "To hell with the both of you—I won't be part of this."

"That's a shame," Maldoon said. "Considering it's your challenge that's to decide the winner." His arms were too long. Smoke seeped between his fingers, steamed from his nails. "How did you put it? That your freak of a horse is faster than our *chest-beatings*? Well."

For a big man, Maldoon sure can move. His hand plunged through Cord's breastbone, twisted, and pulled back out again before my mind registered the thud of flesh meeting flesh.

"Oh," Cord said, a man-shaped balloon deflating against the card table. His eyes were still open, his lungs still sucked in and expelled air, his hair still curled to the nape of his neck, sweet and waiting to be grabbed—but *he* was absent. While I stood there gormless, the heart had gone out of him.

The Mayor held it, not a squelching veined mess in his palm, but a transparent silver-blue ghost. Pulsating though it seemed made of glass, filled with hourglass sand instead of lifeblood. Grinning, he shook it like a tambourine to the banjo's manic rhythm, then tipped it upside-down. A cascade of crystal grains spasmed a counter tempo with each beat of Cord's displaced heart.

"Now his chest matches his head," Maldoon chuckled. "Empty, unless you're around to fill it."

"Fuck you," I said. My mouth went dry and my own ticker pounded hard enough for the both of us. Cord blinked vacantly at me. Not smiling, not laughing, not pulling me close for a kiss. "Set the terms."

"It's as easy as three county lines." Carrying the heart in front of him like a king's orb, Maldoon sauntered over and took me by the elbow. Though every part of my body shrank from his touch, his hold on me was unshakeable, reinforced by the strength drawn from his soul leaf cigar. He'd pay for it later, this magic few sane men ingested; already his skin looked more wizened than it had an hour ago. But for now, his will was supercharged and he had the grip to prove it. A busboy ran ahead of us as I was manoeuvred to the front door, which the young fellow, compelled though I hadn't heard so much as a whisper from Maldoon, held open until we had passed.

"What's the catch?" Outside, the shadows grew long, stretching across the hitching post and striping Springwell's pure hide with fingers of evening soot. My windcharger neighed a greeting as I unhooked my empty satchel from the pommel of his saddle; then his nostrils flared, snorted as he caught a whiff of the Mayor. "Three county lines—then what?"

"It must be crippling," Maldoon said. "Carrying such a world of distrust on your shoulders."

I stared at him until he continued.

"No tricks," he said, sighing, a real martyr in blue cowboy boots. "No catches." He stroked Springwell's muzzle, then handed me Cord's hourglass heart, watched avidly as I strapped it into my bag. "You and the horse cross three county lines before your man loses his gumption. If you make it before the sands run out, he lives. If not, well." He took both my hands in his, traced patterns in my palms with his thumbs. "Soon as he's planted in Cobb's boneyard, you'll be trading your black veil for happier white."

Stomach churning, I squirmed free of his grip. Instantly, a map of Plantain and surrounds came to mind, my delivery routes described in lines and dots of imagined ink. On a good day, Springwell can fly us from here to Reverend's Hollow in forty minutes, fifty tops. And if we deke around Portage, we can cover twice as many districts and be back in just over an hour. "How long have I got?"

"Long enough."

Springwell screamed as I gripped his shoulder joints and pulled myself into the saddle. Air exploded in his pinion sockets, taut sinews snapped, and plum-coloured bruises bloomed wherever I laid a hand to soothe him. "Shhhh," I said, my eyes filling with tears. Panicking, I rubbed his muscles more fervently. It didn't make sense—instead of healing his shoulders, neck, back, every caress left them all bloodied. "Hush now, honey." His wings drooped as I smoothed his marginal feathers, each stroke crushing delicate bones and streaking his pale plumage red.

"What are we supposed to do now? He can't fly like this, you fucking bastard." Crying openly, I scrubbed my palms along my thighs and tried to rid them of whatever magics Maldoon had planted with his godforsaken thumbs.

The mayor shrugged. "He got four legs, ain't he? Use them. No one ever said nothing about *flying*."

With that, he slapped Springwell in the rump then stepped aside to avoid rearing hooves and the spray of horse-kicked soil.

We'd just cleared the saloon yard's fence when I heard Maldoon's shout. "Ms Grace—" Ignoring him, I urged Springwell forward. The first arrow nearly threw me from the saddle as it thunked into my ribs. I was no less prepared for the second or third, but when they struck I was so winded I couldn't even whimper, much less respond.

"Three for three! Now you'll know when you saved your man's heart." I swear I heard him laugh then, far away as I was. "Sorry, did I say *when*?" He hooted, voice ringing like chapel bells. "Darlin', you know I meant to say *if*!"

𝄞

Plantain county ends and Chippewa begins somewhere between the honky-tonk and the summer carnival fields. Folks sit outside on warm nights like tonight, sharing a toke or nursing a pint after a hard week's work. The drunkest ones holler for us to join them, but most ignore me and Springwell as we bolt across the roadhouse's gravel lot, sprinting for grass and that first intangible line.

Cord's heart is still beating—I can feel it pulsing a sparrow-rhythm against my hip—though my skirt has grown heavy with a galaxy of sand. Looping the reins around the saddle horn, I take my eyes off the track for no more than half a second. Just long enough to flip the satchel flap; to see we've already pumped through a third of our time; and to miss the family of raccoons scooting out of a copse of ticket-seller's booths at the edge of the field, their bandit eyes glinting as they cut across our path.

Springwell spooks. Muscles contracting, wings flopping as he fails to fly, he runs across the fairground. Weaves between skeletons of sideshow tents and scaffolds and ballyhoo platforms. Banks hard to the left; circles right. Hooves slip on grass littered with the faded relics of cotton-candy days; scraps of manufactured happiness that dissolve with the summer, leaving folk with sugar-spun memories and a hankering for something more substantial.

I yank the reins hard as I can, try to impose some direction on his insane dash—but porcupined with arrows, 'hard' is a relative term. Springwell plunges ahead. We chew through a mile of parade grounds until he spits us out on the far side. Silver shoes ringing against pavement, the windcharger finally slows as we reach the highway, where we find ourselves facing, then passing, a familiar plywood cowboy.

The sign's lit up so bright you'd have to be blind not to see its peeling *Welcome to Chippewa!* blazed across the falling dark. I'm numb with pain from gut to gullet, but I would've known we'd crossed the first county line even without the cowboy's painted greeting. There's a change in tone coming from my back—a bit less *clackety-clackety*, now more of a subdued *click-click*—that lets me know one arrow has vanished.

Thank Christ, I think, risking another glance in my bag. Cord's heart flutters. Crumbs of his lifetime escape, trickle down my leg, slide into my boot. They settle in a soft pile beneath the arch of my foot.

Three for three, Maldoon had said. Three arrows for three county lines.

"C'mon, darlin'." Chest heaving, Springwell canters to catch his breath. His wings shudder, instinctively reacting to my command. He whinnies and stamps, picks up speed. The road is a dark gash across fields shading from dusk to nightfall. Every so often streetlights flare, then drown in my windcharger's liquid eyes— eyes that should be spangled with stars, not crusted with dirt. Free of black flies and reflecting the topsides of clouds, soaring high out of the Mayor's reach.

"C'mon now, Spring—"

We can't let Cord die.

"C'mon—"

I'd sooner kill Maldoon than marry that horse-maiming son-of-a-bitch.

"Giddup!"

As Springwell launches into a gallop, he veers to the left. Races past a tractor puttering along the roadside, heedless of jutting hitches and balers. Sharper and sharper, he turns until we're facing the direction from which we just came. He barrels full-tilt down the road to Plantain, every inch of his body aching for rest in the warm stable Daddy built specially for him. "Oh, no you don't," I say, tugging uselessly at the reins, striping his haunches with the whip. "It's the prairies for us, darlin'."

But he isn't having it and I'm about as strong as a sack full of feathers. "Turn around, for Christ's sake!" He forges on. I've used up all the adrenaline desperation had to lend, so there's nothing for it but to think quick.

Cord's blank stare. His heart sand. The musky scent of his skin. The touchable curls of his hair.

Concentrate. We won't reach Reverend's Hollow from here, but if we make for the bridge we can cross the wedge of Kaintuck land jutting between Chippewa and Portage, knock the other two county lines off the list. Head back to the saloon well before moon-up.

Hold on 'til then, babe. Hold on.

Once more, the Chippewa cowboy looms in the distance. Still smiling that timber smile, he exclaims, *Y'all come back now!* while his painted lasso threatens to make us do as he says. Set for home, Springwell's pace doesn't slacken one iota, broken wings and wooden threats notwithstanding. Soon, we've navigated the carnival grounds and can hear strains of bluegrass lilting from the honky-tonk's open windows. Despite our troubles, I feel my soul lift at the sound of that sweet Plantain music.

And I feel my back straighten, ever so gently, as the second arrow disappears.

𝄞

Me and Springwell crossed that fucking line between Chippewa and Plantain about twenty more times, but the third arrow didn't budge. Wasn't until I let the horse have his head, holding on as he sped back into town, that I reckoned what the Mayor was up to. *Take a single goddamn step into a different county, that counts as one. Go back where you come from, cross that same fucking line from the other side, and that's two.* So simple—once you remembered never to take Maldoon at his word.

He never said *cross the county*, just like he never said anything about flying. He said, *cross three county lines.* Cord's life reduced to semantics and a failing, hourglass heart.

I could take Maldoon's shoestring tie and garrotte him with it.

Every building, every vertical surface, taunts me with his unnatural hair, his too-old face. Hundreds of printed eyes glint, dozens of inked mouths sneer as we tear past shops that are now well and truly locked down for the night. Open windows glow with warm light, casting lace and gingham shadows from upper storey apartments onto awnings and gutters below. Steak and onion breezes waft past us, gut-wrenching aromas of dinners cooling on tables, being enjoyed by husbands and wives. Boyfriends and girlfriends. People who've only recently started to date.

My satchel is too light. It beats about once every thirty seconds.

"Giddup, darlin'." Springwell's ear twitches at the sound of my voice. "Hang in there." His gallop echoes toward the saloon, bounces back to us interrupted. Main Street is empty. It's just me and my steed; us and the paper Mayors, their flat gazes universally vigilant. Observing my failure, keeping watch on Maldoon's county.

I can just imagine the smug look on his face, like the one he wears whenever he deigns visit 'his' town. The expression that heralds his self-appointed claim to all and sundry in sight.

Jesus H. Christ.

All feeling rushes back and with it energy, pain, and anger. So much anger. "Go, Springwell! The fucking bastard – go!" It feels like the windcharger's strong legs are wading through quicksand. I stand in the stirrups, lean over his neck to help him surge forward. Hollering, I drive him until my thighs are shaking, my ribs razorblades of agony; until Springwell chokes on each breath, his lungs bellowing in and out with sharp whines. "Go!"

I curse myself for not seeing it. The catch Daddy warned me about so long ago, when Maldoon won the election.

Never cross a man who smokes his own soul leaf cigars.

There's no point hitching Springwell outside the saloon. Good luck to anyone who tries to steal a windcharger with mutilated wings and legs shivering for rest. I fling the door open, send a cigarette girl flying into a couple of dumplings in overalls near the bar. She squeals as one pinches her arse while the other pinches a pack of smokes from her tray.

"Back so soon, love?"

Sitting at a red velvet booth in the far corner of the room, Alimunny Maldoon cleans his fingernails with a toothpick. A full rack of spareribs has been picked clean before him; grey bones lie congealing in pools of hickory-smoked fat on the plate. Four punters are blowing their wages at the blackjack table to his right, but none of them is Cord. "Where is he?"

The Mayor looks at me, puts the stick in his mouth. He shifts it from side to side with his tongue, lifts his eyebrows, and shrugs. Looking at the couples swirling and dipping to the band's rollicking two-step, he asks, "Care for a dance, Ms Grace?"

"For Christ's sake, Alimunny—"

My heart pounds when I see him. Cord is propped up on the bandstand; head flopped toward the young kid playing accordion, boots pointed at the girl whose singing voice is rich as maple syrup. I'm on the move before Maldoon manages to slide his gut around the table. I cross the floor and plant myself in front of him, right where anyone not too deep in his cups can see, and grab the silver-tipped end of his shoestring tie. The floppy bow loosens at my touch; the cord slinks, snake-like, from beneath the Mayor's collar. I throw the black string to the ground, straighten it out with the pointed toe of my boot.

If Maldoon fancies himself Plantain County personified, I reckon this here's closest thing he gots to a line.

I cross it.

Without looking back, I keep going until I'm so close to the stage I'm liable to get kicked by the foot-tapping musicians. The Mayor's stare burns into my back as I lift the glass heart from my satchel and smash it into Cord's chest. Breaking, it resounds with a bass twang, an echo sprung from the hard-packed earth, not the crystal tinkling I expected. The sound fades as Cord's big hazel eyes focus. Silence catches the third arrow as it drops from my ribs, absorbing it into nothingness.

The band plays on.

"Three for three," I say, waiting for Maldoon's challenge.

He doesn't offer one. Instead, he tips his hat, condescending in defeat. "Well played, Ms Grace." Swinging his cane, the Mayor of Plantain, man and county, ambles over to the blackjack table. Taking the croupier's spot once more, he searches his pockets, sparks up another cigar. Casually picks up the well-shuffled deck, starts laying the cards in pairs of two.

"You sure crossed me good," he shakes his head, almost as if he didn't believe it. Almost. "What's say we go double or nothing?"

A smoke-stained smile stretches across his face. All mouth, unburdened by the gleam of a soul.

♪ ♪ ♪

The Short Go: A Future
in Eight Seconds

The Short Go: A Future in Eight Seconds

Can y'all see? There's quite the glare coming through the canopy, bright as all hell over the clearing. Here, I'll shift over so y'all can grab yerselfs a patch of shade. Yeah, Pilchard always runs rodeos at high noon—the sun gets the wolves in the ring proper riled, while the heat lulls their packs to sleep in the forest. Don't worry none about them though; the Minotaurs got the dens of them feral ones covered. Only wolves them big bastards let into town is the ones Pilchard orders caught for fine events such as this. And I'd warn y'all if we was about to come under attack—which, by the way, ain't happened since I was knee-high to a grasshopper—I'd *know* it 'fore them night-loving beasts could skulk from the trees and take their first bite of human flesh. Trust me.

Now, where was I?

Y'all got here late, but there's still a bit of time till Hésus Solares is ready to ride the short go. He's doing good so far, real good— but it's how he goes after today that's important. Being champion of this here rodeo is only one step for Hésus when it comes to winning Twyla Blue for his bride.

And he'll do it—hell, he already has. He just don't *know* it like I do.

Now's yer chance, go'on: get the scoffing out of yer system. Most folk 'round here laugh when they hear tell of my knowings, so why should I expect less from strangers like yer kind selfs? A few chuckles won't make a whit of difference, not with my ears ringing so's I can hardly hear you.

Screaming at me as they do, quick and unexpected, true knowings have a way of leaving me ragged. Cyclones of words and pictures that rattle the silver in my teeth then lift me like tumbleweed, sending my mind skittering across time and space and all them flimsy barriers between *actual* reality and what regular folk take for granted as real. For a few seconds, no more, I float breathless, surfing zephyrs in the late summer sky, looking down on the forest, the clearing, the Minotaurs ringing our tree-shrouded town. I'm the soil gone to dust beyond the woods, the rough bench beneath my fingertips, the hot sun beating down on our deer-hunter skins. I'm all three hundred souls turned out for this here rodeo, the bettin' money in their pockets, the moonshine in their bellies. I'm salt soaking through the judges' Stetsons, blood pounding through competitors' veins, cigarillo air meshing with lungs. I'm Hésus's beating heart, yers, mine—everyone's, except the Swangirls', them whose tickers is made of memory and the thinnest wisps of their father-god's breath.

Inside and out I'm everywhere when the spell's on me, 'til I know the way of things to come, right down to their very guts.

Look: that's Hésus over there. The scrawny kid with the thatch of black hair, waiting between the birch tree and the great sugar maple, wrapping and unwrapping that rope around his left hand. Nah, he don't wear gloves like the rest of them riders. Says he likes to feel the cut of the hemp across his palm; the pain keeps him alert, slippery blood forces him to hold all the more tightly. Here we go: them Swangirls is called Hésus back to the gate—oh, don't bother crossing yerself, boy. You of all folk should know Jesus ain't got no say when it comes to cowboys and rodeos.

That's right: Hésus ain't learned that yet, ain't aware of what he already done in the future. Alls I can say is I seen young Solares's unfoldings clear as the view we got of Pilcher's wolfring over there, loud as the Alabaskan cheers coming from these bleachers we's setting on. Just like I know the Minotaurs won't break the treaty our granddaddies dealed with them, unless we do so first—and we will, mind, but that's a story for my daughter's daughter to tell long after I'm dead and buried. And it's the same way I know them Swangirls, beauties all, won't never have wings strong enough to sustain flight. Sure, they look tough from here, herding wolves into separate bucking chutes, pairing riders with their allocated mounts; wending around tree trunks holding up these here bleachers, ducking and weaving through catcalls and good-natured jeers; all with their muscles cut and bulging inside chaps, white feathers bristling from graceful backs, torsos pale and bare as truth, tits displayed without shame to the crowd. But their wings is too small to lift human limbs, too delicate to be more than decoration. They're light on their feet—see what I mean?—but they sure as hell can't fly. You just keep an eye on them a while and *then* try to tell me I'm wrong about things I see.

Sit for a spell. I *know* Hésus Solares will wrangle three wild critters 'fore he makes Twyla Blue Pilcher a good husband. Them twister-visions I got said he'll ride one beast to woo, rope another to wed, and lash a third to recover the love he thought lost. C'mon, now. Our rider's mounting up; the courting's about to begin. For eight seconds, Hésus will show his heart's set on Twyla Blue. While he hangs tight, risking life and limb to prove he's a fit mate for his gal, I'll tell y'all how things will be after he's won. Direct from my mind to yers, I'll think the future to y'all, slow it down some lest it passes by 'fore y'all can blink. How's that sound?

Eight seconds, then, for him and me. For y'all, it'll seem a sight longer.

There goes the bucking chute gate.

Start the clock.

$$\text{♩}$$

Looks like he's waving at her now, don't it? With his right arm raised and flailing, left hand gripping the rope them Swangirls knotted 'round the wolf's waist and balls, and Twyla Blue perched on the edge of her seat watching Hésus from the friends and family box. Such a pretty lass, not so thin as most girls 'round here, more blonde and round and fair, 'round for them eyes of hers—long and black as a Minotaur's snout, but twice as wet. She's staring hard at young Hésus's twisty-turning form, pinning him to his lupine seat with the weight of that dark gaze. Knuckles white in prayer, she's hoping he'll hold on—'cause if he don't there ain't no way they can make their courting official—

and she's memorising his moves so's she can recreate them in the bedroom once they're wed.

Seven seconds to go.

Believe you me, Hésus'll feel that wolf's fur bristling between his thighs, chafing through his jeans, as the beast works his muzzle into a lather trying to buck the boy into the dirt. It's a nasty rash he'll have come morning, but guaranteed Twyla Blue will be the first to visit him at sunup with a love-gift to pledge her troth: a jar of willow bark cream to soothe his skin, mayhap a pair of soft cotton drawers tailored to fit his narrow hips.

He'll accept her offering. Ain't no other reason he's out here, riding beneath a blazing sky. I can't tell you the number of times he's dreamt of touching her, holding her, filling her up. Since they was both little, 'fore he even understood what that ache in his chest meant, 'fore that dull throbbing slipped below his belt and tormented him day and night, he's imagined the two of them together.

He can't wait to see her naked.

So he'll take the cream, the unders, and whatever other trinkets Twyla Blue gives to show she also gots an interest in the goings-on in his pants. And soon as he does, Pilcher hisself will give Hésus a tiny metal key to unlock the silver chain looped 'round and 'round Twyla Blue's hourglass waist, cinching her from navel to tits like a corset.

"You ready for this, son?" Old Pilcher will ask, speaking the same words in the same tone his father-in-law used on him so many years ago. "You got it in you to be a man to my girl?" And, just as quick as Old Pilcher did when folk still called him Young, Hésus will nod and put key to lock. The silver lasso Twyla Blue's wore since she first got her bloods will slink to the ground with a metallic whisper. Her chemise will billow, concertinaed with fabric wrinkles, showing how much room there is for her belly to stretch. To grow a strong Minotaur baby.

Six seconds.

𝄞

Poor Twyla Blue. Such a lovely face to be creased with such worry. Darlin', yer man's nose is bleeding but it ain't broke—that bronco's rearing head sure cracked him a good one, ain't it? Cartilage smashed against skull with a *whack!* right in the kisser. Makes my own honker twinge in sympathy.

Roping a bride's Minotaur ain't half as hard as riding a wolf for three go-rounds.

Armed with his fiancée's lasso, face coloured in paint made from a paste of bone chalk, crab-apple pulp and rich Alabaskan clay, Hésus will put on a good show of stalking a stud buck through the forest.

He won't see most of the herd. They'll be hidden behind sycamores and pines, thick arms covered in sap and soil and maple keys, camouflaged by nature and oncoming dusk. Downwind, Hésus will smell them, taste their musk on his tongue, inhale the earthy scent of their spoor. He'll hear their snuffling, great gusts of air bursting from wide nostrils, giving away their positions. Near and far, they'll remain out of sight. Hoof beats will resound as Minotaurs wrangle wolves to uphold their part of the bargain, clearing a safe path for Hésus to enact his hunt.

As day dissolves into night, one bull will finally show his proud face.

Lord only knows how the herd decides who the lucky begger'll be. Mourning doves and jaybirds will sing the chosen Minotaur toward the man wielding a love-spun lasso. There'll be a scuffle as Hésus puts chase, his red and white mask catching the last glimmers of sunset, his boots loud as he tramps through the undergrowth.

Buoyed on the promise of winning, driven by the thrill of the hunt, exhilarated as hard-earned sweat trickles into his eyes and down his chest, Hésus will launch the rope at a creature more than twice his height. With his first throw, he'll snag the Minotaur's mighty horns, pull the noose—a short jerk and a flick of the wrist—and bring the beast low. Adrenaline will surge through his body as he plants a foot atop the bull's prostrate form. He'll laugh and bellow, in victory and relief.

As the sweat cools on his brow, as his breathing slows, he'll see the future transformed, though not the same way I do. *A man*, he'll think he's become. *A husband.*

He'll feel fit to burst—damned if he wouldn't take Twyla Blue right then and there.

But he can't, of course; a point he'll remember as he reaches down to offer the Minotaur a hand up. The bull will take it and say, "Congratulations," 'fore swinging Hésus over his shoulder, carrying him like a sack of wood shavings to hasten their run into town. "Where's my cow?"

Ain't sure if you ever noticed, but when it comes to Minotaurs it's all balls the size of melons and thick cocks dangling for the world to see. Being a strictly male species, them hairy bastards is always ready to rut—they just ain't got no women of their own to fuck, no she-Minotaurs to bring forth calves.

Five seconds—our boy's hanging in there.

As he will be tomorrow, flopped over the broadest shoulders he's ever touched. Hésus will first suffer vertigo, then bone-wracking chills as he looks at the longhorn he's just roped. Gasping for breath, he'll feel powerful muscles stretching and contracting beneath his ribcage as he directs the Minotaur past the bullring, down Trader's Row, and up the hill to Pilchard's house. Hésus understands the arrangement all Alabaskans have made, explicitly and as a matter of course. But hanging upside-down, clinging for dear life to the sweaty haunches of an twelve-foot Minotaur, he'll struggle to see its benefits.

A fair trade, they'd agreed, the settlers and the Minotaurs. A treaty on behalf of generations past, present and future. To live here in Alabaska, instead of ploughing fields drier than my dear Mamma's ashes. Our town rich with oak for furniture and houses, water for fishing and brewing, enough deer and rabbit to feed a family of six like kings every day of the week. Better than fighting off packs of wolves every night, or spending daylight hours prying great bulls like this one off their screaming wives. The cost of staying, unmolested: first breeding rights for a community free of wolves. One night with the bride—they's fertile beggers, them Minotaurs, one poke's all they ever need—buys a town suited for bearing and raising *all* children. Them with bovine features, and them without.

Most would agree it's still a good deal.

But tomorrow, spots will swim in front of Hésus's eyes as envy chokes his heart. He'll grip that bull's headgear same way he's clinging to the bucking wolf's rope, down there in Pilcher's rodeo ring. His face'll scrunch as it is right now; cheeks flushed, expression stuck midway between determination and disgust that he's going to hand-deliver the first partner ever to get between Twyla Blue's thighs.

His girl—*his wife*—will be stretched all to hell on that monster's pole, then torn to shreds as she births a bull-headed calf.

Damage done in no more than four seconds.

♪

Twyla Blue's firstborn will have her eyes.

See how she's looking now, all teary and excited, hardly blinking for fear of missing a second? Craning her neck to see around the folk walking to and from the makeshift bar Jolly's knocked up near the entrance? Every skerrick of her attention is riveted to Hésus, a mixture of love and pride and something darker, something of which she's yet unaware. Hate, maybe. A shining instance of hate because he brung her to this point, he changed her life, he made it both sweet and unbearable.

Well, that's how he'll look, Twyla Blue's cow-headed boy, soon as they swab the blood and placenta from his pelt, rub the mucus from his peepers. Delight and resentment articulated not in words but in the shady cast of his exaggerated features.

Hésus won't notice the similarity: he won't have looked close at Twyla Blue for months, much less her bastard son.

He'll tell hisself it's the work what's keeping him distracted. Takes time, it does, building a cottage for two on the fringe of these here woods. It won't be nothing fancy; rough-hewn logs, tar and shingle roof, foundations made of stone. It'll be simple, but solid enough to support happiness and to fend off the fear of wolves. While Twyla Blue's belly waxes huge, Hésus will mark out a small room for his own young'uns. He'll erect a fireplace framed by a timber mantelpiece, and leave one nail jutting out, high and centred on the wall, upon which they'll hang their wedding gift.

Horns pointed up to catch all the luck Twyla Blue deserves, a huge granddaddy skull, the Minotaur's blessing, will overlook the Solares-Pilchard nuptials.

This is another thing Hésus will avoid looking at.

Twyla Blue will wear white on their wedding day, for it will hold true that she's never yet lain with a man. With sprigs of holly in her hair, clutching a bouquet of sumac and lace, she'll talk about young'uns, the ones she and Hésus will make. Doughy babies with fat thighs and rolls dimpling their knees, plump pink sausages to make old folks coo. She won't talk about the calf, not ever, after the morning of the ceremony has passed. Two hours 'fore they say 'I do', Hésus will rearrange chairs in their home's new front room, place tables against walls to clear up space for an aisle, and he'll hear his bride tell her nameless kid that she'll visit him one day in the forest. He'll hear the clippity-clop of the young Minotaur's hoofs on the kitchen's wooden floorboards, and the squeak of the screen door as it opens.

"See you," Twyla Blue will say as she sends the creature away.

Hésus's stomach will churn, though he knows it's not true, though he's aware none of the mothers do visit.

But he'll wonder if she might.

He'll feign exhaustion on the night of their wedding.

"Such a busy day," he'll say as he rolls over and faces the wall. "And we have our whole lives ahead of us."

Twyla Blue won't change out of the special nightdress she bought, white like her wedding gown but spangled with tiny red hearts. She'll leave it on in case he changes his mind. The flutter in her chest will slow to a molasses crawl. She'll wait as the room is gilded silver. To pass the time, she'll think about the need for curtains, the patterns she'll stitch along their hems. Soon enough she'll doze, her dreams catching on sharp needles, drowning in vinegar brown eyes.

When her breathing evens out, Hésus will turn and watch his wife sleep. He'll see moonlight striping her body, outlining her unique dips and curves, and the shimmering beams will remind him of spit. Fat cow tongue saliva, smearing wet the places he should've been first to lick. Twyla Blue will sigh and stir. Hésus'll pull up the sheet to cover everything but her head. Hoping a thin veil of cotton might hide his changed desire.

Three seconds to go—and here come the Swangirls, right on cue. They ain't no regular rodeo clowns, saving cowboys being trampled should they take a tumble. Nah, they's supposed to run across the arena like that, flapping their feathers, hooting and hollering, egging the maddened wolf on. *Little fates*, folk sometimes calls them; if the girls' shaking and shouting makes the wolf buck his rider, it's a sign the love match weren't meant to be.

Hésus the wolfrider is certain Twyla Blue is the gal for him.

But I been Hésus's heart. I been inside his secrets, his inner workings. I *knows* the heft of his coming disappointment. Less than a week after he weds his missus, a time not so very far from today, he'll feel stifled and restless. That old ache in his chest will be back—but where 'fore it was a balloon that made him soar through his days at the mill, floating on visions of Twyla Blue, now it will seem a burden too heavy to carry. A rancid weight beneath his ribs, squirming with maggots of doubt.

Fantasies will worm through his thoughts. He'll imagine going to work in the morning and never returning. But he can't leave, can he? Such a move is unheard of. What would a miller's son do in treeless fields beyond the forest? His axe is useless for ploughing. Stalks of barley are much too slender for building cabin walls. And how will he fight wolves clustered in packs, roaming the edge of the woods? He hasn't the Minotaurs' strength and, let's face it, he hasn't their balls.

He'll dream of flying then, over branches and leaves, away from horns and treaties and snapping jaws. But each night as he slips into bed, consistently late enough to ensure Twyla Blue's already asleep, he'll find hisself crashed back to earth.

Just like them Swangirls, Hésus will learn he simply ain't got the right wings to take flight.

And at the public house, four days after he slips a pearl ring on Twyla Blue's finger, Hésus will realise how much he and them white-feathered ladies gots in common. They's all of them caught up in the workings of love, he'll reckon. All of them let down by appendages a shade too small for their purposes. One chick in particular—look, there she is: the beakless one with devil-red hair, running fierce after the wolf, lashing its rump with a cat o' nine tails—will show Hésus she gets where he's coming from. In a voice soft as the down behind her ears, she'll chat with him at the bar, then join him for a whiskey or ten. It ain't worth scowling over: she ain't the first of the little fates to lead an Alabaskan man home to her nest soon after his wedding night, and she sure as hell won't be the last. How else do y'all think them girls add to their broods?

Of course he'll go with her, our young man over there, face a mess of blood and left hand white for lack of it beneath the rope, forearm straining to master the wolf that started it all; of course he will. And when he fucks that Swangirl without even asking her name, when he uses her rodeo whip to lash frenzied stripes across her lean arse, when he buries his problems deep, deep inside her, he'll think of Twyla Blue. As the winged girl gyrates with pleasure, Hésus's confidence will grow. He'll stop picturing his wife as she was before: pure and tight and his alone. Instead, he'll believe he can make her writhe the way the Swangirl is; he'll make her feel good; he'll kiss her the way a Minotaur can't; he'll run to her on uncloven feet; and together, they'll love.

Oh yes, oh God, oh yes, they'll love.

He'll feel wonderful, never better, for a few minutes. The Swangirl will offer him a towel, point him towards the shower. Warm water will erase all evidence of his deed. He'll scrub his face, rinse his hair. Relaxed in the comfort of being clean.

Then, as he softens, as the dregs of soap and sex echo down the drain, he'll feel terrible.

If he gets home right away, Twyla Blue will never know. He'll never have to see the look on her face when she hears about what he's done. *I can't lose her*, he'll think, stepping out of the tub. Not now he feels he just got her back.

He's made a mistake, that's all—

A mistake.

It must be a mistake!

Six and a half seconds on the clock.

Not eight to win—six point five for the loss.

He's fallen.

This can't be.

This. Simply. Can. Not. Be.

Everything's a blur—can you see Twyla Blue? Speak up—good God, what a noise! There's a *knowing* coming on me hard and fast—twice in one day; incredible, incredible. Oh Lord, where is she? What? I can't hear you. She's leaving the stands? With a bag full-packed?

I can't breathe. Don't y'all worry about me, what's happening with Hésus? Is he winking at me? Sure he is—look at him! Shit, the fucker has gone and messed with my knowings! How'd he reckon

to do that? Ain't happened but once or twice in my long years—
did he throw hisself off that bronco on purpose?

He must've.

He must've.

I *know* things. Goddammit, I *knows* them.

He's leaving the bullring? Yeah, but more—oh, more—I can see
him now. No, not out there; in here, in my noggin. I'm him and
he's me and we're taking Twyla Blue, the both of us, the him of us.
We're stealing her away; unwon, unearned, unproven.

Oh, Lord. We're eloping.

Don't know who's marrying us; don't recognise his face.
A stranger, must be. One of yers? Christ, we're being wed by a
visiting fool.

My head's paining me something fierce—no, not *his* head, *mine*.
Hésus is just dandy now, *soon*, screwing Twyla Blue, his premature
bride, behind his daddy's mill. Crowing with pride and stupidity;
a black-haired raven thieving the Minotaurs' due.

Give me some water, won't y'all? A mug of ale? Anything,
I'm crumbling with thirst. This *knowing* I gots don't feel right.
Banshees is wailing and now I'm down in the ground looking up at
a leaden sky. Not floating, not feeling life and love pulsing through
me, not coasting on warm summer breezes. The air smells of wood
smoke and ash, the wind tolling with funeral bells.

Not for Hésus and Twyla Blue, though, them paramours is
happy as lambs. There's grass stains on his knees and her back.
Cicadas singing matrimonial hymns so loud in their love-stoppered
ears they won't hear the tread of wolves.

Everywhere, everywhere, wolves.

Christ Almighty.

I think that y'all better go.

$$\text{♪ ♪ ♪}$$

To Snuff a Flame

To Snuff a Flame

Let's get one thing straight from the get-go: Lola Mae ain't wicked. Sure, she ain't none too happy caring for her brothers and sisters, 'specially now Annie's due to add to their brood, but that don't make her rotten. Hell, I ain't too fond of the little beggers meself. Seems every young'un after Retti, Annie's first, has been a thorn in my backside. Hooting and hollering next door from sunup to shuteye, playing at sheriffs and injuns and all fool sorts of make-believe. Always getting lost in the woods between my land and theirs, then crying "Doolittle! Mester Doolittle!" till I comes and sets them aright. Reminding me every day, with their noise and their pranks, their tears and their giggles, that I'm nigh on thirty and still ain't got no young'uns of my own.

Lola Mae ain't the mothering type. Never mind that, at fourteen, she's the same age her Mamma were when she birthed Retti. Now *there* was a sight to behold. Pretty Annie nursing that beautiful child, looking for all the world like Mary cradling the baby Jesus. Excepting, of course, that Retti weren't a boy. And, far as such things go, I reckon Trick must've felt a bit like Joseph when the two of them got together—a craftsman sweet on a woman whose belly were already good and filled with another man's seed. Like old Joe before him, he watched without a word as the babby growed into a shape that looked nothing like his.

Don't go feeling sorry for him, mind. Trick knew what he were up to when he rode down to Portage to steal a tumble with Annie. I can't hardly imagine what he done to convince her to leave her man and take up with him instead. Raises my bristles just thinking on it. "Your daddy's going to skin you clean," he'd probably said, "soon as he gleans you gots your bustle on wrong." Then he would've laughed and pulled at her dress till the fabric stretched taut across the five month swell of her middle. Annie would've blushed and said, "Ain't nothing I can do about that now, is there?" And that's where Trick would've got her.

He'd have took lengths of hemp and twine he'd brought from his workbench, twisted them together in a serpentine weave, then wrapped the rough magee belt 'round Annie's waist. Concentrating till tattooed bracelets glowed 'round his wrists, he would've whispered, "*Shift,*" or some such command—then watched as the belt tightened. Within seconds, her stomach would've cinched flat. With the babby gone all Thumbelina, Annie's bulge would've repositioned to fill out her hips and tits with its extra bulk till she looked like a pinup girl from the pictures. Problems is solved easy as that, for one with Trick's talents. And a girl like Annie—who ain't got no magics of her own apart from the looks Ma Nature gave her—well, she would've been beside herself seeing the weaver at work. So powerful, so confident. He left no sign of a babby and got his way, simple as breathing.

Gives me chills thinking on it, even though spring is already chewing the hardest edge off winter. There's been melt enough to widen most paths through the woods, allowing easy passage. My boots make nothing more than a dull thumping sound as I walk. Last year's harvest of leaves, black with decay, is mixed with pine needles and slush until all sounds is muffled. Lola Mae's tread is silent before me. She's so focused on her work, a whole posse of Marshals could creep through the bush without her noticing till it were too late. Even I could walk over right now and sweep her up in my arms while she folds and criss-crosses the pine needles, sticks and brambles she's gathered. I could lift her capelet, throw it over her face so she wouldn't know who it were that nabbed her, then nibble on her exposed neck, lick the salt from her skin. It'd be so easy.

It'd serve her well to be more careful.

I hang back, two whoops and a holler over, let her be. Soon enough she'll learn it ain't wise to wander alone in this forest.

In places the canopy is thicker than shadows, so Lola Mae parks herself in a patch of light. Her fingers is long and fine: they dart in and out, knotting and bending branches so quick it's hard to see what she's doing before it's done. She gots her back half-turned, but in her hands I can see a knobbly twig animal—one what looks to be a squirrel—made from grasses and straw and bits of thread. Too young and inexperienced to have earned tattoos, as she concentrates woven cornsilk bracelets change from pale yellow, to red, to glowing white on her wrists till her creation is lit up like a solstice bonfire. She ties a length of twine around its neck, tugs it tight to make sure it holds, then whispers, "*Shift.*" Bracelets flash with a firecracker snap. The air fills with the pong of sulphur, then the squirrel chitters and comes alive.

What you up to, girl?

"Go'on." She tosses the squirrel into the nearest tree, but keeps a firm hold on his tether as he slithers out of sight. After a minute or so, she asks, "What you got up there, Chip?"

"Leaves, leaves, leaves," comes the high-pitched answer.

"Get me a nest," she says. "Two would be better."

Pinecones and maple keys, shreds of birchbark and cobwebs rain down on Lola Mae as she waits for the squirrel to return with her supplies. The string bobs back and forth, then stretches taut in her hand.

"Ain't got enough rope."

"You better not be messing with me, Chip," Lola Mae says. "You ain't here for a Sunday stroll in the treetops, you know."

"Ain't got enough rope."

"Fine," she says. "Hang tight." Scanning the edge of the path, she uproots a few long blades of grass and plaits them around the lariat. Again, her dark brow furrows, her bracelets blaze, the air thickens with the stench of sorcery—and the rope grows about twenty feet longer.

Shoot, she's got skills. No matter how many times I seen her weave *shift*, never ceases to amaze me how nimble that little girl's fingers is got. Trick sure learned her good. Past dozen-odd years, I seen him show Lola Mae the ins-and-outs of such magics enough times to know what he must've done to hook Annie. Far as I can tell, *shift*-weavers gots the knack to work two ways: some fuse their power to any old thing—grass or twigs, strings or wools—and so long as it's flexible they can knit theirselves a glamour tight enough to stick for good. Others take things a step further, lead their threads straight into folks' minds by way of charms and other doo-dads. Little milkweed baubles behind a girl's ear leave her high for a day or so, changing how she sees things till their magic dries up and gets washed down the drain with vanilla-scented soapsuds. Boleros for cowboys convince them their balls is that much bigger than the prairie injuns', even as tomahawks gets lodged between their shoulder blades. Hairdos twisted *just so* by one with the right hands, the right tattoos, the right bracelets, can hook folk on illusions running from hair to roots to brain, make them want it all for real. Make them desperate to get back to that false life when the spell dies.

Most of them weavers ain't strong enough to work the hoodoo what fucks with the user's head so hard, so they stops at the minor twisting—messing with appearances, creating handsome facades. Most ain't got the nerve to run deals right under the Marshals' noses, to sell such pretty opiates and flaunt the law for all to see. Most ain't as greedy as Trick.

He does whatever it takes to fill his coffers or his bed, a habit what started long before he swindled Annie. That bit of conjuring he done for her ain't stopped Retti from being birthed—Annie would've never gone so far as that, no matter how much her daddy scared her. But she did go so far as let Trick take his payment atween her legs the way he wanted. Without a second thought she let him lasso her with sugared talk of the future.

Then he fashioned her a pendant, one she ain't never took off since.

Bleary-eyed on Trick's weavings, she stepped on down to the courthouse with him. As though marrying a man ten years her senior would turn her more respectable than getting hitched to the kid what knocked her up. Not that Trick cares about such things, truth to tell. But if a man finds a set of tits like Annie's here in Two Squaw, he'd be a fool not to hang tight to the body what carries them. And Trick ain't no fool.

He weren't never unkind to Retti, I'll give him that much—though his affections for that child was a summer breeze compared to the tornado he gots for Lola Mae. Now, them two was cut from the same leather. She's *his* first: his shiny bright. Born with her daddy's gift flowing through her veins, she wears his olive skin and stares out his fox-clever eyes. And unlike Retti, who weren't strong enough to survive her third year, Lola Mae ain't no soft pudding. Soon as her fingers could bend a reed, Trick started learning her to weave *shift*. One of the first *glamours* she done was as a five-year-old over at the coal miner's honky-tonk—she braided her long black hair in a circlet 'round her neck, *shifted* herself a woman's body, and got up on stage to sing a set of Patsy Cline tunes. The audience were so enchanted by her crooning, none noticed Trick's doings backstage. Atwixt the daughter's singing and the Pa's fast-talking, enough *shift* got sold that night to keep Trick's tail out the mines for a month.

Only hiccup in his plan came when it were time to take their earnings and head back to Two Squaw. The two of them had quite the quarrel, between the rows of coats and rifles in the cloakroom. I overheard them as I were strapping on my gun belt, fixing to get my Stetson from the hatstand.

"Ain't time for you to grow up yet, darlin'," he'd said, holding a wad of Lola Mae's fingernails, hair and spit in his fist, set to ram this antidote down her gullet if she looked set to resist him. Jaw clenched, the woman looked down at her high heels, at her knees showing beneath a hemline cut two inches above proper, at the tiny bone buttons pulling the dress tight over her tits. She were a real strapper. There were power in that shape: Lola Mae could see it in the way the miners was staring at her all night.

"It's a piece of you, or a piece of me you gots to swallow, girl." Trick weren't brooking no nonsense—reckon he would've had his hands full with an irate Annie if he came back home with Lola Mae all changed like she were. No matter that the girl's spells weren't nowhere near as durable as his—no doubt she'd be a young'un again before moon dark, even without the remedy he was trying to force through her clenched teeth—but it were clear Trick were using the opportunity to learn his girl a lesson.

"You gots to pick your battles," he'd said. "To turn a permanent *shift*, you gots to want it, *need it*, real bad." He held her jaw with one hand, pressed the pellet to her lips with the other. "And this ain't the time for doing that kind of undoable, star."

Lola Mae stared at her daddy long enough for ol' Duke to finish his banjo solo in the next room and launch into a new tune. I buttoned my jacket to the rhythm of a familiar song, readjusted my pistols as the snare drum kicked in. Duke's reedy voice caught Lola

Mae's ear, set her to smiling. Trick's fingers cut deep into her rouged cheeks as she eased her mouth open and gulped down those bits of her true self. She lost her curves and height and fancy clothes soon as they was ate, went back to being Trick's shiny bright babby.

It's a strange kind of love, what they share. I knowed its like meself, so it's easy enough to recognise. One what makes folk sacrifice anything to get what they's yearning for. One what make a little girl reckless enough to go into the forest alone, just to save her daddy. One what makes that daddy suffer all manner of indignities, if it means she'll always be his. His alone.

Instead of flaunting her that night at the honky-tonk, getting cowboys hooked on the sight of her, Trick would have done better to keep her magics secret, 'specially since she ain't licensed to do half the stuff she can. Not that I'm set on turning her in, mind. But anyone else 'round here catch sight of her doings and she'll wind up in the pokey. Just like her Pa.

Still can't hardly believe them Plantain Marshals nabbed him, after all these years.

Trick swore he weren't going to dig the Devil's nuggets till his lungs blackened him into an early grave. To prove it were true, he started running *shift* over the border atwixt Plantain and Portage. Taking his business out of Two Squaw; away from kin, away from me. Fooled hisself into thinking it weren't greed, but his family's needs what kept him tripping over county lines. As if making dirty deals in another province were somehow safer for them all than if he'd stayed in the mines. Way I see it, now that Trick spends his days pacing the length of a Two Squaw cell, damned near *anyone* can hit him where he's vulnerable. And there's all kinds a reasons a man would see fit to harm that weaver's folk, as a means of repaying his so-called good intentions.

Meantime, Lola Mae's running loose in the bush without her daddy's protection, getting up to all kinds of mischief. I keep to the shadows while she steps further into the light. With a shrill whistle and a yank on the rope, she reels the squirrel back in. I crouch to get comfortable as I can in the scrub.

Not a minute too soon. Before I even muddy my knees, Annie's come to the gate. She's peering into the forest, trying to spy her daughter between the tree trunks. Eyes rolling like a spooked pony's, she whimpers and cradles her overgrown belly. Clings to the fence rails that run 'round her property, the only barricades separating her from the dark.

"Git in here, girl!"

Lola Mae jumps. She drops the squirrel, and the nest he's brung her, and loses hold of his leash. All-fired to make his escape, the little begger legs it across the path and runs straight for my hideout. I'm resting so still, he don't see me till I clamp one hand 'round his hindquarters and slam the other 'round his trap. Wriggling like a good thing, he's mad enough to spit hornets. I keep a tight grip, hold him close till he's a sight more biddable.

"Them wolves is going to git you. They got my babbies, they's going to git you, too." Annie lowers her voice, mumbles: 'Sweaty teeth, so many, many teeth. Gobble you up, girl; gobble, gobble, gobble—" Then, so loud it echoes: 'Gobblegobblegobble!'

"Save part of your breath for breathing, Potpie. Hooting and hollering like that ain't going to scare nothing away."

Potpie, I think. Horrid nickname for a bird what used to be such a stunner.

"Oh, Lola Mae, all them *wolves*. They gone and ate up Retti, didn't they?"

No they didn't, darlin', I think, swallowing thickly. I know Annie ain't been right in the upper storey since she became Trick's wife—became his best customer, more like. That don't make it no easier seeing her buffaloed like this.

Lola Mae gathers the nest and slides it into her satchel. She makes a cursory check for the squirrel, then echoes my thoughts: 'No, Mamma," and wanders towards the house.

"Retti's been ate, and now they gone and took Jaybird too!"

My head whips up. What does she mean, Jaybird's took?

"Don't get your spurs in a tangle," Lola Mae says. Tucking the squirrel under my arm, I slowly approach the cabin, keeping the rustling to a minimum. "Hush now, Potpie. Jaybird's dandy. He's paying Daddy a visit—I seen him off meself this morning."

Annie don't look convinced and I can't say I am neither. Something in the girl's calm reminds me of Trick when he's aiming to bulldoze a client. And now she's trying to pry her mamma's hands from the veranda rails, trying to usher her inside. But Annie won't budge. She runs down the steps, into the yard, stares into the forest beyond the fence. Lola Mae sighs and follows Annie's gaze.

Wrinkles corrugate her forehead as she looks; her eyes steady, like she knows someone's watching.

"Hey, Chip," I whisper, keeping the women in my sights. "Do me something."

The squirrel looks up at me with his black button eyes. "I ain't yours to play with. Let me go."

"And I ain't going to higgle with no overgrown rat. Have a gander through them's cabin window over there, and then we'll see what we'll be seeing. Don't you even think about fussing, you hear?" I wrap my hands 'round his neck, tighten them just short of throttling.

Much as he can with his collar squeezed, he nods. Then he's off my lap in a flash, a black blur of motion across the sodden ground. The twine linking us unfurls like yarn from a bobbin—two, six, twelve, fifteen yards of it—then he slips between two slats in the fence. A handful of seconds later he's splayed and skittering up the cabin's wooden siding; clodhopping across the windowsill. Dancing back and forth along its length, he admires his reflection from all sides in the glass. "Purdy," he chitters, leaning back to take in the full view. His high-pitched voice carries far on the cool air—I barely have to strain to hear it. "Mighty purdy." He fluffs his tail, looks into the cabin, claws at his face. Then shouts, "Sparrow!" and leaps off the ledge, dashes across the yard and up a fencepost, chasing the oblivious bird.

"Get back here, damn coot," I whisper, yanking and spooling the rope till he complies. When the line atwixt us is drawn up short, the squirrel hunkers down in front of me, chest heaving from his efforts. "What did you see?"

"Sparrow."

"No, before that."

"Window."

"Inside," I hiss. "What were inside the fucken cabin? You seen any kids in there?"

The squirrel squints. "Kids. Bed. Rug. Fireplace. Baskets. Branches. Wicker. Wool. Nests. You want nests?" *All the supplies for weaving* shift, I think, shaking my head. *So Lola Mae's fixing to pick up Daddy's business, is she?* "'Icebox. Kid. Cradle. Table. Chairs. Kid."

Were that four, or five? Lola Mae gots five siblings—'How many were that, Chip?"

"Kids, bed. Kid, chair. Kid, cradle. Sparrow. Sparrow!"

And he's off again.

The rope whips a red line across my palms as the squirrel cuts dirt after his prey. I've half a mind to let him keep running all the way into someone's crock pot; but the other half wants the skinny on what's happening to Annie's young'uns. And since I ain't going to traipse up no weaver's front steps meself, I'm going to need me a critter like him a whiles longer. I hoof it after him, trap him between me and the fence.

Keeping low, I jerk the twine so hard he's pulled clear off his feet. He rights himself quick-smart; coils his tail and rises up on his hind legs, ready to spring either to the trees above my head or back to the pickets behind him. The cord goes slack as the squirrel quits moving. Instantly, everything but his ears and nose, which is twitching something fierce, is frozen. His eyes is wide open, staring at something over my right shoulder.

My muscles tense and for a second I'm a human squirrel: hunkered down in the bush much too close to Annie's house, arms crooked in front of me, wary look in my eye. Heart pounding in my mouth, I turn my head slowly, neck straining as my chin brushes my shoulder—take in the sight of a polished Winchester, a ten-gallon hat, and spurs spinning like windmills on the back of the cowboy's tooled boots not ten yards to my right. His pointed ears perk up as Lola Mae says, "C'mon, Potpie." The girl flicks her hair, glances into the woods. Between leaves and branches, her gaze meets his.

"Let's get you inside," she says, wrangling her mamma's bulk away from the gate, back to safety. The Marshal's long pink tongue curves out his snout, wets his lips. He bares his yellow teeth in a wolf-faced smile, steps away from the hundred-year oak. Nods as she gestures him to wait. His eyes is the only features a man would wear: the rest of his face is pure lupine.

Hoo-ee. Trick sure done a number on them Plantain Marshals before they caught him. Seven lawmen was set on his trail, chased him from their jurisdiction into ours here in Two Squaw. Trick rode at full gallop, burned the breeze 'til his horse were nearly buzzard bait. By some accounts he were heading for Chippewa country, hell bent to get there with his haul intact—God knows what dark doings he could've got them injuns into, if'n he ain't got nabbed—but I reckon he were heading home, where the lone Sheriff ain't never gave him much trouble. As he fled, whether home or away, his tattoos streaked lightning. He tossed lasso after *shifted* lasso, aimed them at his pursuers in hopes of roping their heads. A flick with his wrist and Trick could've tightened the noose to change their minds and their direction, by magic or brute force. Whichever worked first.

But either his concentration were off on account of his speed, or he'd seen the only real chance at freedom came from buggering the Marshals up real good: *shifting* their bodies, never mind their souls. One shot felled two men, sending them to the bone orchard with their necks broke, their faces half-stretched and hideous, adding murder to the tally of Trick's crimes. The other five was merely struck glancing blows: the weaver's rope slid off scalps, thighs, forearms. Everywhere a loop touched, them cowboys was changed. *Shifted* half-wolf, not full. Instead of making them think they was dumb animals and losing them in the wild like he'd planned, Trick's magics made them stronger. Wilier. Faster.

Ain't nobody can outrun a half-wolf, a lesson Trick ain't soon to forget.

Now Lola Mae pretends she ain't looking back at the Marshal as she ushers her Mamma up the porch steps, but it's obvious that's what she's doing. I lean to the right, peer around to the front of the cabin, see her take a final peek at the woods before she opens the door and goes inside. My knees crack as I shift position and settle back on my heels. Without looking at him, I can tell the wolf is tense and eager to be on his way. He quietly clears his throat, spits into the undergrowth.

Get yer fucken hide out of here, I think, hoping the cowboy will pick up on my vibe and skedaddle. Pins and needles is stabbing my legs, but I gots to hold still and keep out of sight so long as he's nearby. Gingerly, I reach a hand out to the pickets and twist my body to ease the ache in my gams. Inch by inch I drag my right leg straight. The wood creaks as I lean my left shoulder against the fence, waiting for the blood to circulate proper again. The Marshal still ain't paying me no mind, so I take a risk and stand. Staying well away from the window on this here side of the cabin, I hold onto the posts for balance as my legs come back to life. The wood is sturdy, some of it freshly hewn. I rub my palm across its rough grain, enjoy the scent of sap and oil the motion dredges. Looking at the space Lola Mae just vacated, it occurs to me that Trick ain't built this barrier just to keep the wildlife out. It were to keep his family in.

All men is wolves when it comes to plucking a lamb like that girl. Don't have to be half-changed like that sorry Marshal to know the best way to hurt a man is through his women. Through his young.

Lola Mae comes to the window, signals patience to the wolf outside. I shake my head. She ain't never learned that lesson: she don't know what such a man wants, what he needs—how he can use her to get it. No, she ain't wicked.

I lick my lips.

Not yet.

𝄞

"What you doing out there? Snuffling 'round my yard like a bloodhound."

"Jesus Christ!" My heart near busts out my chest at the sound of Annie's voice. I look to the grand old oak tree: cowboy's gone. With a sigh of relief, I turn to face the cabin, and Annie. The window screen makes her fair skin look grey; the roof's eaves cast a diagonal shadow across her face. Her mouth is hidden in darkness, but her eyes is bright. Feverish, like she's seeing something more than what's there. I straighten my shirt, brush the dirt from my pants, then move closer. "You just shaved ten years off my life, woman."

"Wolves is going to git you sooner than that if you ain't careful, Simon Doolittle." I can't tell if she's smiling. Don't really look like she is. "How come you ain't come up to the front door, anyway? Paid me a proper visit."

I tilt my hat and look down, hope my beard's thick enough to hide the flush in my cheeks. "Don't mean no disrespect—"

"Them sniffer-dogs of yours got loose again, ain't they?" Annie gestures at the squirrel's leash in my hands. "Why can't you just hang onto them, Doo? Why you always gots to chase them over here?"

— 173 —

I shrug and check to see where the squirrel's got to. "Can't say."

"Serve you well to hold tight to thems that's under your care."

"You ain't got to tell me that twice," I say. The twine twitches as the squirrel runs for a sapling and starts scaling its trunk. I slam my foot down on it, hear a rustle and thump in the undergrowth as the critter falls back to the ground. "Look, I best be getting back—"

"Stick to the path, Doo. Them wolves is fierce—they gone and took my Retti and now they gots my Jaybird. Such good little'uns they was, such sweethearts. Wolves is going to eat up all of my young, gobble them all up. Gobble, gobblegobble—"

I can't stand to hear any more. "Get off the *shift*, girl. Like as not, Jaybird's down the quarry scaring up tadpoles, or over at Pa Mason's shooting raccoons. Stop and think on it for a tick."

"Oh, them teeth—chomping chomping chomping. My poor Retti; poor, poor little Retti—"

"Enough! The Good Lord took that child from us years ago, remember?" Annie continues babbling, so I gots to yell: '*Remember?*"

But she ain't listening no more. She's well on her rant now: ain't nothing going to stop her short of Lola Mae weaving her up another hit of *shift*. The girl's magics ain't as strong as Trick's, but they's good enough to bring wicker babies to life, to convince Annie she ain't lost none; to thread spiderwebs around furniture and rafters, letting her mamma see a golden palace 'round her instead of a one-room shack in the woods; to knit shackles around Annie's heart and mind, saving her feeling any regret, any pain. But they ain't so powerful that the spells is permanent—'round here only Trick's strong enough for them sorts of conjurings. And when Lola Mae's latest *shift* starts wearing off, reality rushes in, so fast Annie's poor mind can't always keep up.

"I gots to mosey," I say, waving the limp rope where Annie can see it. "Ain't none of my hounds over here. What say I drop by the station, see if there's word of Jaybird's whereabouts? And you let me know soon as he turns up, you hear?"

At the sound of her son's name, Annie's eyes focus. "You watch yerself out there, Doo. Watch yerself."

"Yes'm," I say, tipping my hat. Then I circle 'round to the back of the cabin and start reeling the squirrel in. He wriggles and resists with all his might. "Let me go! Let me go!" I cuff him upside the head. Not hard enough to knock his stuffing out, mind; I can't afford to rattle his pea-brains any more than they already is. But I whack him till he shuts his gob.

"Listen here, Chip," I say. I take the dagger from my belt and wrap the leash around the blade, knotting it tightly just below the hilt. "I gots to get me some supplies from home before I can venture out." I stake the knife into the ground, leaving just enough rope to let the squirrel negotiate a path to the windowsill. "There's a handful of peanuts and a whole apple in it for you if you keep an eye on them ladies in there till I get back."

The squirrel hushes as greed overwhelms his self-preservation instincts. I can almost hear the rumble in his belly, see the drool on his buck teeth. His cheeks puff in and out as he says, "After that, I'm done?"

I take a look at the bits of twig and hay already wearing holes in his elbows and knees, the blades of grass sprouting from his tail, and reckon he ain't got long for this world one way or the other.

"Sure," I tell him. "Keep watch and keep quiet. This'll be over before you know it."

♪

Between bites, the squirrel's talking bullshit.

"So the girl—"

"Lola Mae," I say, gesturing for him to keep his voice down. It's unlikely they'll hear us, far as we are now from Trick's cabin, but I ain't taking no chances.

The squirrel nods, scoffs down another peanut, swallows. "Lola Mae takes the Potpie," he gulps and stuffs his cheeks full of apple. *Annie*, I think. *Her name's Annie.* "To the rocking chair, sits her in it. The girl runs her fingers through the Potpie's hair, rocks her back and forth till she closes her eyes."

I take the fruit away from him. "Go through the next bit again, and slow it down this time. What you're jabbering just don't make no sense."

The squirrel runs his paws down his cheeks, scrubs apple juice into his mouth. He smacks, eyeballs the core I'm holding just out of reach. He starts again: 'She takes a shiny stick out her apron—not a stick. A pin. No, it gots a thin piece of floss dangling from it, so it ain't just a pin." His nose twitches and he unconsciously licks his chops. Clearly, he reckons this insight is worth a peanut. But I keep the apple and the bag of nuts firm by my side—'round these parts folk don't get no reward without working hard for it.

"The girl leans over the lady," he continues, beady eyes locked on the food. "Leans right over her face, says, *Rest now; settle now. This here's for your own good*, and coos like a mourning dove till the Potpie shuts her peepers. How 'bout we get us a mourning dove? So fat, so slow, so fun to chase!"

"Concentrate, you little shit." I pull the twine—it's fraying a bit now, but still holding. "Forget about the fucken birds. Tell me about Lola Mae."

The squirrel rubs his throat. Grass pokes out where the rope has chafed. "The girl flicks the needle in and out, up and down. Back and forth, back and forth. Tangles that floss through the lady's eyelashes and leaves bits of red behind with each pass. Then she snaps the thread with her teeth. Kisses the woman's forehead and whispers something what makes the lashes grow and grow till they wrap like a blindfold around the lady's head."

"And you're sure Annie ain't done nothing about it? She ain't complained or nothing?"

"Nope." The squirrel scratches his belly till his fur peels away in places, revealing the dirt and hemp Lola Mae used to build him.

"Stop that," I say, and pass him the apple to keep his hands from tearing a hole in his guts before he's told me everything I gots to know.

"Nope, she weren't making no fuss. She asked for a blanket so the girl gave her one. Then she snuggled down and dozed off while a little kid turned into a key." The squirrel licked his paws, ran them over his ears. "Nuts."

"What?"

"Nuts. Now. I been good."

I take a deep breath, sucking in the smells of damp leaves and wet earth, then exhale. Wait for the critter to gorge on another peanut, then prod him with the sharp end of my boot. "Who was it she *shifted*? Lilah? Or one of the twins? Was it Mabel or Twig? What did she say, again?"

"Peanut." The squirrel holds out his scrawny arms.

"Fuck the peanuts!" I toss the whole bag to the ground, whip the apple at the rodent's head. "You trying to tell me that Lola Mae's sewed up Annie's lids, and is *shifting* her kin into keys?"

"I ain't telling you nothing, cowboy." The squirrel turns his back, forages through the scrub for the food. I reckon he ain't going to cooperate no more, so I scope around for a branch thick and sturdy enough to bash the unholy creature back to Hell. But he starts talking again, his high voice gone even squeakier in imitation of Lola Mae, staying my hand.

"*You gots to do something for me, cricket.*" The squirrel stops, stuffs a chunk of apple into his face, thinks about what Lola Mae said next. I imagine the girl talking to Lilah—it must've been Lilah, what with Jaybird already gone—and try to glean the meaning behind her instructions. "*Stop squirming; this won't take a minute. Hush, child. It don't hurt: I done this a million times. Just stay calm and be good for the cowboy when you see him, you hear? Jaybird'll meet you there. Ain't you keen on seeing him again?*"

"She's sending the young'uns where?"

"I told you," the squirrel says in his own voice. "She ain't *sent* nobody; she gone with them. With *it*. The key what used to be the little blonde girl. She braids that child's hair, whispering and whispering the whole time. Psssh-psssh-pssssh, hissing like wind. Lots of fine plaits snake out the kid's head by the time Lola Mae is finished. Then she leads her outside, sits her down next to a grapevine basket."

Again, the falsetto: '*Them wolfboys what ran* shift *with daddy is wanting to bust him from gaol near as much as we do,* Lola Mae says. *But there's five keyholes and they only gots one key. So.* She pushes a sumac-leaf band through all them braids she wound, talks like the trees again, and the little sister vanishes. Lola Mae bends over, lifts something small but oh-so-heavy into the basket. *Good thing we gots magics to help.*"

"A likely story," I say, my stomach dropping.

Them double-crossing fucks.

Trick ain't never partnered with no-one, so the cowboys she's talking of is gots to be them no-good, wolf-turned, Plantain Marshals. I can't hardly wait to find out how they convinced Lola Mae they was working *with* Trick 'stead of *against* him when he were took down. "She knows Trick sells to all sorts of mix breeds and shifties—must've reckoned them cowboys ain't looked no worse than the rest of them folk her daddy uses."

"Don't know if that's true or ain't it." The squirrel sat back, rubbed his full belly, which were starting to split at the seams. "All I knows is Lola Mae leaves the lady with the eyelashes behind. Leaves them other two girls and the babby boy. Takes up the basket, hoists it onto her hip, then hauls it up to her shoulder. And just as she were about to trek deeper into the forest, one of them cowboys steps out of the shadders to meet her."

The squirrel burps and pulls at his collar. "I ain't seen where they gone after that—this goddamn string's too short. Besides, right about then I were getting so so so so hungry. Couldn't do nothing else without some grub."

"Well, now you got it, ain't you?" The critter looks up at me, and I swear he's smiling. "All right," I say, standing up. "Guess I'll be seeing you."

I creep up to the path, steering clear of Annie's window, and leave the little begger to deal with untying the cord hisself.

♪

Lola Mae's walking through the thickest part of the woods, right where anyone could snatch her. Every so often, a steam train blows its top in the distance, but otherwise the path is quiet. Few jaybirds gossip overhead; ain't much chickadee-dee-deeing neither. Just the whoosh of the wind, and the creaking of the big basket Lola Mae sometimes carries, sometimes drags behind her.

The journey seems to be taxing her heavily considering her parcel looks to be empty. No sign of Lilah anywheres: squirrel was right about that much. But where's the cowboy? I step careful through the trees, using them for cover any time Lola Mae stops for a breather. Like now: she wipes sweat from her forehead with the hem of her capelet, lowers the hood till it's a flaccid peak on her back. She flips her long hair out the neckline, fans her cheeks to cool down. A sunbeam breaks through the canopy, picks her out the surrounding gloom.

A lamb, ripe for the plucking.

I gots to get to her to the station quick. I can't help but grin: it's less than a quarter hour's walk from here. *I could have her in front of Trick before supper.*

My pulse races, but Lola Mae don't look the least bit afraid. Her posture is straight; she's alert but not skittish. Looking around, she keeps her brown eyes peeled. I tread slow-like in her direction: heel, ball, toe, heel, ball, toe. Avoiding dry branches and crackling leaves.

I'm no more than ten feet away. I can smell the vanilla scent of her hair—I step closer and hear the cadence of her breathing. Another step: almost near enough to suck the sweat from her upper lip. Another step.

Across the path, saplings shiver. Winter-bare limbs bend as a rough paw pushes them aside.

I spin on my heel, press my back against the rough bark of a sugar maple. Sink to the ground soon as I catch a flash of the cowboy's red vaquero shirt. My heart's pounding so hard, I'm afeared they's going to hear it. But Lola Mae don't pay me no mind as she steps lightly toward the Marshal, leaving the basket behind her. I force myself to calm, take deep breaths in and out. Then, edging ever so slightly 'round the trunk, I take a gander at what lies inside it. Sitting on top a gingham handkerchief is a picayune key, just like the squirrel said. Its shank and pin is copper; the bow and bits made of blonde hairs and ten-year-old bones.

"Where's the rest of them?" The cowboy slurs the question, his wolfish lips still not fit for shaping human words. "Dwayne reckons you gots all the keys we—your daddy—needs. Why can't you bring more'n one at a time?"

'Cause she can't carry four young'uns all at once, I think. *She ain't quite got the knack of spreading their weight across the atmosphere yet. Four's too heavy to lug without breaking her back.*

But Trick learned his girl good about using deception to cover weakness; ain't no way Lola Mae's going to own up to her failings. She looks the Marshal straight in the eye, and lies. "You know Potpie: always worrying about the young'uns. Always fussing about wolves and such." She smiles, takes a step closer, glances up at him through her thick lashes. "Wonder how such ideas get into that muddled ol' head of hers?"

The wolf snorts. "Best get a move on, girl. Sheriff'll be back soon."

"I know," Lola Mae says. "Ain't saving none repeating yerself." She points to the basket. "Key's in there. Be gentle, mind. Lilah's a shy one and bruises easy. Don't be dropping her or shoving her in a pocket or nothing."

I hold my breath as the Marshal collects the key. Close my eyes, as though me not seeing him means he won't see me. He grunts as he bends over. His claws scritch on the dried grapevine as he reaches into the basket. A series of pops runs up his back as he straightens. As he heads back to Lola Mae, I swear I hear him lick his chops.

Steady on, cowboy, I think. *That filly ain't yours for the taking.*

"Won't do us no good getting cotched 'cause we ain't gots the timing figured. Reckon?" Lola Mae nods. "Japeth'll meet you by the footbridge in two sweeps of the dial. And enough fucken around already: bring the rest of them kids—them *keys*—when you come. It's the only way we'll get to your Pa."

"All right, Willie," Lola Mae says, a dimple curving her cheek. She curtseys, tilting forward and dipping just low enough to let a touchable expanse of her tits balloon up the front of her dress. The Marshal were in such a hurry to be gone, he only took a quick glance at her wares before melting into the dense woods.

Lola Mae gathers her basket, much lighter now without Lilah weighing it down, and skips away humming a old-time tune. My pulse slows as she pulls out of sight. *Give her a minute, Doo,* I tell myself. *Buy yerself some breathing room.*

So I wait for her trills to drop away. Wait for her boot heels to scuff out of earshot. A scrawny brown hare leaps from the scrub to my left, and I nearly jump out my skin. He pads over my foot then bounds toward the patch of light Lola Mae were standing in earlier. "Damn fool," I mutter—and shut my piehole as I catch the sound of a footstep crunching on gravel.

It's soft, but loud enough to scare off the rabbit.

I peek around the tree trunks and see Lola Mae, basket slung like a rucksack on one shoulder, inching her way back up the path.

Girl's got Trick's devilish eyes on: squinting and focused. *Weaver's shiny bright may be ignorant, but she ain't stupid. Seems she trusts them foreign cowboys less than I does.* She raises her dun-coloured hood, blends into the bush. Bracelets two torches on her wrists, she twists and knots her hair, *shifts* her body to slip between, over, under any branch or stone or damn-fool critter what might give away her position. Tugging at her cuffs to cover the glare, she follows the trail Willie left as he ploughed his way to the forest's heart, aims for the station.

Adrenaline surges through me till my balls is aching. *I gots to catch her up.* Gots to run; cut her off at the pass; stop her going in there without me. But she moves so much quicker than I do, so much quieter. My soul's hollering, *Go! Get her!* but I gots to be measured. Sweat trickles into my eyes, and I blink her in and out of view till I nearly lose her. Swiping my arm across my forehead, I cross the path. Plunge into the woods.

Never has a ten minute walk to the stationhouse felt so goddamn long before. I circle around to Lola Mae's right, wait for her to move forward. She keeps low. I keep lower. She takes ten steps. I take eight. My body don't know what it wants to do: run or fuck, or both. She's smaller and fourteen years younger'n me, but she gots the bearing of a lifelong hunter. Poised, stalking the joint one graceful step at a time. Reckon her thighs ain't shaking like a nanny goat's; bet they ain't burning like Japeth's firewater. I gots to brace myself against a tree, try to catch my breath. Feel my belly turn to water.

Lola Mae might wear her daddy's looks, but she gots Annie's stamina.

My balls clench.

I take a step closer, then two. Four. The station peers out between the boles of knotty pines and blue spruce. Part log cabin, part cave, it's the strongest lockup we gots for folk like Trick—never mind it looks a regular shanty from the outside. Out front, them walls is older than the sky and twice as weathered; half the crooks 'round here reckon it wouldn't take but a fart to blow a hole clean through them. Of course, only blind men and little girls gather all their knowings from the face of things. Each log supporting that granddaddy shack gots a flint skeleton, and indoors the gaps is all chinked with paper, gunpowder and coal. Any fool tries to shoot his way out of that joint, he'll be blown from yesterday to the sweet hereafter before catching even a whiff of outlaw air. And ain't no chance for posses to bust cowboys out the cells, neither. Back in the way back, the station's arse-end got *shifted*, joined to the rock behind it. A few plate-sized windows half-sunk in the ground let a bit of light and air into the rock caverns, but ain't no way a man's getting in or out that way. Forget bars and steel: even Trick ain't gots magics enough to move half a limestone mountain, which is where Two Squaw lawmen has always gaoled swine like him. Ain't nowheres else for ten counties strong enough to hold his like.

Lola Mae stops just shy of the clearing. She scans the horses hitched to the porch rails. I can practically see her counting them, doing the sums. *Only three dappled rides, and there ain't no stable. Five keyholes in Trick's cell needing five keys; four lawmen and one daughter to turn them all together, to break the spell keeping her daddy bound.* A line darts up between her eyebrows. *Four Marshals should mean four horses, not three. Ain't no Marshal going to ride double 'round these parts.*

Takes all my energy not to giggle. *Not even a nose as perfect as hers can smell this setup.*

The station door opens and wolf-faced Willie comes out. He lights his smoke and goes to double-check the contents of his steed's saddlebags. Cigarillo dangling from one corner of his snout, he fastens the leather buckles with one hand and cradles the Lilah-key in the crook of his other arm. Seeing that everything is in order, he heads back inside. Beside the front door, Willie drops his smoke to the ground, snuffs it beneath his boot heel. His tongue lolls out, pink and grey gums stretched in the curve of his grin.

I turn to gauge Lola Mae's reaction, but she's gone.

Fucken Christ, I think. *That girl can creep like an injun when she wants to.* I ease forward a few paces, stepping careful in case she's only moved to get a better vantage—but after a minute I gots to admit the bird is slipped away without me noticing.

"Goddamn," I say, straightening up. "Goddamn!"

I near-about knock the stationhouse door off its hinges as I slam my way inside. Japeth jumps up from the table, sending his chair clattering across the floor. He snatches the pistol he were in the process of polishing, even though we all know it ain't safe to shoot in here. "What the hell, Doo?" he barks. Doyle blocks the passageway leading back to the cells, guard up as though this here were his home station. Such nerve. He yips and snaps lest anyone tries rushing him to get to Trick. Willie startles, drops the key he had half-lifted to his gaping mouth. All three Plantain Marshals' ears and tails sag when they see it's me. Their gruff voices grow gruffer to mask embarrassment. "Move like that's liable to get you bit," Willie snarls, bending to pick the key off the packed dirt floor.

"I ain't paying y'all to run a game behind my back," I say. "Deal was—"

"Deal was," Willie says, "we keep our paws off the girl and take the young'uns as payment. And so we done: we ain't broke no oaths."

"But we was supposed to take them all at once—"

I don't know what I were expecting, but there ain't so much as a squeal when the Marshal crunches the key in half, chews, then pops the rest into his maw. "Be straight, Doo. Weren't no reason to believe them magics would work like you said, if'n we ain't tasted the goods early."

Lilah's fixings have an immediate effect: Willie sheds extra skin and hair like a leper soon as he swallows. He don't spare me so much as a second glance. "Hightail it out of here once you ate your medicines, Deputy," he says to Doyle. His snout shrinks with each word; lips retract, turn puffy and pink. His neck lengthens; ears slide down the sides of his head. As he speaks, his voice loses its growl. "Leave that fucker to Doolittle here or let him rot, for all I care. Meet me and Dwayne up near Chillins Bluff once ya'll been righted. If y'all ain't there by dusk, we's heading back to Plaintain without you."

"This ain't what we arranged," I says. "You was supposed to wait for my say-so before glutting yerselfs on Trick's flesh and blood."

"You'll get yers," Willie says, grabbing his Winchester and a satchel of grub. He brushes stray whiskers from his cheeks, runs a hand through his hair, sets the ten-gallon on his human noggin. "I done my bit. How you deal with Trick's whelp after she's done with Doyle and Japeth ain't none of my never mind." Hoisting his gear, Willie nods at his deputies. They grunt in reply. Finally, he looks me straight on.

"Much obliged for the tip," he says, picking his teeth. "Feels mighty nice, wearing me own skin again."

The Marshal lets daylight flood in as he leaves. I squint till the door swings shut behind him.

"Fuck you, Willie," I says. Turning to the other wolfboys: 'And fuck y'all, too. You want to change plans? Fine. We change plans. From now on, ain't nobody going to meet Lola Mae 'round me."

"Now hold right there, Doo," Japeth says, still cleaning his pistol. "You was the one said she shouldn't see us together, that she'd get—what was that five-dollar word again, Doyle?"

"Suspicious."

"Yeah, you said she'd get *suspicious*. She gots to think we broke in here without your say-so, ain't that right?"

"Right, but—"

"And we's stuck with you so far, ain't we?"

"Only 'cause Dwayne and Willie ain't as stupid as you two—"

"That ain't right," Doyle says, his voice a deep rumble in his wide barrel chest. He approaches, slow and steady, towering over me even from across the room. "We was waiting, like you said— even though, far as I reckon, we might've just ate up that precious girl of yers, left town without fucking Trick over the way you want to." His breath is hot on the top of my head. It smells like hunger, like venom. "You can't blame a man for protecting his interests. Ruin the girl, Doo: we won't interfere. But in the meantime, we ain't gots to trust you."

I take a step back, but stare the wolf straight in his eye. "Lola Mae ain't going to bring all them keys at once, you know. No matter what Willie says, she'll drag this out long as it takes her to figure a way to screw you over."

Doyle shrugs. "Ain't no rush. Plantain ain't going nowheres, even if Dwayne and Willie is." He sneers, leans his muzzle close to my cheek till I'm near choking in the stench of his threat. "And you ain't getting through to Trick while I still wear this face."

"Nor me," Japeth pipes, clicking bullet after bullet into his gun.

"Fine," I say, my mind racing. *Let the fuckers think they can out-man me on my own turf—I'm still the one running this racket.* "Like I said, the girl will take her time with them *keys* you ordered." I turn to the window, run my nails along the rows of gunpowder grouting the walls. Rubbing the smudge of black between my fingertips, I search the woods for any sign of Lola Mae. The powder is smooth as I imagine her skin to be; gritty as her spirit. "She'll bring Mabel next, which leaves Twig and Hen back at the cabin. Unguarded."

I look back at Doyle. "Anyone hears Annie shouting's bound to reckon she's had a bad hit of *shift*."

The Marshals check their weapons, grab their hats and bags, make for the door before I finish speaking. Neither of them gives me a second look as they walk out. I follow them, watch them saddle up.

"Two Squaw ain't home to neither of you, you hear? This here's the last time I want to see your ugly mugs, wolfish or otherwise."

Japeth spurs his horse onto the forest's trail without a backward glance. Doyle stares down at me, squeezes with his knees to keep his mount in check. "Sheriff," he says by way of farewell, spitting a gob of tobacco on the dirt between my boots. We lock eyes as he takes the reins in one hand, his rifle in the other.

I ignore the way his long paws wrap comfortably around the gun's neck, the way his claws brush against the trigger. His nose is wet, his jaws dripping with anticipation. My voice is tight, but steady. "Either one of you bastards lay a finger on Annie, and I'll slit your hairy throats while you sleep."

♪

Lola Mae believes me when I tell her Japeth is held up at the station. No reason she shouldn't. She's growed up next to the Sheriff her whole life, and I ain't never gave her family no trouble they knowed about. Long as Trick kept his dealings in this county, long as Annie stayed happy, I held back. Even when our babby died, our little Retti, I let things unfold as they would, kept my deputies from the weaver's door. All for Annie's sake.

In the odd moments when her eyes was clear, she'd say, "No-one makes me feel like you, Doolittle." Her safety a star pinned on my chest, a tarnished steel guarantee Trick'd be kept out the clink. Now, I may be a fool when it comes to Annie, but I ain't stupid. I know I can't give her what he does—Trick gots more magics in his eye tooth than I gots in my whole self. I know she won't have me while he's around; won't take me if I done away with him, neither. So year passes year, and I work on my plan. On my timing.

Even fools can be patient.

I been waiting so long I can't hardly remember a time when I weren't. Waiting for them fates to turn the path my way, like they did when me and Annie was kids and she were mine for a little while. Waiting for Trick's cock to wander. Or for his magics to burn out. For his greed to send him over county lines. For some other lawmen to catch him, like them Marshals from Portage and Plantain finally has, for them to drag him to my gaol. For arrangements to be made what leaves me blameless in Annie's eyes.

I look at Lola Mae, see her struggling to carry the Mabel-key in her basket. I don't offer to take it from her. It won't hurt if she's tuckered out by the time we reach the cells. I fall a few steps behind to hide my smile. Now that Trick's took care of, ain't nothing stopping me from learning him what a lifetime of hurt feels like. What it means to see his soul stolen, wasted by another man. I ain't never forgot how much Annie loved me. Nor how she left with our babby full blown in her belly. Nor how hard, how fast Trick ruined her. I ain't never forgot a speck of it. Not once.

Of course, Lola Mae don't know that.

"Nearly there, darlin'."

"I know." She takes my hand, looks up at me through the fan of her lashes. *Good God*, I think, and my mind drifts back to the first night I tumbled Annie. Laid out on a stack of hessian sacks in her Pa's shed, she peeled her shirt off, then her skirt. Batted her eyelids. Tilted her chin up exactly the way Lola Mae's doing now. Gooseflesh dimpled every inch of her till I warmed her skin smooth. *Jesus, Mary and Joseph*. Their identical smiles leave me gasping.

I pick up the pace.

The station is dark when we arrive. I hurry Lola Mae into the front room, flapping my hat to shoo the blowflies and to distract her from noticing the horses' absence as we pass the hitching post. "The boys must be out back," I say, flicking a switch to fire up the bare ceiling bulbs, and another for the row of hanging lamps in the hallway. "They's been testing the fit of them keys you brung—"

Lola Mae stops short, her face a weird mask of shadders beneath the harsh lights. "But Willie said—"

I clear my throat. "You think I ain't aware of the goings-on in my own station, darlin'?" I smile reassuringly. "Willie and his boys filled me in—didn't they just?—knowing I can't stand the sight of your Pa in here any more than you can. Letting him suffer like this; well, it ain't neighbourly."

She sniffs, lifts an eyebrow. Hikes her basket up, hooks it on her elbow, watches silently as I unlock the door separating the civil folk from the felons.

"They ain't turned them keys or nothing," I continue. "Just made sure the two you brung slide in as easy as the one they already gots. You know: getting ready for the fourth, for the real deal. That's all." I hold the door open for her. "Reckon your daddy's aching to see you."

"I reckon," she says. I keep smiling until her frown relaxes.

Most of the cells lining the long corridor is empty. Carpeted with straw and fitted only with a slop bucket and a rough mattress, the small rooms smell like piss and boredom. Back here, all the walls is damp, patched with mould. I move closer to Lola Mae to avoid rubbing against them as we walk to the far end. A stale breeze reaches me as we turn the corner—Trick's cubicle, the largest in the joint, has two windows up near the ceiling, the only comfort I cared to give him after the Marshals dragged him in. Next to me, Lola Mae fidgets with the basket, her eyes focused on the barred door to her daddy's cell. I squeeze her hand, my palm slick with sweat.

My mouth starts to water. I imagine what her thin cotton dress is going to look like with my palm prints smeared all over it. I picture the look on Trick's face—the horror, the disbelief—as I bend his shiny bright over and kiss her wet places. Picture his rage as I pin her wrists and tear into her, right in front of him. Hear his strangled fury as the gag in his mouth and the metal cuffs binding his wrists prevent him from *shifting* hisself to her rescue. Already I can feel the hallway shake as if Trick was throwing his bulk against the bars, desperate to bust free as I leave a wicked mess dribbling down Lola Mae's legs. As I leave him powerless to undo what I done.

I'm so excited I could whistle. Takes all my energy to walk normal the final few paces to Trick's cell. "Put yer basket down, darlin'."

Lola Mae ignores me, pulls against my grip soon as she sees her daddy. Gaol ain't been good to him. Kept out the sun for so long, Trick's tan skin is now the shade of bleached hay. His black hair, normally twisted in a single long plait, is straggled and greasy; it droops from his cheeks and chin in a bootlegger's beard. The whites of his eyes is yellow and so is the rims of his nostrils. His arms and legs is wasted thin: elbows and knees jut from holes in his clothes as he sits, injun-style, on the bare floor. Though his fingers is free, his tattoos is scratched off and bloody. Ain't nothing near to hand for Trick to *shift* apart from his bandanna gag, and even it's tied so tight it's bit into his skin. Wind gusts through the two recessed windows above his head: the stench wafting off him, sour cheese and unwashed crotch, turns my stomach.

"Trick," I say. He slowly unfolds his legs, makes to rise.

Again, Lola Mae tries to wriggle from my grasp. I tense my muscles, imagine my bones is steel. She stops tugging, turns away from the cell, faces me. Twists her arms behind her. "Daddy," she says, pressing her body to mine, so close I can feel the sharp edges of her pelvis, the warm curve of her tits. "Sheriff Doolittle's brung me to help you. Ain't that good of him?"

Trick huffs like a dog. Stands as though any weight on his feet pains him. Shuffles closer.

I reach around Lola Mae, run my free hand down her arm, wrench the basket away. Squeezing the bony flesh of her wrists, I trap her hands and throw her against the bars—so hard I can hear her teeth clash, hear her skull connect with iron. She winces as the cold bites into her back, but she don't cry out.

Leaning closer, I bury my thigh between her legs, force them apart. Her face is shaded under the brim of my hat, but her eyes is bright as they meet mine. Gaze unwavering, she asks, "Can't we thank Doo, Daddy? For all he done?" Reaching out with her ankle, Lola Mae catches hold of my calves. Draws me even closer.

In the cell, Trick bends forward in a bow. Bends so low his features is lost in a tangle of hair. Hides behind his daughter.

"Look at me, damn you," I say. Trick kneels, not looking. I can't hardly breathe. My right hand fumbles at Lola Mae's skirts, the left keeps her writhing arms pinned against the bars. She stretches up on her tiptoes, presses her soft cheek against mine. My hips is thrusting into hers, and I ain't yet got so much as a finger in her drawers. She's moving, arcing up, pulling. Trick grunts, but stays down. "You fucken bastard," I growl. "Look—"

Lola Mae licks my earlobe.

"—at—"

Nibbles it.

"—me."

Bites till I see fireworks.

Trick stands. His face is lit up like it's the height of summer. A blaze of red is ripped into his scalp where a length of hair is tore out. Blood trickles down his forehead, into his eye, but he don't blink. His gaze is fiery, reflecting two slashes of red-yellow-white light.

Stars flash across my peepers. The girl's got me moaning and I'm near fit to burst. Lola Mae brushes her lips against my cheek, whispers: 'What kind of fool you take me for, Sheriff?'

Something slippery snakes round my left forearm. It clings, tightens: breaks my concentration. I loosen my grip as Trick reaches through the bars, locks onto my hands. At the same time, Lola Mae drops to the floor like a sack of flour. On her way down, she rolls free, her bracelets glowing sunset.

"No," I say.

The girl flicks a braided length of Trick's hair round my other wrist, holds tight to the end. Pulling till my hands is crossed in front of me, she mutters under her breath, then loops the makeshift rope again 'round both of them. Trick's grip don't loosen a smidge: I'm as good as stuck in tar.

"*Shift*," Lola Mae says, working her way behind me, pulling my beard, weaving it through the long blond strands what's escaped my ponytail.

Everywhere the *shift* touches my skin—forearms, face, and now 'round waist and thighs—feels like I've been branded with a hot poker. My skin bubbles, stretches, then contracts. The air fills with the stank of sulphur. My nose sniffles for a hint of burnt flesh—there ain't none. Inside my head, I hear my bones creak and snap, crunching into a smaller shape. I crumple to the floor, all the gitup gone from my arms and legs: they's curling, shrinking, turning to iron. All of my uppers is glued together in one thin shaft; my feet jut out, press flat into crooked teeth. My jaw peels open wide in surprise, not in pain. It don't ache too bad, this *shifting*. Not near so much as the hurt of failure.

A hole pierces straight through my head. Beneath my eyes, I can feel air whistle clean through my skull where my nose and mouth used to be. When it's all said and done, I make a clank-clanking sound across the stone floor as Lola Mae tips her basket, rolls me into it.

"Good thing there ain't five keyholes—nor even *four*, hey Doo? All we need is one key and now I gots meself two." Lola Mae winks down at me. "You should oughta watch that hangdog tongue of yers, Sheriff. Slobbering 'neath Potpie's windows, trailing it down the path after me, letting untruths slip when you gots your mind in yer trousers." I ain't got no expression at all on my twisted iron face, but the girl giggles like she knows I'm blushing. "You think I ain't seen you?" She shakes her head, uses both hands to lift the Mabel-key to the lock on Trick's cell. "I seen you plenty. Give me a hand here, Daddy."

Lola Mae's laughter turns to tears soon as they get the door open. She hugs Trick so tight I can hear the air whoosh from his lungs; he loops his arms over her head, squeezes back. He looks stronger with his girl tucked safe in his embrace. My tiny steel heart clenches. I wonder if Retti would ever have come for me the way Lola Mae done for Trick. If my little girl's face'd be slick and shiny with happiness, just from being with me. If she'd work at the knot of my gag till her knuckles bled. If she'd kiss my bearded cheeks, knowing that beneath the lice and grime, I were still her Pa.

Probably not.

I can't close my eyes, so I look away while Lola Mae *shifts* the cuffs from Trick's wrists. From my vantage, I can't see much: the dripping ceiling; a patch of crumbling stone 'neath the window sills; grass poking through the rusted bars; and a shadow that twitches, hops, grows into that damned fool squirrel. He pokes his head in from outside, then darts away as Trick's shackles clang to the floor. A second later, Lola Mae is pulling Mabel out the keyhole, passing her to Trick, then running after him as he strides out the cell, snapping up my basket as he goes. Just before I get dragged down the corridor, I see the squirrel's noggin reappear. See him scramble over the ledge, and down the cell's rough walls.

The basket shreds and bumps over the uneven floor, taking me for a wild ride. "Slow down, Daddy," Lola Mae says. "We gots to find Jaybird and Lilah afore we go."

"Keep up," Trick grunts, not slackening his pace a whit. He pulls me all the way to the stationhouse's front room. With assured movements, he takes a Yellowboy rifle from the wall, passes it to Lola Mae. Grabs a pair of Cimarrons, a pack of ammo and a holster from the gun cabinet, tosses them to the girl too. While she belts the weapons on, he finds hisself a pack, a set of Colt revolvers and a Ruger. Pockets some shells then hangs my basket from a hook the shotgun left empty, halfway up the wall.

There's a smash, then another. Trick's broken the two hurricane lamps we gots for emergencies and by the sounds of it is spilling their oil on the floor. He ransacks the single small cupboard I allow myself, finds a stash of beeswax candles I ain't never saw reason to get rid of. Crossing the room, he peels away layer after layer of wax, leaving a stub at the bottom about a finger's width high, trailing a long tail of wick.

"Go'on outside," he tells Lola Mae.

"But what about Jaybird and Lilah?" she asks, planting her feet firm.

"Go'on," Trick barks. "You done a fool thing bringing them young'uns here, star. Meet me where the path splits for Portage and Plantain—then we'll see if there's a speck left of them worth saving."

Sheepish, Lola Mae says, "Fine," and leaves without shutting the door.

Trick looks down, into my basket. "You just had to team up with them fucken Marshals, didn't you? Couldn't leave well enough alone." He digs into the gunpowder grout between the logs above my head, creating a hole big enough to hold a single, shortened candle stub. "Ain't y'all never going to learn?"

Taking the frayed end of the wick, the weaver bends and knots the fibres till they's shaped like a little flame. "*Shift*," he says.

Nothing happens. His tattoos flicker then darken, too damaged now to make so much as a spark.

If I had a mouth, I'd hoot, *Halleluiah! Ain't no fucken limp-dick* shifting *going to burn me*—

The sound of a match striking flint cuts my celebrations short. Cupping the flame carefully in his hand, Trick touches the match to the tip of the wick. It flares, then burns steadily toward the wall. "Ain't everything gots to be magic," he says as he hefts his pack. "You oughta know that by now, Doo."

He don't even bother to close the door as he leaves.

Watching that fire eat its way downwards, I wish I still had hands to fold in prayer. I hope the Almighty will take me, even though I can't make no final confessions, or that them other gods might look kindly on my situation and welcome me to their halls. *Whatever happens*, I think, *please let me find Retti when I get there.*

The ceiling tilts.

"Shiny!" the squirrel shouts—and I'm tumbling to the floor, my basket sent swinging with the momentum of the critter's leap. My head pounds harder than it does after a barrel-full of moonshine, but my vision don't swim. I can still see the fuse burning, flame getting closer and closer to the station house's tinderbox walls.

"Pretty, pretty, pretty," the squirrel chitters. He's in rough shape: already short an ear and missing half his tail, his aim is off as he jumps back down to the floor. He lands in a heap beside me, dropping part of his hindquarters as he scurries my way. "Smells like peanuts!"

The instant he chomps into me, he crumples. The life snuffs from his eyes; his head caves, his body shrivels till he ain't nothing but a pile of grass, straw and dust. As I begin to stretch and *shift*, I thank the little begger for being such a glutton. We's both made from the weavings of Lola Mae's magics: just as I were his antidote, he were mine.

I reckon his long-toothed bite were just about enough to save me.

My head, my face, my limbs expand. Hair grows where a minute before there weren't nothing but metal. Eyelids stretch over my peepers; tears well and spill down my cheeks. Every piece of me fills up with blood and guts and breath and snot and all the things what make a man—all the things except what's most important.

Atwixt my legs, my balls is twisted 'round the grip of a cold hard key. My cock welded to its shaft.

That's it, I think. Lola Mae's first permanent work. Now she's gone, and *I ain't got nothing left.*

No more chances. No young'uns, not even the makings for them. I stare at the ruin atwixt my legs, then up at the candle what's almost burnt clean through to the wall. I can smell the gunpowder, know it ain't going to take long for the place to go up in a ball of hellfire. My eyes swim with heat and tears and visions of Annie.

I wonder if she'll miss me, if I can't find the gumption to snuff that flame.

Depot to Depot

Depot to Depot

Haros can't remember the accident.

He wants to—he *tries* to—but he can't hear the screech of tires across asphalt. The car's windshield shattering. The frantic hiss of his brakes. The teeth-aching squeal of metal against metal. His left palm has rope burns from pulling the semitrailer's horn, but he doesn't know if it made any noise. The Allman Brothers still blare from the radio; he thinks he'd been singing along. Nineteen hours into a twenty hour drag, on a route he's travelled hundreds of times, the hatchback appeared out of nowhere. He's sure of that, damn sure. One minute, the road was empty; a river of black blurring into the night sky. Here and there, his headlights caught lone trees dotting the margins of endless wheat fields. At that speed they were mere flashes; emaciated, glowing people with arms outstretched, waving from a not-so-distant shore. No deer threatened to leap across the highway's two lanes—he could spot those suicidal fuckers a hundred feet away—and at three in the morning you'd be lucky to hit a raccoon. Everything had been still. Sleepy. Cold air rushed in the open window, slapped his face. He thinks he might've blinked.

A few seconds later the car's high beams were tearing his eyes open, its crumpled carcass ploughing a ten-metre gash into the crops. Vaguely, he recalls a high-pitched clinking—like dozens of ice cubes dropping into empty tumblers. Walking back and forth between the truck and the roadside, he sees a trail of broken glass, feels thousands of diamond shards crunching beneath his steel-capped work boots. A glittering parabola describing the car's trajectory after it ricocheted off the truck's cab.

Lord, he thinks. *Not again.*

He'd almost made it this time: there and back with no incidents. And so close to the warehouse ... it wasn't fair. *Fuck*, he thinks, making another trip over to survey the wreck. *Fuck*. He pinches the bridge of his nose, rubs thumb and finger around his tired eyes. So tired. Cybill's been telling him to quit for months, saying he'll lose his pay-outs if Al fires him first. *Just one more haul*, he'd reply, ignoring the risk; forgetting the number of times he's said the same thing. *One more and we'll have enough to get married, good and proper.*

That's what he tells her, the terms of his contract coating each word with lies.

"You got room for us in that truck?" The woman has a toddler on her hip and an arm around the oldest husk of a person Haros has seen in ages. White fluffs of hair top a balding head; a shrivelled face drips wrinkles down the neckline of a button-up shirt. Only sign she's a she is her long floral skirt and the stockings elephanting into old lady sandals. Clinging to her granny is a young girl who looks a few years younger than Cybill's kids, about ten or eleven at most.

He looks at them, at the mess of their vehicle, and sends a prayer of thanks to whatever God is listening at that hour that no-one else has yet driven past. "I don't know, darlin'—"

Deaf to morals and ethics, his instincts tell him to hop in the rig and floor it. Clouds block most of the moonlight and his cap obscures the parts of his face not already covered by his beard. He keeps his gaze averted so they won't see his greyish-blue irises; Cybill thinks his eyes are what people notice first. *They're memorable*, she says. *They're fierce.* He's not so sure. Line him up with a handful of other truckers, pull faded black Styx t-shirts over their beer bellies, hang sleeveless jean jackets on their shoulders and dangle a few coins like novelty buttons from their vest pockets— no-one would be able to tell him from the rest of them. And with no witnesses ...

No. Running isn't really an option. Such things always catch up with him—time and distance are flimsy protection from responsibility. If thirty years on the road has taught him anything, it's taught him this: out here, it's depot to depot. No matter how long the haul, you finish what you start.

He opens the passenger door, takes his lumbar support belt from the seat. Cinching it tight around his thick waist, he clears his throat. "Where you headed?"

The women follow him to the back of the refrigerated trailer, watch him check the bolts on the double doors. How long has he been idling here? No-one will profit if the meat defrosts before he can deliver it, least of all him. He's only just repaid Al for the last time—a detour across the border to a *hacienda* filled with the tightest women you ever saw. Two days round-trip and such a change in temperature he lost ninety grand's worth of grass-fed beef and his job along with it. Neither was his fault. He had no choice: he couldn't leave the minivan's passengers stranded with their only means of transport destroyed, steaming its last breath on the gravel shoulder. What the girls looked like had nothing to do with it. Al had thought otherwise. Of course, that was before Haros found Cybill, and more than a year before his boss put him back on the books. Now, he was reassured by the sound of the trailer's coolers humming, the roar of his engine reduced to a waiting purr. As long as the cargo is secure, he reckons, so is his future.

"Listen, mister." The woman's voice wavers to stifle tears, talking through shock. "We ain't got the right insurance." Unconsciously, she adjusts her hold on her wriggling son, starts again. "This trip wasn't planned, so to speak. Losing the car don't worry us none, right Mamma?" Granny shakes her head as wrinkles curve up her cheeks. "And we can't stay here—who knows what'd happen to us."

Haros keeps quiet, heads towards the hatchback and gives them a few minutes to think about what they're saying. The lasting implications.

"So, look." The woman pauses as he looks through the crushed window panes, tilting his head as though listening. "We'd be awful grateful if maybe you could, you know, give us a lift?"

Rattling the driver-side's door, he feels like bolting but knows he can't. Knows he won't. He exhales, then turns to look at her directly. "You know where you're headed?"

The woman nods slowly, watching Haros work. Again, she nods and tells him what they'd had in mind.

The east coast; a beach. He curses under his breath. Granny—her name's Daena, he's told—used to go there with her family as a kid. *She wanted to see the sun rise over the ocean once more before she meets Jesus*, the daughter says. The woman: Sissy. Nowhere near as good-looking as Cybill, but friendly enough to spend a few hours with. He helps them all into the cab, shows them where they can sit.

No more than three hours until dawn. "That explains the speed." Did Haros say this out loud or in his head? Then, or now? Sometimes it's all a muddle. "Give me a sec to clean up here," he said. He *knows* he said.

His hands are stained by the time he's done. A properly frozen side of beef sounds like wood when struck—he hopes all his cargo will pass this test once he arrives. Brushing the dirt and filth from his jeans, he takes a moment to calm himself, to adjust his timelines. *Just a few extra hours*, he thinks. *It's better than days.* Now, sitting safely in his rig, the wooden beads of his seat cover pressing into his sore back, he finally smells burnt rubber. Smoke. Spilled fuel. Char from a barbeque.

He'd smelled nothing at the time.

"All set?" The cheer in Sissy's voice is forced. The family is settled: Daena and her daughter bracket the little girl, Penny, while the youngest member is passed from lap to lap. "Tha's a *truck*," the boy says, nodding and pointing earnestly.

Crescent moons of sweat are acrid under Haros' arms. He turns up the air-conditioning even though the window is still down. Rubs the red from his eyes, grips the steering wheel. *Just a detour*, he tells himself, glad the key is already turned in the ignition. *Back to the sea.*

♪

A faded tattoo runs the length of his right forearm: a long twisted staff pushing a skiff from elbow to wrist; the sun and moon merging like a yin-yang symbol where other folks might wear a watch; the whole thing framed with writing in some language Sissy's never seen before—all upside-down Vs and pointy Es. Angles so sharp they could cut.

She watches his red-rimmed fingers brush the black hair around on his arm; now casting the image in shadow, now revealing it.

"What's it mean, mister?" she asks.

"Haros." He spits the word from his throat, guttural emphasis on the H. The look she throws him is pure confusion. "Not the tatt," he says. "The name. Haros. Call me Harry—most do."

"Like you, Harry-berry," Sissy says, pulling the boy closer, pressing her cheek against his soft curls. Her sing-song tone leaves a taste of bile in Haros' mouth.

"Tha's a truck." The toddler shrinks from the hug. Pudgy hands reaching for the pile of change in the ashtray, he eyes the driver warily.

"Ma, tell him to stop saying that." Penny squirms between her mother and Daena, pries the silver quarter from little Harry's fingers. Sissy blushes and apologises. "He always fixates on the last thing he sees."

Haros understands; he's dealt with plenty of kids. The woman smiles then, and repeats her question.

He suddenly wishes they'd all just shut up. Taking a deep breath, he contracts his diaphragm; tries to smother the vines of anxiety sprouting from his stomach, groping from his oesophagus to strangle his heart. The odometer ticks over as he exhales.

"Stint in the navy," he says, which is mostly true. It was a long time ago. He'd captained a boat, nothing too grand, no more than a handful of passengers in one go and him the only crew. The work was cold but regular. Always, he knew what to expect. He picked folks up, dropped them off; it wasn't brain surgery. The gig got him a berth on the vessel, hot meals when his guts rumbled, a few coins in the bank. No surprises. For a while, it'd sufficed.

The squall changed everything. He'd grown so complacent pushing bodies around in the water that it shook him to the bones having to pluck one from the waves instead. At first, he'd thought she was a mermaid—all delicate skin and weedy hair—but she was just a little girl. Swept overboard, she was half-drowned but still full of fight. Every inch of her twelve-year-old frame screamed it wasn't her time to die. And Haros had agreed.

He'd jumped in. Dragged her out. Returned her to her family, saved them premature grief. He hadn't felt like a hero; it'd been a fluke. He was paid to make deliveries, not retrievals. The child was an aberration. But for the first time, the thought of doing his job gave him chills. For the first time, he ached for dry land.

Two days after selling his boat, he got a letter of thanks from the little girl's family. Nearly three decades later Cybill rediscovered his name, tracked him down to repay him herself. And after sharing his bed that night, she'd stuck around. It was a first: having a constant friend, a stable lover. So much better than the roadhouse tarts he used to bring home—so fulfilling, he sometimes isn't sure which of them is more grateful she didn't drown that day.

Now she works at the diner near their place, brings home leftover cherry pie on Sundays. Makes him egg salad sandwiches and packs them in a mini cooler with a couple cans of cola and a mickey of rum. "For the truck stop," she warns, teasing him with the bottle and a cheeky grin. "Not a drop before you've pulled over, you hear?"

Haros' mouth is dry.

He could offer his passengers a bite to eat, but doesn't. Ordeals like the one they've been through tonight have a way of stealing the appetite. And they've other things to deal with than hunger.

"Wonder what the cops will do when they find our car," Sissy says.

Penny perks up. "I bet they'll measure the skid marks on the road and dust for fingerprints and see if there are different colours of paint in the smashed up parts." She pauses to catch her breath. "And they'll look it up on the computer, find out which dealership makes those paint colours and search for licence plate numbers that match." Excited now. "They'll narrow it down to a few different people who've bought those cars and then they'll see who has a record." She smiles at Haros, smug and accusing.

"Hoo-ee, girl! Look who's got some school learning in her." Daena's dentures click when she talks, whistling the 'S's. Penny falls quiet, her face red. Embarrassed by Granny's ignorance or because she's got most of that shit knowledge from late-night TV. Far as Haros knows, real cops take much longer to figure things out, if they ever do.

Especially when there's so little evidence.

♪

A gas station glows on the horizon. Haros doesn't usually make stops so close to his destination, but tonight is an exception. The rig's too crowded. The travellers won't stop talking to him. Won't stop staring. He can't look at them directly, their faces grey with the night's final hours. Mile after mile, he feels their gazes boring into his skull. Penetrating. Questioning.

Every time he blinks, he sees the four of them inside their hatchback.

Eighteen wheels spit out gravel on the road's soft shoulder then rumble to a halt under a cluster of spotlights near the station's gas pumps. The tail-end of a Johnny Neel tune crackles out of a hidden PA system. The singer's nasal melody falls into the pot of black coffee a young waitress carries between tables on the sidewalk outside. Focused on the lengths of their own journeys, not a one of the diners spares the rig a second glance.

"Stay here," Haros says, grabbing a handful of change and throwing the door open. "I need to piss." Bluish light fills the truck's cab; garish and too bright. He squints and adjusts the peak of his cap.

In his mind, the car's high beams are still blinding.

In some ways it was easier on the boat. Less mess, fewer conflicts. He turns the bathroom faucets on full, splashes his face until the front of his t-shirt is soaked. Water gushes down the drain, the sound echoing around the tiny concrete room. He closes his eyes and imagines himself as the vortex in a whirlpool. The calm point after the gales, a hush after the noise. Empty and rudderless. Alone.

In a flash the space fills with bodies. Bloated. Bloody. Mangled. They rush in, waggle their familiar heads, their silenced mouths, then disappear with the tap's squeaking shut. He grips the basin, waits for his heart to stop racing. When he can bear to reopen his eyes he ignores his reflection in the mirror. The fluorescent ceiling light hums and flickers, its glass littered with fruit fly corpses. *How do they get in there?* He doesn't bother switching it off as he leaves.

Damp and standing out in the fresh night air, he is overwhelmed by an urge to call Cybill. To tell her everything. To be absolved.

Though he knows it's useless, he pats at his back pocket to find his phone. Flips it open. Still dead. He spots a rusty public booth at the far end of the parking lot, heads for it. A series of dimes and nickels chinks into the bashed-up coin slot as he presses the receiver to his ear. *Please wake up*, he thinks. His hand so jittery he screws up the number, and has to start dialling again.

He leans against the cold glass, oblivious to the graffiti and gobs of dried spit marring its surface. One ring; he shifts from foot to foot. Two, three, four; there's a click followed by Cybill's voice. He swallows the lump in his throat and hangs up without leaving a message.

Staring at his stained boots as he walks back to the truck, he hears the buzz of walkie-talkies before he sees any cops. State troopers, what looks to be a whole fleet of them, line up at the bowsers. It takes all his willpower to keep from breaking into a run.

"Hey—" The lawman is stocky and holds his chest out like an eagle. "Hey, you."

Shit. Haros shoves his hands into his pockets, tries to look casual as he picks up the pace. He keeps his eyes forward, focused on the truck. On the folks inside it.

Footsteps on gravel behind him; walking then jogging.

His pulse races. Sweat trickles down his back.

"Hey!" The cop grabs Haros' arm, spins him around—then snatches his hand away as though burned. The teamster's body is so tense it prevents him from striking.

"That your rig?"

Haros nods. "Why?"

"Quite a ding you've got there," the trooper says. "Ain't safe driving around with half your front lights smashed."

Fucking do-gooders. Haros thinks quick. "Yeah," he replies with all the pleasant he can muster. "Twelve point bucks'll do that."

The cop whistles through his front teeth. "Shit. You keep the meat?"

No-one 'round these parts would leave something that valuable behind. It wouldn't be right for him *not* to have picked it up. Haros swallows. "In the back."

"You planning on using it? I mean, my cousin's a butcher—" The policeman saunters over to the trailer, keen to have a gander. "Mind if I take a look?"

Clenching his fists, Haros wonders how hard he'll have to belt the cop to knock him out. Adrenaline courses through him until he's short of breath and his temples throb. He's never hit a soul in his life. Not with his hands.

Beep! B-b-b-beeeep! Styrofoam coffee cups teeter on the police cruiser's roof as the cop's partner wails on the horn. "Problem, McAllister?"

"Nah," the trooper calls over his shoulder. "Reckon this feller's got a side of venison up for grabs." The grin he shoots in Haros' direction is crooked and shows too many teeth. "Don't you, buddy?"

Turning to a pair of officers in the neighbouring car, the partner chuckles. "Opportunistic fucker, ain't he?" Still laughing, he calls out, "We got to roll, Sarge. You can do your wheelin' and dealin' off the clock."

"Shit." McAllister slaps Haros on the shoulder, pats him like he would a dog. "Sorry, pal. Maybe next time."

Incoherent farewells garble from the trucker's mouth before he finds himself back in the driver's seat, slamming the door. Gripping the steering wheel until his knuckles whiten, he puts his forehead on his hands and fights the urge to weep.

"Everything okay?" Sissy whispers because the kids are looking dozy, and she thinks they might drop off if she leaves them to it. Granny's staring out the window, face aglow as the first hints of pink bleed into the sky. The air in the cab crackles with static. Seagull cries fill Haros' ears. He tastes seaweed and salt; smells rotten fish, earthworms, the electric zing of an oncoming storm. He shakes his head to clear it. For a second it feels like his callused hands are gripping an oar.

"We'll get you there soon," he says, the engine roaring to life beneath his heavy foot. "Just in time to catch that first wave."

♪

The gods are smiling on Haros: the beach is empty, tinged with a wash of mauve and red light. He drives over the curb; across grassy knolls that will be covered with families of sun worshippers in a few short hours; and onto a thin strip of white sand newly exposed by the retreating tide. The delivery truck's tires sink into the soft surface and kick up showers of grit as the heavy vehicle inches its way to the waterline. Tongues of foam lap at nine of the eighteen wheels when Haros kills the engine. Half in the ocean, half on land. He takes off his boots, plants them high up on the shore with their toes pointed to the parking lot. The sight of them, safe from the sea's greedy reach, calms him. Reassures him he'll make his way back once he's sent his passengers on their way.

Opening the trailer's hatch, he takes the pail stored inside and fills it with seawater. He tosses a whole bucketful into the back so the corpses, already partially frozen and coated with frost, will come away from the floor without sticking. Again he dips the bucket, douses the bodies. And again, until their contorted limbs begin to move, to float on the rivulet of red now dripping out the door.

An orange slice of sun, as tremulous as his passengers' ghosts, emerges from the navy horizon. Haros tightens his lifting belt, prepares to put it to work.

"Come on," he says, hoisting little Harry's stiff grey form from the back of the truck. The boy's spirit lingers, clutching his mother's hand. Haros plunges into the water, gasps as it numbs his ankles and thighs, shrinks his balls. Rum and cola fumes heat his throat as he exhales, but does nothing for the rest of him. "Come on," he repeats, dropping the small body like a plank into the swell. Sissy leads her son over, helps him straddle his half-submerged torso like a surfboard. The boy squirms beneath the weight of Haros' hand.

"Don't let him get off," Haros says, going to retrieve Penny, then Sissy, then Daena. He's drenched by the time the spirits are settled, legs wrapped around their conduits, faces pointed to the east, features radiant under the sun's yellow touch. From the corner of his eye, he can see Granny as she was a lifetime ago: rounded and smooth, hair thickly chocolate, a shimmer of joy on her cheeks.

"Yes," Daena says under her breath. "This is it." Of their own volition, her feet start kicking, propelling her away from the shoreline. The children, afraid of being left behind or keen to show off, lean forward to follow. Uncoordinated, they nearly slip from their bodies.

"Use your arms, not your legs." Haros demonstrates, up to his knees in the surf, his hands flat and outstretched, churning the air. They laugh at his efforts. Even to him, the motion looks awkward, unnatural. He wishes he had a paddle to lend.

"We got nothing to give," Sissy says, watching her family's progress. "No way to pay you for this."

Haros shrugs. Reaching down, he fumbles with frozen fingers at the woman's lifeless neck. With a short grunt, he tugs until the chain draped around it snaps. Straightening up, he holds the necklace aloft letting the small golden medallion slide off into his palm. He raises the pendant to his vest, sizes it up next to the others he's got pinned there.

"This'll do," he says. Dawn's rays refract off his new bauble, the glare blinding.

He doesn't remember their passing—knowing where they've gone is never part of the deal. But as he trudges over to the truck, he takes a last looks for signs their fragile flesh-boats have gone off course. Finds none.

The stiffness in his back lifts with the morning.

He listens while cleaning all traces of their blood from his trailer. Soon enough, the splash of their saltwater voices merges with the rush of waves. *One delivery down*, he thinks. Seabirds wheel overhead, eyeing his remaining cargo. He concentrates on scrubbing quickly, so the beef won't spoil more than it already has. *One stop to go.* He prays the roads stay clear until he gets there.

Just once, he'd like to reach that depot on time.

Commonplace Sacrifices

Commonplace Sacrifices

In the end, it was a fingernail that saved you. Now let's be clear: I'm not talking about some tricky-tricky metaphor, some la-di-dah imagery here. Last time I checked, none of your teeth had skins that could catch you. Time wouldn't get nicked on your behalf. And while the seat of your pants mighta conspired to get you into this mess, years back in the happy-happy *before* days, it sure as hell didn't help scoot you through the exit now. Nope, no fancy words would help you escape. But a grimy fingernail, rip-torn from the tip of my naked Peter Pointer—well, *that* would open doors.

This final offering was real, kiddo, and it was a masterstroke. I know you won't mind me saying so.

Not now, anyway.

It had taken a while for the hocus and the pocus to align, for the big hand and the little hand to shake in agreement, for the elements to alchemise just *so*. Years of practice have taught us—haven't they just?—that timing can save you a bruising when you're dealing with the likes of him.

I knew I had to get it right. You were sagging like an empty bag of flour, and I was running out of parts. I mean, it'd been a busy year for the two of us. My stocks had run too low. Only a couple of stumps were left to hold me up; a pair of wingless stalks sprouted uselessly from my back; my hands no longer boasted a full complement of digits. There were no more lids, no more lips, no more lashes. Just a nail, and a sparkling opportunity.

My eyes tick-tocked between the sparkle and my finger while I worried. About you; about what I had seen yesterday; about the rough edge of my nail and how I could use it to let you see now what I had seen then. And how all of it combined could help you—help us—get out of here for good.

Removing the Pointer's half-moon was a tidy feat of engineering, what with a bottom incisor and a canine my only tools for the procedure. I gnawed, gouged into the cuticle, worked my jaw until the nail flapped like a pet-door from the end of my finger. He watched TV beside me, oblivious; you were doing laundry in the basement.

There wasn't much blood when it finally came loose. At least, not enough to do anything *really* useful. Just enough to let a few drops drip onto his dewy Gouda cheek; enough to trickle down the deep crease blurring the boundary between his mouth and jowl. I sucked on the shard, rolled it on my tongue, and nearly laughed it out my nose when I saw pustules take root, then bloom on his cheek, where my bloody splashes had kissed him.

Good ones, I thought with a grin. Deep, blind, under-the-neath pimples. Guaranteed to start throbbing the moment they're touched. I leaned over his dishwater face to prod them a bit—just a little poke to get the agony started . . .

But then you walked into the living room, carrying two weeks' worth of laundry, still wearing your Buy 'n' Save uniform. Flyaway hair had sneaked its way out of the tight braid you'd tied at 5:30 this morning, and your hands were cracked from handling thousands of other people's dollars at the cash register all day. Static charges followed in your wake as you dragged your feet across the carpet; energy lost through your soles.

I waited until you drew closer to his op-shop recliner before I took aim. I chewed with anticipation: what a surprise I had in store for you!

This is it, kid, I thought. Just keep on walking. Keep on going . . . Keep on, keep on, keep on—don't hesitate—that's it—now's the chance! I haven't stuck by you for thirty-two years only to—

Wait. Settle down.

Your cough caught my attention. Your husband didn't so much as blink, didn't even acknowledge your presence; but the sound shook me back into the moment, forced me to calm myself.

Focus, I thought. *This is it.*

He was bound to be angry when the laundry basket tumbled from your outstretched arms—why didn't you come in when the clothes were filthy? *Man oh man*, that would've been so much more fun! But never mind. Clean or dirty, I had to take this opportunity. I mean, he was in here all the time but you, understandably, weren't. So it had to be today; it had to be *now*.

All you have to do is take a few more steps, just past James' toys over there, and across to the sofa-bed . . .

I worried at the nail in my mouth, scuffed up its enamel, burred it 'til it was Velcro-prickly. When you reached my intended mark, I spat it on the carpet in front of you.

Even though I'd been holding my position for a few minutes, my aim was impeccable. Not to brag or anything, but it was a magic shot. The nail bounced once, twice, on the dusty carpet then stood up like the unearthed rib of some prehistoric beast. You trod square on the miniature spike, and I held my breath until it was firmly embedded in the soft arch of your striped sock. When you took your next step—sorry, kid, that laundry's never going to make it to the table—I could see that it had been absorbed into your foot. I gave it a second, then two . . .

"Jesus!" Clothes popped from the basket, cotton and wool confetti prematurely celebrating your release, while you hopped over to the tartan sofa-bed, clutching your foot.

Stage one: accomplished, I thought. Clapping wildly, I splattered a few extra drip-drops of blood onto his face for good measure. Meanwhile, you flopped onto the sofa, frantically massaging your foot, quietly seething *ow ow ow ow ow* through clenched teeth.

"What the hell's wrong with you?" he asked, not really caring for a response.

You grunted, "Charlie horse," without looking up.

He gave you a scowl then sneered at the boxers that had landed on his forearm. He clunked his canned bourbon onto the coffee table, flicked the shorts away as though the contact had somehow soiled his plaster cast.

You want soil? I thought. *I'll give you soil.* Climbing up onto his drink was challenging without my leathery wings. Don't worry; you needed them last week more than I did. It's fine, honest. They'll grow back. Besides, with a bit of wobbling I managed to squat above the can's gaping mouth. I flexed my pelvic muscles and *pushed*—and if I'd held anything back, I would have pissed myself laughing, hearing him cuss his face red while booze frothed onto his grease-stained track pants.

Paying his rant no mind, you kneaded the sole of your foot, rubbing in the remnants of my gift to you. Your face was focused, darkly intent. For a moment I feared the nail had been too powerful. That it would absorb all of your attention, and then you'd miss it.

Please, kid, I thought. *Don't miss it.* Look down now. Come on come on come on—look down *now . . .*

There! Your eyes drifted to the stubby wooden leg of the sofa-bed. Yes, that's it!

No! No no no—don't look up at him—look down! Look look look; that's right, keep your eyes down until you see it.

Did you see it?

There—yes, there. *Right there*—Yes! That's it!

A small frown. You slid off of the couch and crouched next to its leg, your aching foot forgotten.

Reach out, kid—it's in your grasp!

Your eyes plucked its tiny brilliance from the carpet before your fingers, or your mind, could grasp what it represented.

I slid off the coffee table and danced a jig my ancestors taught me back in the old country. What a celebration we'll have now, kid. Hold on tight!

That little glimmer is your get-out-of-jail-free card.

♪

"It's not that." He reached for his sweaty beer and took a deep draught. His Adam's apple, barely visible through the stubble creeping down the stump of his neck, bobbed with each gulp he took.

Pennies! I thought as I looked at the tabletop in front of you. Hundreds of lucky pennies were flattened and pressed into the antique wood, their charms entombed beneath two inches of discoloured resin. *What sort of a sick bastard would do this?* Who would smother luck under layers of tree-tears? Who would repress something so marvellous, show it off like a prize, but keep it forever out of reach? Disgusted, I flopped into the parmesan dish in the centre of the table, self-medicated in a bath of crumbly cheese.

"Nice table, huh?" he asked, then took another swig of beer.

You swirled your pasta onto a fork that clashed with the rest of the cutlery, and kept quiet.

"It's just that . . ." He paused, deciding how to continue the conversation he'd initiated. "It's just that you look fine from here—" he lowered his hands to the level of his gut "—to here—" and lifted them to cup his concave chest. "But from here down," he pushed your heart into your throat as his hands gestured toward his lower body. "Your thighs? Well . . . They're just not *attractive* anymore."

The pasta in your mouth turned to paste and your jaw clamped down, hard, in mid-chew. You tried to squeeze the pulpy mouthful down your spasming throat, tried to force it past the lump expanding there, tried to swallow so that you could breathe. You looked hot. Beads of sweat twinkled like a crown at your hairline, and a warm trickle of snot winked as it slid from your left nostril. Kalamata olives wavered on the plate in front of you, swimming in cream sauce and tears.

You reached for the cloth napkin on your lap and raised it up to your dripping nose. Stiffly, stiffly. Everything still, apart from the liquids human bodies excrete when distressed.

"How's everything going over here?" the waiter asked, his stained apron camouflaging the faux in his enthusiasm. You kept your face averted and hoped mascara wasn't running down your cheeks while the men chatted, laughed.

I sprang out of the parmesan dish, bounded across the table, skidded to a halt in front of your meal. Finally, I'd realised what I could give you for your birthday! I had been thinking and thinking, scratching and wondering about it all day—and I'd only *just* managed to come up with the right present for you, with a few hours to spare before the day was no longer yours to celebrate.

Using my fingers to dig into the soft skin at my temple, I coaxed my left ear away from the side of my head. Peeling it banana-like, I clutched the flip-floppy flesh in my hand, pulled and tugged it free from its riggings while the rightie wriggled, waited for its turn to be plucked. Once both ears sat bloody in the palms of my hands, I threw one and then the other into your glass of Riesling—what precision! they didn't even make a splish-splash—then watched as they swelled like greedy sponges in the pale yellow liquid. Giggled as they grew large enough to intercept his words.

Tears plinked onto pressed pennies. You tilted your head back and forced down the offensive mouthful of fettuccini. The fork wavered in your hand, reminding you that it was ready for action. You stared at it and tried to regain your composure. With a deep sniff, you reached out and neatly placed it on the placemat to the right of your pasta dish. Oil seeped into the faded linen, surrounding the discarded utensil with a deep maroon halo.

You clasped your hands on your lap, changed your mind; reached for your wine instead. I gave the stem a gentle nudge as you lifted the glass to your lips, and waved goodbye to my ears as they slid into your mouth. Drink deep, kid. Deep but steady, now. Steady.

Fine webs began to weave themselves across your tender ears seconds after you'd swallowed. Strand after strand of pearlescent strength looped around lobes and over helixes; clear fibres spun along antihelixes, into ear canals and back out again. The sturdy filaments of your birthday present wandered through delicate golden hoops dangling from your ears, blending invisibly with their saltwater pearls. Up and down, in and out, around and back again; the web was impenetrable within minutes. As the last thread fell into place, end fused with origin, shining and sturdy as infinity's figure of eight. Your face relaxed as the webs leached into your tender skin. Taking up your fork once more, you looked up at him.

Steady, I thought. *There, there.*

♪

James sat on the carpet, creating plastic worlds beneath the dining table. His six-year-old legs, extended in a V-shape and clad in pilled flannel, were formidable barriers around a hoard of dismantled Lego. I sat astride one of his exposed shins and tried to pilfer a square —an alien head would be better—to add to my own growing collection. Ah, but he's a savvy one, your James is: the instant I reached out and hooked a piece with my toes, he raised his leggy boom gates and threw me to the floor, crying

"Oh, there it is!" I flipped over just in time to witness the coveted piece being snapped onto a higgledy-piggledy contraption.

Clever, clever, I thought. Breakfast dishes clinked overhead as you cleared the table. Spoons and bowls and coffee cups joined in discordant symphony to accompany my foiled heist.

Spoils to the victor, I thought, swinging myself up onto the chair you had recently vacated. Laurels should always be awarded to valiant conquerors. So I slid across the varnished pine seat, plucked my last eyelash, and balanced it on the crest of James' primrose cheek. It was only fair. He'd earned it with his sneaky-cheeky cleverness.

"Look what I made, Mamma," James said. He brandished his construction like a trophy over his head. Craning his neck as he reached up, he pushed the Lego vehicle up onto the table and shoved it well away from the edge. One by one, he clamped his hands parenthetically around his toy, then hoisted his slight figure *up.* His dark hair, so much like his father's had been, back when the two of you were in lah-lah-love, poked up over the table's horizon first. It caught the morning light spilling in from the living room window, glinted like velvet. Seeing your son's pride, you paused, and put the stack of dishes back onto the table. For once you didn't mind that the living and dining areas were compressed into one uncomfortable room.

"C'mere, sweetness," you said. A deep brown eye, heavily-lashed, peeked up at you and crinkled with an unseen smile. I scuttled off your seat as you reassumed it, then shimmied my way up the table leg while the rest of your child's dimpled face sprouted next to the dishes. Moving clockwise around the table, always keeping one hand on his creation, James tip-toddled toward you. A curl of scrambled yellow in a pool of condensation caught my hungry eye as he clambered up on to your lap, so I snacked on its goodness while James exhibited his fragile handiwork.

"It's an awesome—" You widened your eyes, tilted your head toward the Lego.

"Velociraptor catcher," he supplied. "With fangs and lava-shooters."

"Well, of course. That's what I thought it was. "'Cos it doesn't have wings, so it couldn't have been a pterodactyl trapper, could it?" He shook his head in agreement while his pudgy fingers fiddled with rotating pieces.

"Besides, you wouldn't need lava for pterodactyls, would you?"

"Nah, you need a shooting star machine for them, Mamma."

You drew James closer to you then and gave him a kiss on his left cheek. He giggled, squirming until he faced you directly. *Magic*, I thought. I leapt across the table and balanced on one toe atop the sugar bowl. A little nudge shunted in the right direction is all it would take to draw your attention to James' cheek, so I blew you a kiss and—

"Oh, James—how exciting! No, not the shooting star machine—I mean, that's exciting—but no, that's not what I meant. What a lucky boy you are: you've got an eyelash on one of your cheeks! And if you can guess which one it is, you'll get a wish!"

Fairy lights of joy shone in James' eyes.

"Pick a cheek," you said, turning your head away, so as not to influence his decision.

Very serious now, James closed his eyes. He concentrated, bunching his face up the way he does when forced to choose between chicken nuggets or grilled cheese at Pete's Roadhouse. Chips or cheese? "You can only pick one," you'd say. Wish or no wish? It was a momentous decision.

Choose well, buddy, I thought. *There's not much I can do if you pick the wrong one.*

Honouring the solemnity of the occasion, James slowly lifted his hand, extended a reverent finger, and pointed to his right cheek.

A heartbeat passed—one of yours, not his. Your boy's chest fluttered; your own was measured, a reliable metronome. Two beats. James's eyes flicked open on the third, interrogating.

"Did I get it right, Mamma?"

Slowly, slowly, you took his wavering finger and pressed it into the lash. "You're right!" He rewarded your excitement with an exuberant, gap-toothed smile.

Here comes the good bit, I thought, moving closer to see the outcome.

"Now make a wish. And when you're ready, blow the lash off your fingertip otherwise it won't come true."

James gazed with due deference at the lash teeter-tottering on his finger, and held his breath to avoid disturbing his prize. Exhaling carefully, he closed his eyes once more.

"Stop filling the boy's head with all that airy-fairy shit, Sal. You're turning him into a fag. That's why he can't kick a football, why he cries all the time—look! See what I mean? He's at it again. You're making him soft with that shit, I swear."

James opened his drowned eyes to glare across the living room.

"Make your wish, my beautiful boy," you whispered, placing a slender hand on your son's head, turning his face toward yours. He blinked several times; I captured as many of his tears as I could, drank away his salty hurt.

On his still-extended finger, James' wish waited.

With intense focus, your boy drew a deep breath, puffed his vulnerable chest out, and blew.

As James wheezed, a nimbus bloomed on his fingertip. Prismatic beams scouted across his hand and wrist; luminous way stations dotted his arms, laced around his legs, and girded his torso with their warmth.

Well chosen, I thought. *Such a clever boy.*

Constellations appeared all over his body. Light draped, cloak-like, across James's shoulders. A mask of illumination shone across his tear-stained cheeks, shielding his eyes, growing into a helm that protected his thoughts. Sunny gauntlets and noontime greaves sheathed his scrawny limbs, while moonlight laces secured his armour in place. Thus attired, James stood perceptibly straighter; ready to confront and conquer any breed of monster. Resilience burnt just a bit brighter in his reinforced eyes.

His father's gaze was successfully repelled. It slid away from his son and lodged once more on the box sitting on the milk crate across from his chair. Hollow projections flickering from the backside of a transparent screen attracted all of his attention.

♪

"I can't get any bloody disability payments, and the fuckers won't take me back 'til September. Liability, my ass. I could do that job with two busted arms, for Christ's sake. Half the guys are jerking off all day anyway—so how's my working with a broken arm any different?"

"I could work," you offered. "I mean, now that I've got my diploma and all. I could start applying for some jobs, see how it goes?"

"Oh, you could, could you? Well, doesn't your shit just shine? What are you saying? 'Cos what I'm hearing is that Princess went to night school, and now she thinks she's hot shit. So what? You trying to tell me if I had a degree, I wouldn't be in this situation? A goddamn piece of paper wouldn't've saved my arm from the press, would it? Nice fucking sympathy you've got on you, Sal."

"All I meant was I could get a job at the grocery store, or the bakery. Maybe. Whatever. I was just trying to help."

He shook his crimson head. Bridges of spit stretched between his lips as he shouted. "Why you so keen to get out of here all of a sudden? What've you got up to while I've been slaving away at work all day? You hooked yourself some toy boy in town? That why you're so hot about getting a job?" His tongue flicked to the corners of his mouth between each accusation.

You kept your voice quiet, but it wasn't enough. "Stop being such an arsehole. It's not my fault you're sore."

Uh-oh, I thought.

"It's not your fault, eh Sal? What about that kid you brung me? Hey? What about that? I'd wager my good arm he sure as hell *is* your fault. Said you were on the pill—my arse! And what about—"

He just kept going, broken record-like. You know how he gets when he fixates. Eyes a-bugging, nostrils a-flaring; there's no reasoning with him when he's doing his crazy-crazy impersonation. But who am I to tell you all this? You were there. I don't really need to subject you to the whole episode again, do I?

You know, kiddo, I would've stopped him if I could have. I swear it. But my powers can only stretch so far, even when I'm fully equipped. And even then, when I've got two arms, all my fingers, at least a toe or two, and my wings, preferably—*even then* there are some realities my parts can't prevent.

I cried as I watched. I stayed by your side, suffering in my impotence while you suffered because of it.

When it was all said and done, and you'd retreated to the sofa-bed, I curled up in the purple curve of your eyes while you slept.

It was the least—let's face it, kid, it was the most—I could do. I would have crawled into your heart, insinuated myself into your mind, erased the memory of the whole episode, if only. Instead, I bathed in residual tears. Soaked up the aftermath until my body was tumescent with your violet pain.

Your face was nearly set to rights by the time dawn squeaky-cleaned its way into morning. Superficially, at any rate. I'd have to work a few more nights to erase the haunted look in your gaze, the echo of violence in your features. James didn't notice the swelling when you offered him a bowl of Cheerios for breakfast. He simply asked you to pass him the box, then dug around in it for the plastic prize. An innocent smile twinkled in your direction when he retrieved a pen filled with invisible ink.

When you congratulated him on his find, he asked if you'd like to use it to fill out your job applications. He was sure your new bosses would think it was pretty neat, having a magician as an employee.

𝄞

Your uniform drooped as you waited for the elevator to drag its arthritic bulk down to the ground floor. The paper bags in your arms matched the expression in your eyes. Rebellious tins of kidney beans, obnoxious rolls of toilet paper, and apples with the shine of street-brawlers were defeating the bags sneaky-like. Tearing things up from the inside.

The lift's heavy steel doors mimicked the firm line of your mouth: pressed shut with no sign of opening. I *popped* up to the apartment while you scuffed your dingy sneakers along the imitation marble floor downstairs, waiting.

His plaster cast peeked out beneath the folds of her skirt as she straddled him on the sofa-bed. Startled, I *popped* back down to the ground floor before my brain could register the contorted shapes on the couch, before my footless legs had even brushed the surface of the coffee table as I materialised in the living room.

But you weren't downstairs any longer. The light above the closed metal doors teased me, boasted that you'd reached the second level. I *popped* into the grocery bag propped between your right hip and the mirrored wall. Your reflection rolled its eyes as the ancient tenant from apartment 204 inched her walker into the elevator. Her irises seemed to consume the thick Nana Mouskouri glasses she wore, and she blinked twelve times between each laboured footstep.

"We're going up," you said, hoping to dissuade the cornhusk doll from entering the tiny lift.

"That's fine, dear," she replied. "I've still got a few rides left in me, never you worry."

Stop stalling, Nanna, I thought. There's a humpy-bumpy sort of ride happening on the sofa upstairs, and Sal's got to get up there quick-smart if she's going to catch the bastard!

The brunette moaned when I *popped* back into the apartment. She sighed dramatically, flipped her long hair around in circles like some ridiculous porn star. He didn't notice her theatrics, focused as he was on his inner eyelids, on the swell of her arse in his hands, on the churning of her hips on his.

Out in the hallway, I gauged the elevator's progress. Fifth floor. The contraption was, officially, the slowest of its kind. It would have been quicker if you'd sat on that old bag's walker and let her drag you up the stairs. I *popped* back in to see you. Your eyes were fixed to the numbers above the door as if by staring they could somehow power the antiquated machine into the next century. The old lady's lungs rattled. She coughed up a honeycomb of phlegm.

Back to the apartment. An extended grunt and he was finished.

Shit, I thought. He never had been one for lengthy tumbles, so I don't know why I thought he'd start today. She peeled herself off of him, leaned over to unravel the panties strangling her left ankle, hoisted these dainties up and pulled her skirt back down. I watched as the sparkle left her—*it's always disappointing for you girls, isn't it?*—and saw the glimmer settle at her stilettoed feet. She asked for a glass of water; he tossed her a beer and an envelope instead. She chugged down the first, pocketed the latter. And then she left.

The latch on the fire door clicked shut as the lift doors groaned open on the seventh floor. Your floor. But you were too late.

I could have cried.

He was snoring like a bull on the sofa-bed when you unlocked the front door. Kicking it shut with your heel, you dropped the grocery bags on the dining table and then crossed the room. You stared down at him, entranced-like, for a minute or two. Your face was impassive, but your hands were all ball-y and white around the edges. They quivered to some inaudible rhythm. Then you reached down and grabbed the crocheted blanket folded on the back of the couch, and draped it across his satiated form.

I only noticed it once you'd left the room. *Hoo-ee!* I whooped with delight.

The trollop had left her sparkle behind, ground into the carpet next to the couch's leg. Waiting for you to find it.

♪

The tiny diamond was pinched between your fingertips as you half sat, half knelt on the guilty sofa-bed. It wasn't diamond, really. More like cubic zirconium: I'd bet my last finger on it. Whatever it was made of, rock or chiselled glass, its tiny glare held you in thrall. I stared at you while you stared at it; he stared at the TV. We held our breaths in unison.

"Whose is this?" you said, finally. Your voice was sandpapery. The words raced out of your mouth before they could be shaped properly.

"*Next time on Holiday,*" blared the television, "*move beyond the comfort of your own backyard! Cut loose and visit the wilds of—*"

"Whose? Is? This?" Louder this time. The tiny prism refracted light from the tips of your fingers as you thrust it into his line of sight. The earring shone, highlighting his rough jaw; a miniature detective's lamp pinpointing its shady subject.

Indecision flickered across his drooping face. He feigned disinterest, but his usually sedate eyes had adopted a frantic shift.

"Dunno. Must be yours, hun."

"It's not mine." Your heart turned all feathery as you spoke. Your voice shed years, jumped octaves. A smile flew across your lips, practically singing as you repeated, "It is *not* mine!"

When he opened his mouth to make excuses, to try and convince you to stay, to spread the guilt of years on you like rank butter, I dove in. I jumped into his seething gob, filled it with every inch of my misshapen body. I rammed my legs down his throat and propped his jaw wide with my arms. I inhaled every lie he tried to utter, and bought you the time you needed to speak.

𝄞 𝄞 𝄞

Wires Uncrossed

Wires Uncrossed

In the stillness before dawn, Boeing rolls over in his bunk and eavesdrops on people's thoughts. The words are atomised, electronic fragments. Buzzings along fibre optic cables. They're spoken, then broken into Humpty Dumpty jumbles. Eggshell phrases speed overhead, travel from mouth to ear until spiral cords and numbered boxes put them back together, give them meaning. For two weeks he has concentrated as hard as he can, but Bo still can't understand everything they say. He can hear the steady hum of their emotions, though; their sad rhythms, their happy cadences. He closes his eyes and tries to listen carefully.

Sometimes it's too much. There are nearly as many telephone poles as squat mobile homes in Kaintuck Estate trailer park. Reaching above the rooftop forest of TV antennae, the timber posts are the only real height on a cornfield horizon. Nearly all of them carved, inscribed with ragged graffiti and local couples' initials. Between the tips of their arms, a trapeze net of wires curves from one end of the lot to the other. All night the crosshatched lines are alive with news, carried from miles away. Secrets revealed two counties over are sent to Kaintuck for safe keeping. Falsehoods spread like lightning, spearing at least twelve trailers before Bo rubs the dreams from his eyes. Hundreds of thousands of words whisper, shatter, sob. So many voices for one boy to take in, pouring from the wires.

Bo holds his breath and strains to catch a hint of Mamma's hot chili voice among the rabble. There are plenty of wives calling husbands, but none of them are his mother.

It ain't natural, Charlie had said, when he'd told her about it a fortnight earlier. He had focused on her long brown ponytail while he spoke. It bounced on her backpack, kept time with her skipping-walk. Bounce, swish. Bounce, swish. Her hair was never still; her heels never touched the ground.

I'm serious, Char. Late spring had freckled the bridge of her nose. He followed the vertical stripes on her t-shirt, down to her cut-off shorts. Her legs were muscular, golden. (She wasn't his girlfriend, no matter what the other kids said.) He couldn't meet her eyes when he admitted, *I think they're getting louder.*

Bounce, swish. Swish, turn. Stop.

Charlie dropped the dandelions she'd collected from the side of the road. She'd reached up with her weed-stained hands, turned his face like she would a dog's. Looked at him directly. *Keep talking like that, Bo Stearman, and they'll send you to the Reverends to get your head read.*

He'd known she was probably right. So he'd smiled, told her he was just kidding. Thought it best if he failed to mention the foot-long tendrils that had sprouted out of his chest.

Now, lying in bed, he watches them undulate like sea anemones, waving back and forth under the current of his breath. He gouges the itchy flesh at the base of each phosphorescent strand, digging for relief. Static sparks as he scrapes at his skin, filling the room with the scent of raw ozone.

"Shhhhh," he says to calm HeeHaw, who is whimpering and sneezing in the bottom bunk. The dog has been acting odd for days; unsettled and overly whiney. Nestling deeper into his sleeping bag, Bo obscures the weird glow the tentacles emit. (*That's what they look like,* he realises. *Tentacles*). Naming them doesn't make them itch any less. Doesn't make him feel any better about what he's done to earn them.

His cheeks prickle with shame.

What would the Revs say about these, *Charlie?*

He presses a pillow tight against his torso, revisits an invented scenario he's replayed a thousand times since Mamma left. This time, when he goes back to that night, he imagines he's not alone. That the Reverends have come to absolve him of responsibility. That they've taken it all upon themselves. In this new version of events, he's got two of them at hand, bursting with advice. One, a gap-toothed man, is too tall to sit properly on the bottom bunk. The other, a green-eyed Rev with flaxen braids, is leaning against the doorframe, cowboy hat in hands, waiting for Bo to make a move. The men will talk over his head and around him. As if he weren't there at all.

Rev One: *She's been blubbering all day—shouldn't Bo go out and comfort her? For the sake of appearances?*

Rev Two: *He don't understand. Besides, he gots his headphones on. He don't need to hear this. We'll explain later.*

Rev One: *He ain't actually switched the music on yet; he's only feigning deafness.*

Rev Two: *Ah, that old trick.*

(Sometimes Bo interjects at this point: *I don't know what to say!*)

Rev One: *Hush, boy. Phone's ringing.*

Rev Two: *Time to listen.*

Both Reverends cock their heads to hear everything Mamma says. Bo wants to hear none of it. Let the Revs interpret what they want; sinners are their territory, not his. Not knowing is the only thing will leave him blameless; will leave him without the half-remembered patches of Mamma's furtive phone call; will leave him without the guilt of not having told Pa.

Not telling him how, between sniffles, Mamma had said, "Jethro . . ." She'd blown her nose, mumbled into the phone. "Okay," she'd said, at one point. And, "I've tried to stay—" The person on the other end of the line had interrupted. Bo had heard the smile in Mamma's reply. "I'll be there first thing tomorrow. Around eight-thirty or nine. No—don't worry. Rick will only notice I'm gone when his belly rumbles for a feed."

She'd actually giggled when she hung up.

At this point, if the Reverends had been there, they would've urged Bo to confront Mamma. "Looks better on our record," they'd explain, "if the pointing is done by someone else's finger first. After that's when we take over." So they would've told him to set his alarm, to wake up early, to catch Pa as soon as he got home from work. "Secrets like these are best told immediately," they'd say. "Over time they grow so stale it's impossible to do anything with them. Best get it out in the open now. For her good, and yours."

But Bo's words had dried up that night, left his mouth empty.

No matter how many times he replays this scene, it always ends the same way. The Reverends' advice gets drowned out by the swell of other voices. And just like he did that night, Bo presses 'play' on his walkman, turns the volume up to full blast. He curls up beside HeeHaw on the cold floor. Hits 'repeat' until the battery dies. Until his bones ache from the awkward position he's in.

Until he can no longer deny that his chest is throbbing.

♪

Just outside Bo's bedroom door, the bar fridge's motor kicks in, shakes him from his reverie. The sound rattles around the darkened kitchen, echoes across linoleum tiles into the adjoined living area. It trips over the collection of porcelain figurines Mamma keeps on top of the TV. (Farm animals, mostly; her favourites are pigs wearing overalls and Snoopy dogs flying airplanes). It avoids the guitar abandoned in the corner of the room; skips to the hallway and bumps into two photo frames Pa hung there to replace the one he'd broken. Mamma hates to throw anything away, even an off-kilter frame. So she'd dabbed the damaged one with superglue and slipped a close-up of HeeHaw beneath its cracked glass. *This pup is our baby*, she'd said, re-hanging it between Bo's Grade 6 picture and a faded snap taken at her and Pa's wedding. (Only time Pa's worn a suit; he's leaning over the bulge of Mamma's belly, stealing a kiss.) *We can afford to give him at least this.*

Bo rubs at his chest as the noise whirs, clunks, and finally rests on a crocheted blanket at the foot of an empty double bed.

Two new tentacles have grown overnight. Translucent and already as long as fingers, they itch way worse than the older three ever have. He tries snipping them off with his plastic school scissors. They simply waft like smoke around his cuts; then reassemble, resolidify, as though never disturbed. He wants to obliterate them, like Pa did that time when, to avoid doctor's fees, he took a hammer to his own wrist and crushed the calcium deposit growing there. And with the money he'd saved, Pa had bought Mamma an Indiglo watch. Just because. Soon after, Mamma gave it to Bo. "Irritates my wrist," she'd said.

Mamma doesn't wear any jewellery.

Probably so her boyfriend won't know she's married, Bo thinks.

He knows about romance. He's seen all the Channel 2 films Mamma tapes, seen how it works. Men tuck wedding bands inside their breast pockets before a night on the town. Women drape their figures in slinky black dresses, order martinis with olives on toothpicks. Girls wear curlers (long legs shaved, finger and toenails painted), then sit on overstuffed chairs, and try not to let tears smudge their mud masks when the phone doesn't ring. Boys with leather jackets and too-greasy hair pretend they don't care when really, deep down, they do. Frequently, there's singing. Occasionally, dancing. Always, relationships are guillotined by a receiver slammed down, then resurrected with a carefully timed call.

Like the one Mamma had made that night. *To Jethro.*

He feels around for his watch. When he finds it, he throws it so hard HeeHaw yelps when it hits the wall.

"Shit," Bo says, wriggling out of his sleeping bag. Pa had pasted newspaper (cheaper than curtains) over his bedroom window when they moved in; though dried and yellowed, it's thick enough to trap night inside. Reaching over, he picks at one corner until a triangle of light creeps in. Behind him, the walls change from pure black to pale grey, striated with a wood veneer pattern. Pages he'd torn from magazines to decorate his room now shine in pale orange patches, reflecting the sun's first rays.

He looks to the highway. Two dots of yellow bob along its black length, slowly getting bigger. "Shit shit shit—" Holding the cold metal frame of his bunk, he stretches down with his toes, releases his grip and slides with a thump to the floor.

"Move," he tells HeeHaw, shoving the dog off the lower mattress so he can lift it. Hidden beneath are several long strips of calico stolen from Mamma's sewing box, a handful of safety pins, and a crusty tube of calamine lotion. He grabs the cream, smears gobs of it onto his chest. Listens for the sound of car tires crunching on gravel. Prays the headlights won't streak through the gap in his window paper too soon. Wraps a floral-patterned strip of fabric round and round his chest. Flattens his tentacles, forcing them to lie still. Pins the bandage in place, jabbing himself twice, then throws on a hooded sweatshirt and jeans without checking if he'd drawn blood.

A pot of baked beans bubble on the stovetop and two slabs of pressed ham sizzle in the frying pan by the time he hears a jangle of keys outside the trailer door. Mamma would've had the kettle boiled by now, and a tray of 'tater tots grilled too; but Bo hasn't had much practice getting Pa's daybreak dinners ready. He doesn't always have the timing down.

A blast of cool air follows his father into the living room, carrying a waft of stale coffee and the vinegar of exhaustion. Bo pops two slices of bread beneath the grill as the shower squeals on in the bathroom. The toast is plated, covered in beans and meat, and set on the table thirty seconds before Rick, wearing nothing but a bleach-spattered towel, sags onto the bench beside it.

"Coffee?" Bo stands halfway between the sink and table, hands shoved in his pockets to keep himself from scratching.

Rick shovels a forkful into his mouth, wipes sauce from his goatee with the back of his hand. "Nah," he says, storing food in one cheek like a chipmunk, scooping in more.

Bo watches his father eat. Sweat and steam drip down the man's shoulders and the wide expanse of his back as he hunches over the plate. His forehead stretches to the far side of his crown; stubble clings like dirt to the back of his roughly shaved head. Pa's skull has always been ringed with that two-inch imprint, red and shiny from the security guard's hat he wears for work. Not too long ago, Bo liked running his hand around its almost plastic smoothness, then over the Velcro roughness of Pa's scalp. He loved pushing the bristles around with his palm, feeling them both soft and sharp.

Why did Mamma choose Jethro?

"What?" Pa looks at Bo through mushroom-puff eyelids. Knife and fork clink on the plate. He exhales sharply through his nose, stops chewing. Waits.

"Nothing."

Pa grunts. The chair legs scrape new grooves in the linoleum as he stands. He readjusts his towel, then takes the dishes to the sink for Bo to wash later.

You look tired, Bo wants to say, but instead he just crosses his arms. Beneath his bandages, the tentacles tug and stretch, resisting their confinement. *I got to tell you something.* He tenses his arms to squash the feeling, then goes to the pantry to get some kibble for HeeHaw.

The dog pads into the kitchen as soon as the cupboard door squeaks open. He sits tense and stiff, the way Pa taught him, as a cupful of pellets clatter into his plastic dish. Tail swishing from side to side, his eyes and nose lock on the food. His neck strains as he tries to stay still while also yearning to reach the bowl. The wait is too much: he lets out a double-yip, chastising Bo for taking so long.

"Take HeeHaw out when you go," Pa says. "Fucking mutt kept me awake all afternoon, yapping."

"All right." There's a buzzing in his father's voice that makes Bo spill kibble on the floor. Static and echoes, like those from a radio tuned to two stations at once, crackle through Pa's words. It's garbled, but audible. The discord of everything he's not saying.

"You going to see her today?"

Bo can't miss the emphasis Pa places on *her*. It rises above a wave of other sounds: the picture glass shattering; a heart beating wildly; Rick and Mamma saying *I do*; tin cans dragging on strings behind a burnt orange Mustang, clanking a shivaree. Beneath it all, his mother's name, unspoken within these walls for two weeks, dripping electricity.

Maggie.

Bo shivers and nods, afraid to speak. What if his own sentences come out multilayered? His chest whiskers (please let them be whiskers) hiss and seethe.

Pa walks into his and Mamma's room. He turns down the sheets. "Boeing?"

Bo swallows, nods again.

"Yeah," he says. He keeps quiet for a second, and listens. There don't seem to be any spare thoughts piggybacking the word. "After school."

The mattress springs whine as Pa droops into bed. *No extra meaning there either.* Bo concentrates as the bed groans and exhales under his father's weight. *Just normal creaking.*

"Tell *her*—" his father begins. The volume of Pa's static-messages explodes in Bo's eardrums: *I miss you—Twelve years; twelve long years—Not again, Maggie—Please. Not again.*

Leaden circles of Pa's confusion spin down the hallway, across the linoleum, and into Bo's head. The boy closes his eyes against the onslaught, tries to catch his breath.

He can't find out about Jethro, Bo thinks. The realisation makes him sick. His stomach churns and his saliva turns acidic. His jaw clenches around his secrets.

"Tell her she owes me forty bucks for the last phone bill," Pa says, flicking off the light. He falls silent, but isn't asleep. Bo grinds his fists into the sides of his head. Chest strands pulse, vibrate beneath his clothes. He blink-blink-blinks to keep himself from crying as his father's anger swells, then slowly, finally, begins to ebb.

𝄞

"You busy later?"

Bo takes a drag on his cigarette, looks up through the gaps in the bleachers, and waits for Charlie's response. School seems a million miles away, even though there's only a flimsy set of plywood seats and a football field between them. He exhales. Smoke hangs in the damp air; it strobes grey, yellow, grey as it drifts up through shafts of sunlight to the grandstand overhead.

"Give me your sweater," she replies. "My butt's freezing to the concrete here."

She grabs the back of Bo's hoodie, goes to pull it over his head.

"No!" He jumps up, jerks the shirt from her hands. HeeHaw's collar jingles as his head whips up; Charlie's expression matches the kelpie's. "What the hell, Bo?"

His face burns red. Tugging at his waistband, he sits down again. Wraps his arms around the dog, uses him as a furry barrier between him and Charlie.

"Hush up, HeeHaw," Bo says. "You'll get us in trouble." He looks sideways at his friend, forces a laugh.

"Idiot," she says, rolling her eyes.

"I'm not the one wearing shorts."

This time his smile is genuine. Charlie snorts and Bo's anxiety eases a bit. There's nothing but silence behind Charlie's words, behind her laughter. Her opinions are only tuned to one frequency; her comments are one-dimensional. Honest. When they're together, Bo can't hear anything but what's being said. It's a relief hanging out with her.

"So, anyway." He passes her his backpack. While she settles on top of it, Bo looks for his cigarette. Finds it broken on the ground. "Want another one?"

Charlie shakes her head. "Save it for later."

"I'm going to visit Mamma," he says. "See if she needs anything. Want to come?"

Charlie shivers, draws her knees up to her chest. "No point sticking 'round here all day, I guess." She ruffles HeeHaw's ears until the dog rolls over and offers his belly. "But I got to be home by five. What time's your Mamma get off work? Can she take us home after? Reverends are coming over to talk about the twins' naming ceremony, and Daddy says we all gots to be there for Shelby 'cause Ted-the-arsehole's done a runner."

Bo jumps in before she gets warmed up. Lately, Charlie takes any chance she can get to heap abuse on her sister's ex. He hates to think what she'd say about Mamma.

"Let's take our bikes," he says. "Who knows when she's coming home."

𝄞

"Pass me a cig, babe. They're in my purse."

The acoustics of Mamma's thoughts are more complex than Pa's. There's more feedback in her phrases, more echo. Bo looks at Charlie: she doesn't notice anything unusual, just sits there chatting with his mother in pure, singular tones. Cargo trucks roar down the interstate beside Mr Dewinter's motel, rattling the glass in Room 2A's only window. Between clinks Bo hears the need for nicotine wheeze in Mamma's lungs. He feels the discomfort of her orange polyester skirt and snug matching blouse scratching at the back of his mind. She hasn't worn a uniform since before he was born. It doesn't look good: the fabric makes her look sick. She's lost weight to fit into it. And it clashes with her hair.

Mamma sits on the sill, resting her stockinged feet on the edge of the brown-quilted bed, runners abandoned on the floor. She leans back, quells the window's rattle. Chewing gum pops between her molars as she alternately gnashes it and bites her fingernails.

Bo reaches over the armchair, its yellow upholstery decades beyond cheery, and grabs Mamma's purse. Causing a clatter of keys and lipsticks, he rummages for the cardboard pack that inevitably sinks to the bottom; swipes the cool plastic of her lighter, and hooks it with his fingertips.

Smelling the over-used, but not lived-in, scent of the room emanating from the carpet, he wants to say, *What are you doing? You can't live here forever.* Mr Dewinter has been too nice, giving her a job, paying her in room and board. She should come home. Then he could tell her about the tentacles, about how they itch, about how they hurt, about how they scare HeeHaw. How they scare him, too.

He opens his mouth. Closes it. He inspects her neck for evidence of hickeys. Looks at her mouth to see if her lipstick is smeared. Stares at her hands, her clothes, her unpainted eyes; as if they'll be different now that Jethro's got his paws on her.

A lump forms in his throat, so big it's hard to light Mamma's cigarette. It takes three tries, but eventually he gets it. He passes her the smoking white tube, cherry-tip pointed up, then snags another two from the pack. Gives one to Charlie, and lights the other for himself.

"When's your break over?" he asks, just as Mamma says, "How many of them you had today?"

"Three," Charlie says.

"Five," Bo admits.

"Five," Mamma echoes. She leans forward until she's silhouetted against the late afternoon light. The tips of her curls glow with sky fire. He sneaks another peek at her through the thin trail of his exhalation. Is that a love poem slipping beneath her phrases, spun from words as red as her hair? She taps her cigarette against the bin dangling from her housekeeper's trolley, watches the ash lilt to the bottom of a clear garbage bag.

"You shouldn't smoke these things, you know," she said, taking a long pull. "Stunts your growth."

An image of Mr Dewinter's runty form accompanies Mamma's warning. It vibrates up Bo's chest-strings and stings him right in the heart. Mamma's boss looks handsome when she thinks of him. Hot, even. Like the guy from all those Channel 2 movies; the one who always seems nice, even if he's playing a scoundrel, because his eyes are so blue and his hair so ridiculously floppy. Mr Dewinter's doppelganger runs his hands through his unruly fringe. Smiles a dimple into his cheek as he calls Mamma *Margaret*. Not Maggie.

"What's Mr Dewinter's first name?"

Charlie pipes up. "Andy. Right, Mrs Stearman?"

Mamma raises an eyebrow. "Yeah. Why?"

Two ghostly men drip from the corners of Mamma's mouth. The bald and soft one is Pa, no doubt about it. Beneath his shirt and bandages, Bo's tentacles rasp with friction, sending messages of near-recognition to his brain as he focuses on the other man. He's fair-haired, like Bo. Lean and tall. Rugged.

Fucking Jethro, Bo thinks.

Mamma coughs. Mr Dewinter and Pa dissolve into motes, float into the air. Jethro clings to her lower lip, then peels away like a stolen kiss.

"You seeing him tonight?" The question blurts out before Bo can stop it.

She chuckles and picks a shred of tobacco from her tongue. "Get out of town, babe. Andy? He's old enough to be my father. Besides, he's my *boss*."

Mamma's throaty laugh is infectious. Soon Charlie joins in, giggles, "And what about your Pa? The Reverends would blow a gasket!"

Smoke sputters from Mamma's nostrils as she swallows, falls silent.

That's right, Bo thinks. *You know what you're doing is wrong.* The filaments throb beneath his hoodie with a pitch so high he's amazed HeeHaw doesn't start howling outside. They push against their floral-patterned constraints; tug at something buried deep inside his ribcage; begin to snake in cool lengths down his belly. Pressure pulses across his torso as the strands pull and reach toward the far side of the room. Toward the window, and Mamma. The highway. Beyond.

Bo stands up so quick his head spins. His pulse races and he feels a prickle behind his eyes as he snatches his knapsack from where it slumps on the desk.

"Let's go, Char," he says, holding the bag close.

Mamma looks at the clock, at Charlie. She avoids Bo's gaze. "Guess it's about that time."

An alarm clock beeping underscores her sigh as she drops her feet back into their sneakers; a reminder to both of them that Pa's evening breakfast needs cooking. Bo edges closer to the door. Mamma stays put.

"You know," she says, clearing her throat. "I really miss—"

Songs bursting from a raw, cracked voice; the silken slide of a steel guitar wailing chords of first love, first heartbreak; conversations shared over a meal eaten together, instead of twelve hours apart; the patter of a soft kiss showing she's noticed, needed; the rumble of a man's gentle snores lulling her to sleep; spending the whole night together . . .

Bo stops, his hand on the doorknob. *Don't say his name . . .*

"I really miss HeeHaw," Mamma finishes.

Two of his knuckles crack as Bo turns the handle, opens the door. It would be so easy to run down and smuggle the dog upstairs, or to bring Mamma down for a quick cuddle before she gets back to work. But his bandages are shifting, his tentacles squirming. Tears are burning the back of his throat.

"Bring me that picture of him, next time you come." She starts across the room. "Okay?"

"Fine," he replies. He knows she means the dog's portrait, but as she speaks he sees Pa superimposed over the words, Jethro's smug face not far behind. Bo hears a plane screaming to the earth; crops thrashing beneath wings and propellers; a cello note of regret. And, at the same time, an orchestra of relief. The tones tumble out, crepitate, shatter.

"C'mon, Charlie," he repeats, as if she wasn't already standing beside him. Then they slip out, into the stale piss smell of the stairwell, and close the door before Mamma can hug him goodbye. Before she can feel how much he's changed since she left.

𝄞

HeeHaw laps salt from Bo's face. The boy snuffles and wipes tears on his dog's mottled fur. Shadows lengthen across the motel's parking lot while the pair sit at the foot of the fire escape, two bikes leaning against the brick wall behind them. Charlie positions herself so that her body blocks the sun from Bo's eyes. Her hands lift in a gesture of consolation, but fall short of touching him.

"What happened in there? What's going on?"

The simplest questions are the hardest to answer. But the white noise behind her questions reassures him. He weeps openly, shamelessly. And between hiccups, between tears, he tells her.

About Mamma leaving.

About the voices.

About the five thick cords protruding from his chest.

When he's finished, his legs feel like jelly. Too weak yet for riding, he tells Charlie to go home without him. Three of his appendages now dangle out his shirt front; the brightest one grown so long it trails in the dirt at his feet. He's not sure if she's seen them, doesn't feel like being gawked at if she has. Tears spent, he suddenly feels shy.

"Tomorrow?" he asks. "Same time, same place?" He tries to smile, only half succeeds.

"Sure," Charlie says. Her grin isn't much stronger than Bo's. "I'll meet you here after school." Then she goes, leaving Bo to collect himself. Unclasping the safety pins from his useless bandages, he tries to work out a different way to bundle the strands out of sight. Focused on this task, his breathing evens out. As he twists the tentacles into rubbery skeins and knots them in place, Bo can almost forget about Mamma and Jethro. Almost.

HeeHaw barks until the growths are hidden.

By then, the sun is less than a hand's width above the horizon. On the other side of the highway, running as far as Bo can see from one direction to the other, rows of cornstalks are gilded the deep yellow of suppertime. If he doesn't leave immediately, his father will wake to find his breakfast table empty. And it's up to him to make sure that doesn't happen again.

"C'mon, boy," he says. One last time, HeeHaw flicks his rough tongue across Bo's cheek. The boy transfers the dog's leash from railing to bike handle. In one fluid movement, he kicks his leg over the seat, nudges HeeHaw's rump into action, and launches the bicycle onto the road's gravel shoulder.

Within seconds, they're speeding along next to the highway. The going is bumpy but the street is too narrow in most places to allow him to ride safely on the asphalt. So he stays near the edge, gives HeeHaw free rein. After a day being cooped under the bleachers and tied outside a cheap motel, the kelpie must feel so good now; stretching his muscles and the leash as he pulls Bo's bike, his black mouth lolling open, tongue flapping up and down.

Bo catches the dog's mood. He stands on the pedals, fair hair streaming away from his brow as he cycles. The wind whistles over, around, beneath him, whisking away all trace of tears. In the distance comes a familiar, welcome sound: a biplane's motor sputtering to life with a pure, clear drone.

"C'mon, HeeHaw!"

The dog picks up the pace. Small stones ping off the bike chain and fenders, ricochet into the fields. Bo's wheels are a blur of exhilarating motion, the ground a victim of his speed. Dodging intermittent telephone poles, he pedals so quick he can only hear a faint murmur from the wires. Right now, he's got no time for other people's woes or delights. He pumps the pedals until lactic acid sears his thigh and calf muscles; until his lungs sponge in greedy gulps of air; until the crop duster, its vibrant yellow wings twice as long as the cab, comes streaking up beside him.

"C'mon, boy!"

Out of all the old planes local farmers hire, Bo loves racing the Piper Cubs best. Their pilots are the most daring, he reckons. They fly so low their landing gear grazes the crops; chemicals plume behind them like superheroes' capes. With the wind at his back and a good head start, Bo sometimes reaches the end of the road in tandem with the little aircrafts. And when he does, he imagines he's the pilot, not the scrawny kid on the bike down below. In the cockpit, he's brave and bold and strong—worry is a cargo he refuses to carry. Once the crops are tended to, and just before the sun dips south, he flies higher and higher; rockets upwards until the boy, the dog, the motel, the trailer park and the telephone poles with their strangling wires are all smaller than specks of dust. And then he scrawls messages people have paid him to write— things like *I surrender* or *Be mine* or *Roses half price*—across the heavens. Each letter taller than a skyscraper, louder than pre-dawn confessions.

As Bo rides, his tentacles uncoil from their hastily-tied sling and bring him back down to earth. He doesn't want to stop, doesn't want to lose the race. But he's afraid they'll get tangled in the spokes if he lets them hang loose. Hunching his back awkwardly, he reaches down his shirt's neck and grabs the feelers. Pulls them up and out until all five hang from his collar like a shredded bib.

It doesn't help: they're still in the way. Keeping track of the Piper Cub's progress, Bo takes the long strands in one hand and loops them around his neck like a gauze scarf. His legs pump, up and down, up and down, propelling him forward. Sweat drips into his eyes. HeeHaw pants, swallows gobbets of spit, pants some more. Still, they lose ground. The plane gains an acre's advantage, then the span of a whole field—and with a final burst of pesticide it accelerates, shoots into the lead, and snatches victory out of Bo's reach.

The boy stops pedalling.

Fluorescent lights flicker around Kaintuck Estate's welcome sign by the time he drags himself home. As he passes through the gate, the last few hints of day are withdrawing between rows of aluminium structures. Exhausted sunbeams clock out, give dusk a passing nod as the factory whistle signals a shift change; then crawl up trailer steps, settling in for the night inside bulbs that illuminate windows. All across the park, tired yellow squares hover in the gloom, barely bright enough to reveal bedrooms and lounges and kitchens inside.

Bright enough, though, to show that Pa is already up.

HeeHaw barks at the sight of him.

"Shhhhhhhhh!" Bo hisses, heart pounding. He claws at his tentacles, yanks them away from his flushed neck and starts hauling them back down his shirt. *Why won't they stop growing?* He stuffs their curved ends down his pant legs. Panic churns in his belly as he tightens his belt a notch. *I'll tell him.* He looks up to check if his father has heard the dog. It doesn't seem so: Pa sits in the kitchen, his hands clasped around a coffee mug, staring vacantly at a flowered vinyl chair on the opposite side of the table. Eyes still puffy, despite a full day's sleep. *I'll tell him.*

Bo pauses. For a minute or two, he just stands there watching Pa watch nothing. He waits for his pulse to slow, for Pa to change position. Listens to the ache in his chest. Decides that now isn't the best time for bad news.

"Don't say a word," Bo tells HeeHaw, as he finally creeps up the stairs.

"Not a word," he repeats, gently easing the door open.

♪

"You get home okay last night?"

"Yeah," Bo says. Holding back the sheers with one hand, he keeps an eye out the window for Charlie. She wasn't at school today, and now she's late meeting him here. It isn't like her to bail on him at the last minute.

No, he thinks. *It's more like* her. He passes his mother a saucer to catch the long caterpillar of ash drooping from the end of her cigarette. Mr Dewinter loaned her this 'no smoking' room (single bed, single chair, single Formica table, single kitchenette, single TV/ VCR unit); and though the carpet is already littered with circular burns, Bo doesn't see why they should add to its destruction.

"It's just—" She inhales, then grinds out her smoke. "I was doing the downstairs rooms after you left, and I swear I saw you and Charlie crouched out in the parking lot. With HeeHaw." Her voice lifts after *HeeHaw,* inflecting the words with an invisible question mark. Bo ignores the uncertain, little girl tone punctuating Mamma's comment; ignores how it makes his feelers quiver from their roots all the way down to his socks.

"Nope," he says. "Wasn't us."

He can't explain the lie. Or that, as soon as he'd gone, he'd wanted to turn back. Or that when he'd gotten home Pa wasn't mad about breakfast. He was blank. He had served his own cereal, and eaten it. A deep well of blackness threaded through the greeting he'd grunted at Bo. His few short instructions, "Do your homework; change the dog's water", had been blanketed beneath television snow. The fridge motor had whirred on, clicked off. Pa had emptied his bowl; drained his cup; washed them.

When Bo passed him a bologna sandwich to take for lunch, Pa's thanks had echoed with loneliness.

Bo's tentacles had stretched over four inches trying to absorb the sound.

Mamma sighs, readjusts the pillows propped behind her on the bed. "Pass me the remote. I hate this part."

As she fast-forwards a love scene they've both seen a least a dozen times, a rusted blue station wagon pulls up outside. Bo shifts in the uncomfortable plastic seat, tries to get a better view.

"Speaking of HeeHaw." He reaches into his bag, tosses a picture frame onto the bed. "Here."

A tall, blond man is sitting in the driver's seat. He's looking up at Mamma's window.

Mamma takes the silver picture frame, looks down at the dog's pointed face. "Hey, pooch," she coos. Pressing 'mute' on the TV, she stares quietly at romantic comedy colours reflecting across the cracked glass in her hands.

"Mamma?" Bo's voice is barely louder than a whisper. "What does Jethro look like?"

She blinks. Her gasp explodes with the sound of metal propellers *thwapping* into dirt. "Who?"

"Jethro," he repeats.

"Why do you want to know about him?" Once more, the ghost man trickles from Mamma's lips. Only, this time, the vision flickers like an old film across her t-shirt, across her heart. The shot is close, cropped. Posed for a photograph, he wears an aviator jacket and sunglasses. A pilot's license thrust towards the camera lens half-obscures the cheeky grin on his face.

Bo looks for traces of Jethro's features in the driver's face below. The man is talking now, to someone in the back. He reaches to the passenger's side, takes something off the seat.

"I reckon," Mamma begins, turning the picture over and placing it face down on the bed. "There's something—"

The afterimage of Jethro is insubstantial, made of memory and vapour and half-spoken truths. Bo studies it, then the man outside, as Mamma dismantles the frame, and slips not one but two photos from its skewed casing.

The car's back door opens.

Charlie steps out.

What's she doing with Jethro? Bo's chest-strands all strain to get loose. He clutches his knapsack hard to stifle their wriggling, crosses his legs to pin them down. As Mamma hands Bo the picture, Jethro's spectre transforms. Disappears. Outside, the Reverend gets out of his station wagon, dons his cowboy hat.

Everything goes still, silent.

Bo's eyes blur. He tries to focus on the snapshot, and on Charlie and the Reverend. *What is she doing with him?* Charlie points at the window, tucks a strand of hair behind her ear. The Reverend follows her gesture. His eyes meet Bo's.

This can't be right. There is no floppy-haired lookalike, no cheeky grin. The Reverend's black curls have adopted the shape of his hat. His skin is dark, his face cragged with age. There's no plane here, no pilot's license, no glasses. Bo gapes as Charlie tells the Reverend his secrets. His mind whirls. Looking down, the collection of tints and shadows clutched in his hands resolve into a snapshot of Mamma and a younger, much happier Pa.

"Jethro looked a lot like your dad," she says.

His father has hair. And it's blond, just like Bo's. Slicked with so much grease it doesn't move, even though he's doing a back flip in the photo's foreground. He's wearing a white jersey with a school letter sewn on it, just like the guys in Mamma's favourite movies. Caught in mid-jump, Pa's shirt has slid up to reveal a few inches of taut stomach. There are other girls in the background, but Bo can tell Pa is showing off for only one of them.

What is Charlie doing?

Mamma's hair is waist-length, stick-straight, parted perfectly down the middle. Her cheerleader skirt is so short it's nearly invisible beneath her oversized v-neck sweater; her long, bare legs shimmer in the sunlight. Though her body is turned toward the girl beside her, Mamma's eyes are trained on this handsome, playful version of Pa. A smile quirks the corner of her glossy lips. Two pompoms droop from her hands, their purpose temporarily forgotten.

"But? What?" Bo feels the whinge pierce his ribcage and slide down his wires. He looks outside. Charlie's heading for the motel door. The Reverend's back in his car, reversing.

Charlie called the Reverends, he thinks. "Why? Where's Jethro?"

Mamma's response is stilted. "Same place he's been for thirteen years, I reckon. Planted in Cobb's field. Right next to your Nan." Her eyes linger on the photo.

"I think Jeth might've taken that shot, back when me and your dad was courting." A bluegrass symphony accompanies *courting*; a twang of banjos, mouth organs, accordions, fiddles reverberating with strains of love Mamma can't let out. "Never seen closer brothers, I reckon. We named you after him, sort of. Did I ever tell you that?"

Bo nods, then shakes his head.

"Used to tease him about how much he loved that plane." This time her laugh is laced with synthesised happiness. "Called her his Tinny Titty." She takes a tissue from the bedside table, dabs at her eyes until her giggles subside.

Suddenly serious, she says, "Pa won't like it if he hears we've been talking about Jeth, you know."

Looking out the window, Bo hears all the things Mamma can't say. *Rick's lost all his zing—leaves me to raise Bo by myself—never takes a holiday—thinks he ain't got no family, without Jeth.* He hears it all, but sees Charlie's betrayal heading toward the highway.

"Mamma?"

She holds up a hand to stop Bo from speaking. "I won't tell if you don't."

If I don't leave once in a while, her harmonica wails, *he'll forget to notice I was ever there.*

The Reverend's taillights glow devil-red as he waits to pull out of the parking lot. His indicator points the way to Kaintuck Estate. Flick, flick, flicking away the time it will take him to reach Pa. Counting down the seconds until he can preach about corruption in this community. About Mamma's immoral behaviour.

Except, Bo thinks, *there ain't been no cheating.*

His heart pounds.

There ain't been no cheating.

His tentacles yearn to break loose. They threaten to strangle him; to keep him forever quiet; to keep him always listening.

Charlie knocks at the door. "Bo? Mrs Stearman?"

"I got to go," he says, standing up and shouldering his bag. He has to get home before the Reverend gets there. Has to fix his mistake.

"And Charlie?"

"I don't care."

Mamma points at the picture. "Bring this to your dad for me, okay? Ask him—"

"I got to go," he repeats, clutching the photo so hard its corner wrinkles. "Ask him yourself."

He runs for the door. Pushes past Charlie, ignores her shouts as he flies down the stairs. Without her bike, she can't follow. Didn't matter if she could; he'll ride faster, harder than her. He'll lose her on the homestretch.

He'll never speak to her again.

Tentacles punch holes through his sneakers, burst through his sweatshirt, tear out the knees of his jeans. Three, five, seven writhing wires—still transparent, but swiftly becoming real. One latches onto the fire escape, refuses to dislodge. Bo keeps moving. He jumps on his bike and cycles as if a whole squadron of crop-dusters, all piloted by Reverends, were begging for a race. The wire tying him to Mamma whizzes out of his chest as he rides. It wrenches, hurts, but grows thicker and stronger as the distance between them increases.

The photo flashes through his mind. *Pa never looked so happy.*

An image of Mamma on the motel room bed, wiping her eyes.

Pa at the table, staring. *Not tired. Broken.*

Mamma's lips curled in a smile, pompoms forgotten.

Movie star love.

And no sign of Jethro.

The Reverend will ruin it all.

Pain surges through Bo's body. His shirt hangs in shreds, his jeans tatter like a castaway's. Everywhere, wires snake, crackling with truth and electricity. He hears it all. And knows it's time to speak.

HeeHaw goes wild as Bo speeds into the trailer park and up the path to their lot. The dog snarls and strains at his rope until it looks ready to snap. Bo pays no attention to his pet's raving. *The station wagon—where's the station wagon?*

He hops off his bike while it's still moving, watches it crash into the shopping trolley Mamma once filled with petunias. He falls to his knees, straining for breath.

"Pa!"

Please be awake, he thinks. "Pa!"

The Reverend's car pulls up the drive. Neighbours come to their screen doors, press their faces to small square windows. They watch, silently or with phones in hand, but nobody comes out to help. A few of them nod, knowingly.

"Pa," Bo calls, quieter now because the central tentacle is crushing his lungs, forcing him to lie down. Gravel presses into his spine and the back of his skull; it crunches beneath the Reverend's tires as the wagon slows down out front. The engine dies. An alarm bell hollers *keys still in the ignition!* as the door swings open.

One minute HeeHaw howls like a demon; the next he cowers beneath the front stoop, as far from the Reverend as he can get. Far away from the trunk shooting out of Bo's sternum.

"Pa," he croaks. Finally, the screen door bangs open.

"Maggie?" His father pounds down the steps into the yard. "Bo?"

No static, Bo thinks, seeing distress crease Pa's face, hearing nothing but the sound of a man worried sick about his wife. About him.

"Bo!"

This is love, he realises. No singing. No dancing. Just a girl's long legs covered in tights and orange polyester. A boy's too-greasy hair all fallen out, bristles soft and sharp beneath his son's hand. Both carrying a chest full of pain.

"What the hell happened, son?" Phone lines unfurl from Bo's ribcage. They launch into the air, high above Pa's head as he attempts to scoop Bo into his arms. Two strands solidify into crossbars, stationed near the top of the pole. Two others quickly attach to Bo's trailer, insinuate themselves into the utility box. One speeds down the highway to join its partner at the motel. Bo looks up at his father and says, "It ain't true, Pa. It ain't true."

Next trailer over, the Reverend knocks on Charlie's front door. He tilts the brim of his cowboy hat as it swings open. "Sorry to bother you again, Ma'am. Your daughter, Charlotte, said I might have another word with you. Shelby's out, ain't she?" Mrs Morales welcomes the Reverend back into the caravan.

"What ain't true?" Pa hugs Bo close.

"Nothing," he says, as he hears the Reverend begin, "Good. Then, about one Teddy Lucas . . ."

With a crack of splitting timber, the telephone pole dislodges from Bo's chest. He rolls on his side, watches it send showers of gravel flying as it burrows deep into the earth, right there in the middle of the yard. Its shimmering blue surface turns into veined yellow pine freshly stripped of its bark. A roughly hewn, permanent brown.

Immediately, a hush softens the evening. Particles of conversation disintegrate, blow away on the wind. Wires hum in foreign, untranslated languages. Whispers sneak from trailer to trailer; but now Bo hears them only with his ears, not his mind. HeeHaw settles, places his head on his front paws, and sleeps.

Bo breathes deeply. The quiet loosens his tongue.

"Hey," he says, tightening his grasp on Pa.

"You gave me one hell of a scare there, boy."

"Sorry." Inside, a new phone rings. "Go get it."

"No way—"

Bo cuts him off with a laugh. "Get it. It's for you."

As Pa's footsteps retreat, Bo closes his eyes and stretches on the ground. He reaches out, rubs his palm across the pole's smooth roughness.

The spice of Mamma's voice, he imagines, now fills the silence following his father's gruff, "Hullo?"

Let's talk, babe, he supposes she'll say. *I think we need to talk.*

"Yeah," Pa says. Bo can almost hear him swallow, hesitate.

C'mon . . . Bo sits up. Opens his eyes. Slowly, he stands and leans against the sturdy pole for balance. *Say something.*

Pa takes a shuddering breath. "Please come home," he says. Nothing more. Then he gently lays the receiver in its cradle.

Within seconds, a *scritch-scritch-scritching* noise sounds next to Bo's ear. Curls of wood and sawdust pepper his bare shoulder. Confused, he begins to pull away—and freezes. Then he smiles until his cheeks hurt.

I can't wait to tell Charlie about this.

Gouged deep into the post, the letters 'M + R' appear before his eyes, carved in enduring capitals. They remain raw for only a few seconds. Soon, they're burnished as if they'd been there for years. Worn, but not worn out. Surrounded by the outline of an uneven, but complete, love heart.

♮ ♮ ♮

Forever, Miss Tapekwa County

Forever, Miss Tapekwa County

Verralee trusted the bluebird tattooed behind her mother's right ear.

She couldn't hear what it chirped—those songs were for Kaylene alone—but long ago she'd learned to decipher its colouring, to translate the rhythm of inked wings flapping. Ultramarine feathers blurred with excitement meant Kaylene's tattoo had truths to tell. If he had gossip to share, little black-beaked lies, the *sialia*'s downy throat would flush lurid red, and moulting shoulders would slump beneath the weight of false news. His voice, as far as Verralee was concerned, sounded just like her mother's. His insights were shaped on her tongue.

In the makeshift kitchen backstage, Kaylene's frosted-blonde hair was pulled back, unbleached roots framing the bird's sapphire promises, his sketched body still visible through the steam of canning pots boiling on the camp stovetop. *Smile pretty,* he said with her mother's mouth. *Tilt your head to avoid doubling your chin. Keep your hair out of your face.* Clean pickling jars were extracted with tongs from scalding water. *And don't hold your breath, my girl. Don't repeat your Mamma's mistakes.* One by one, three wide-mouthed Masons were expertly lined up on a small countertop, the workspace identical to six others the judges had ordered made for this year's contestants. Prepared for their test runs.

The glass cooled, waiting to be filled with a practice-round of preserves.

One last time, for lungs' sakes. Pay attention.

He didn't always make sense, at least not at first, but Verralee was used to the bird's riddles. She looked up at the clock: fifteen minutes until the final round. Quickly, she changed into her bikini as the audience, hidden now beyond the stage curtain, babbled in the auditorium. She joined her mother at the stove while the crowd quaffed shots of whiskey, wolf-whistling as last year's winner was paraded around for their entertainment. The tattoo chirruped nonsense—*breathe deep, breathe deep*—and though she still didn't catch his meaning, Verralee believed in that deep Egyptian hue, that lapis lazuli warbling. With his fluttering wings mussing Kaylene's loose French roll, and that grin curling her mother's magenta lips as she spoke, Verralee knew things would turn out fine. One way or the other.

For fins' sakes, pay attention, the bluebird repeated. *Don't you want to win?*

She was—*honest*—and yes, she really, really did.

Goldfish whirlpooled in her stomach whenever she thought about being crowned Miss Tapekwa County. Though she tried not to care—she'd primed herself to be a good sport, even practised her gracious-loser smile—in truth her hopes were sky-high, tied fast to her soul with kite strings. Sometimes she wanted to win so bad, it felt like a hurricane raged around her. Hope yanked at her heart, dragged it up her throat, blocked her windpipe, cut off all rational thought.

She watched polliwogs swimming in the clear round beads of Kaylene's long necklace and knew just how they felt: spinning, spinning in cramped bubbles, stuck in one spot, all heads and tails, half-formed limbs and inhibited growth. She was eighteen now; she had to stretch out of her plain-girl shell, shine like the ageless harvest queens, and prove that her face looked best when not darkened by the shadow of a book. If Verralee won the pageant—and she would, wouldn't she? The bluebird was rarely wrong; only that one time, all those years ago, just that once. When it'd been her mother's turn to compete, when he'd said, without the slightest trace of red at his throat, that Kaylene could win. Not *would*, Verralee reminded herself, *could*. That one simple letter made all the difference: could, not *would*. Like he'd known without knowing that tattooed Kaylene, stunner though she was, would never transform into a true Miss Tapekwa County. But once Verralee won, her smooth olive skin coloured only with spray-tan and dabs of makeup, her hair dyed a black so convincing it almost looked natural, she'd see things and go places her mother, in losing, had missed.

She'd be one of Town Hall's main girls. They'd take her to Nationals, staged on an island on the far side of the country, where ladies with flower jewellery and grass skirts danced beneath palm trees, where they cooked pigs in coal-filled holes in the ground. Where she'd perform, too, under that foreign sun, and when they liked her best she'd be given a special crown; one she could bring back to Tapekwa County after her nation-wide tour. Goldfish churned at the thought of how pretty she'd be then. Officially.

The bluebird said it would be so.

Kaylene plucked one tadpole bead from the strand around her neck, popped it into a jar, handed another to Verralee. *You watching?* asked the tattoo, as his high-heeled interpreter filled the vessel with jellied liquid. She spoke secret words that didn't come from his beak. *Last chance, Vee. Then it's all you.*

Verralee paused, frogling in her palm.

It's all you.

That's what Simon had said yesterday, holding her hand, pressing her close, his glasses knocked to the ground from the urgency with which he hugged her, begging her not to compete. *You'll be different,* he'd said to the only girl he'd called his own since the eighth grade. He didn't ask her how hard it all was, didn't mention the fact that winning might hurt more than losing. *No relationship can survive what you'll become*—but Verralee had cut him off. She couldn't cry the night before the pageant. She couldn't afford the puffiness.

This isn't about us, she'd said.

No, he'd agreed. *It's all you.*

The polliwog rolled into the jar. Verralee splashed in a cupful of water, added a frond of seaweed, then rested her hand on the rim. The rest of the spell, caught between her tongue and teeth, refused to form.

This wasn't just about her, not completely. Not only. Winning this title would make her part of a larger, more beautiful story.

She'd follow in her great-auntie's footsteps, pick up the trail where Kaylene had gone astray. Folk would come from all over to see the display at Town Hall, to bathe in the wonder of *Miss Tapekwa County: Now and Forever*. Just like Verralee had each year, donning her new birthday dress and the polished shoes Kaylene wouldn't let her wear 'round the farm. They'd gaze with reverence at row upon row of dewy faces. Drooping ropes would prevent spectators from touching the winners' sequins and shimmer and shine—but every last one of them would want to. Oh, how they'd want to. Instead, under the guards' watchful eyes, they'd resign themselves to commenting on the changing fashions over the years; on the curve of that one's waist, the glimmer in that one's eyes. All would agree, even without touching or tasting or knowing them intimately, that each girl was the most beautiful in the world. And as they turned for home, back to dry fields and cold dairies and dwindling bales of hay, their bellies would warm with pride. These perfect girls in their swimmers, they'd say, these paragons of aquatic beauty, came not just from God, but from the very soul of Tapekwa County.

What was wrong with wanting to give folk such pleasure?

Verralee shook her head and again looked at the clock. She hoped Simon would continue to visit the show, if and when she won.

Focus, said the bird. *We've rehearsed this a million times.* While Kaylene's tadpole flourished, transforming in the pickling solution she'd charmed, Verralee's sank listless to the bottom. The producers had kept the light dim backstage, but even so she could make out the unmoving shadow in her jar; she could see sparks and phosphorescence illuminate Kaylene's. *You'll always regret it, you know. If you mess things up now.*

True.

The songbird's collar glowed Persian blue, the lines of each feather delicately rendered, thin as the fine crescent scars ribbing both sides of Kaylene's neck. Traces of gills half-formed. Permanent reminders of the only time the tattoo's truth had been one letter off.

Focus, he repeated, after Kaylene cleared the lump from her throat. *You can do this, darlin'. Make us proud.*

Kaylene passed the necklace to Verralee, watched intently as she slipped the length of gelatinous beads over her head.

We've dreamt of this day for years.

🎼

Verralee's arms shook as she lowered herself into the tank.

It stood on a wheeled mahogany platform, the third of seven stationed in a gentle arc across the stage for all to see. Twelve feet high and twice as wide, its faint green glass ballooned like a brandy snifter. Verralee's fingers caught on its scalloped rim, then slid into a recessed ridge that would, once she'd won, support a silver filigreed lid moulded into the shape of a crown. Footlights refracted through the tanks' gallons of liquid, casting rainbows across the ceiling and the lucky few who'd snagged seats in the front row. Overhead, spotlights shone so hot Verralee worried the mascara would melt from her lashes before she had a chance to submerge; so bright she could not longer see Johnny, her stepfather, standing in the wings at stage left.

They're ready for you, hun, he'd said with a wink, his pomade-slick head poking through a split in the curtains. *I'd say* break a leg *but, you know. Somehow that don't seem right.* He stepped through the gap and held the drapes closed behind him, avoiding the stagehands cleaning Verralee's rehearsal space before her performance. Johnny leaned forward, jolly as a clarinet, and kept his voice low.

You look gorgeous, Vee. Real gorgeous. Glad you done yerself natural—the rest of them girls is painted up like a herd of carousel ponies.

Gods love you, Pa, she'd laughed, the sound only slightly forced. He'd blown her a kiss before ducking back out, blissfully ignorant of the fact that the 'natural' look took the most makeup to achieve.

The viscous tonic smelled faintly of lime and was cold on her bare legs. She wriggled her feet, savoured the sensation of chill creeping up from her toes. Her mind wandered as the Master of Ceremonies announced the final task; the pickling challenge, the preserving. *Breathe deep, breathe deep*, the bluebird had said. And she'd intended to, she really had: but now her teeth were chattering as the liquid reached her shoulders; and the chain of tadpoles was squirming around her neck, floating up to her chin as her hair fanned out behind; and Simon, her quiet Simon, all fancy in dress pants and a collared t-shirt, was leaving the auditorium. Fluorescent bulbs over the audience reflected off his lenses, blinding ovals of white that obscured his grey eyes. He stared at her for a moment from the end of the aisle, a gash between rows of threadbare velvet seats.

Her fingers slipped as Simon snuck out the back door.

Water cooled the flush from her cheeks.

Inside the tank Verralee's world blurred. Folk were reduced to diluted colours, glowing patches of liquefied light. Echoes of the band's music grew deeper, more resonant, sound felt as vibration; chords thickened into tangible waves, harmonies licked her long tresses into art nouveau swirls. Air caught in her lungs, nostrils and ears; bubbles jewelled her limbs and gilded her gold lycra bikini. She closed her eyes. Listened to herself sinking.

Though her pulse raced, though the goldfish in her belly fought their way down to her bowels, it was too late to shout *Wait!* or *Simon!* or *I've changed my mind!* But had she, really? Changed it? Shaking the bubbles from her head, she blinked. Plucked the beads from their chain, squeezed pollywogs from their round crystal prisons. *Wait!* she could've called; but she hadn't. If she were the bluebird, her larynx might've reddened at such an exclamation.

The spell Kaylene had taught her frothed from Verralee's mouth, from lips gone cerulean.

She pushed sinuous strands of hair away from her face, like her mother had instructed. *Let the judges see your fine features.* Pain seared through her chest as she ran out of oxygen; it speared through her guts, sent shocks to the tips of her fingers, shredded her inner thighs, calves, toes. *Don't forget to spin; let them see how fresh water accentuates the arrival of your new fins, your new curves.*

To her right and left, contestants floundered in their tanks. Two girls were hauled from the water, their limp bodies thrown to the floor. A third came up for air, just a quick gasp, hoping the panel of judges would be too busy with the drowned to notice her infraction. No luck. The men took to her tank with cast-iron canes, smashed its rippled glass as she went back under for a second attempt at winning the crown.

You get one shot, the bluebird had said. *Breathe deep.*

Verralee wanted to—*don't make your Mamma's mistakes*—but she was afraid her heart might have left the room with Simon. Still, she didn't want to be slapped to the ground like those three—those *four*—girls. She wasn't strong enough for that disappointment. She couldn't bear to let Kaylene down.

This pageant was hers to win.

Just breathe.

She turned a slow pirouette, showed off the muscles in her thighs and upper back. Her arms grew heavy, her head throbbed, her lungs nose eyes veins guts blood screamed for air: *Breathe!* Her neck split and burned, sprouted opercula. *Breathe!* Spots darted in front of her eyes: tadpoles turned frogs turned eels and, finally, turned into a legion of indigo-crimson *betta splendens*. Verralee heard the crowd cheer in delight as around her swam iridescent flashes of joy.

She tilted her head in gratitude, glugged out a prayer.

At last, she inhaled.

Pure Tapekwa water filtered through her new gills. The pressure in her head subsided as she drank in each fluid breath. She exhaled words of binding, phrases of change, and other spells that could only be formed by liquid voices. Delight buoyed her up as the veiled fish latched onto her legs. At her command, the *bettas* multiplied; tripled and quadrupled; burrowed into her flesh; dug into sinew and bone. They gnawed and knitted, knitted and gnawed; transferring their scales, their long silken fins, to create the pageant queen's unique double-tail.

Now Verralee wanted to call out for Simon; *now* she wished he'd return. What a sight he'd have seen through his white-glaring glasses; his girl earning a crown the bluebird always knew she deserved. *It doesn't hurt*, she'd have told him, *turning perfect.*

Painless, her legs blended, her feet flattened, her toes splayed into transparent cartilage. Cold, she lost what made her Simon's love, and Kaylene's little girl, and Johnny's natural beauty. Calm, she buried her humanity beneath a school of clammy skins and gained hips most women would kill for. Blank, she preserved her good looks and became, forever, Miss Tapekwa County.

One last pang, before her blood chilled, at the thought of another girl kissing her Simon's lips. Marrying him. Bearing his children. Maybe he'd sneak over to Town Hall when his wife wrinkled, grew inevitably heavy, sagged beneath gravity and the burden of her husband's heartbroken neglect. Maybe he'd come to stare at Verralee as he'd done today. Silently. Forlornly.

Maybe.

The judges lowered the crown-lid onto her tank. It slid easily into place, glass and silver threading together like frozen fingers clasped.

Verralee looked through clouded glass as the audience applauded. As they gathered purses, jackets, hats and filed out of the hall. As her parents approached, their footsteps inaudible. Black hair wreathed her head, tangled seastrands that caught her kin in its web. She saw her parents, distorted, through the lather of her exhalations. They looked to her like happy, irrelevant dreams, caught and preserved in bubbles from her past. One by one they popped, disappeared, returned to the world from whence such dreams came. She watched the bluebird quiver as Kaylene slowly left, cheeks shining with tears, trailing an ink-smudge of useless advice. In response, Verralee flapped her tail, turned a somersault. As a choir of *bettas* taught her their flooded songs, she bid her land family a water-winged farewell.

Spun another somersault, and they were gone.

Broken glass and fishwater had been mopped up to let the stage's wooden boards dry. Drained tanks had been wheeled away, loaded onto trucks. One only remained, on display for an empty auditorium. Filled to the brim, dusted with a sprinkling of bloodworms in case of hunger, the winner's vessel sat and waited for morning. The stage lights had dimmed, singling her out, but Miss Tapekwa County was not alone.

A transparent, crimson-finned mermaid had appeared right in front of her!

She turned a gleeful forward roll.

So did the mermaid!

Pretty, the pageant queen thought, waving at the glass.

The glass waved back.

So pretty, she giggled, sidling up to her own reflection.

The strange mermaid's smile, when it came, was honest azure. A lovely, forgetful shade of blue.

𝄞 𝄞 𝄞

Afterword

Afterword

I usually don't listen to music while I write.

Anything with good lyrics and an intricate tune distracts me—I wind up singing along, fingers immobile on the keyboard, convinced that if you were to listen *just so* you'd mistake me for Margo Timmins or possibly Karin Bergquist (especially if I'd sipped a hot lemon drink first to tighten the vocal chords). Swept up in my fantasy, I'd be compelled to perform Cowboy Junkies' entire *Studio* album, followed by Over the Rhine's *Ohio* (Disc One), with eyes shut to avoid seeing the screensaver flicker to life while the clock ticked away all the time that should've been spent writing. Just, you know, for example.

Music works best for thinking. The tone of a singer's voice, the wail of background violins, the layering of harmonies and melodies—not to mention style, rich acoustics and cold steel guitars—all conspire to build imaginary worlds in my head. Words aren't necessary for inspiration: an orchestral swell or a quirky glockenspiel can evoke tales just as easily as a deep voice shaping a finely-turned phrase. I seek out albums that, to my mind, match the mood of what I'm working on—and then I listen to them repeatedly whenever I'm not actually putting words on the page. I think of it as 'method writing': plunging myself into a certain headspace the way some actors do before filming; listening for the rhythm of the ideas I'm trying to convey; the beat of my characters' thoughts.

It's fair to say that this collection is a product of such 'method writing'. I listened to so much bluegrass, country, pseudo-country, and folk music while writing *Bluegrass Symphony* that to list everything here would take ages. If I had to narrow it down, I'd say Gillian Welch's albums have probably had the most airtime on my iPod over the past few months—I can hear traces of her nasal twang in most of these narratives—but there are also hints of Amy Millan, Alison Krauss, even oldies like the Nitty Gritty Dirt Band. You won't find any direct translations of songs into story here; it is neither my place nor my desire to adapt the poetic plots of other people's songs into prose. Nevertheless, each of the pieces in this collection is buttressed by a combination of tunes—so I thought I would share some examples of my thinking music with you here.

Carousel

ALBUM: Mumford & Sons, *Sigh No More*. All of it.

I wrote this story because I couldn't get the image of a girl surrounded by moths out of my head. She was sitting on the ground, knees pulled up to her chest, hugging her shins. Around her, the air was thick with fluttering beige wings. At first, I thought she might've been in a bird cage, or in a natural cave high up on a mountainside. It was dark and she was scared. I had no idea how she had been trapped—because I was *sure* she'd been trapped— and I had no concept of how (or if) she'd get out. But as I listened to *Sigh No More*, this initial vision stretched to include dusty fields and, off in the distance, a carnival. This story is also an attempt to reconcile myself with living in a house that frequently has moths as unwanted guests. I figured if I gave them a bit of personality, the next time they invade my space (which is inevitable) I might feel less inclined to crush them.

Down the Hollow

ARTIST: Gillian Welch. Pretty much all of *Time (The Revelator)*; some of *Soul Journey* and *Hell Among the Yearlings*, but particularly 'One Monkey' from the former and 'Whiskey Girl' from the latter.

I started listening to Gillian Welch while driving around Iceland in 2009. Somehow, the sparseness of *Time (The Revelator)* suited the Icelandic landscape perfectly, despite the music's distinct American flavour. Since "Down the Hollow" finds its roots in the Icelandic conception of revenants (corporeal ghosts) I revisited the album while jotting down notes about the story's plot. I branched out, splurged on several of Welch's albums and sampled them while the piece percolated in my brain. Finally, I stumbled on 'Whiskey Girl' which—for the first time ever—I listened to on repeat as I wrote this story. The volume was turned down so low I couldn't hear the lyrics, but the mournful tone of this song undoubtedly got into my subconscious; the effects of its dark chords permeate the mood and pacing of this story.

Them Little Shinin' Things

SONGS: Josh Pyke, *Feeding the Wolves*; Martha Wainwright, 'Bloody Motherfucking Asshole' (from the EP of the same name); Heather Dale, 'Changeling Child' (from *The Gabriel Hounds*).

Several thoughts inspired this story. I've always simultaneously been intrigued and disappointed by changeling tales. The uncanny nature of faery doppelgangers is fascinating, as is the ambivalence faery beings show toward their human victims. Magical creatures who steal babies cannot be nice, as far as I'm concerned; but the abductions they enact might be more meaningful if they had human accomplices. I've also felt slightly disappointed when reading changeling tales because the human children are too often left as absences in the narratives: they are gone before the story begins, or they vanish soon thereafter in order to allow readers to focus on the bereaved parents. Of course that mystery is part of the appeal of the changeling; but I wanted to investigate how these children disappear, and why, without resorting to moralistic devices. And I couldn't ignore Hesteh's voice—she wanted to tell this her way, and there was nothing I could do to stop her.

Fur and Feathers

ARTIST: Johnny Cash—everything. SONGS: 'Furr' by Blitzen Trapper (from *Furr*) as well as 'The Man Who Would Speak' and 'The Tree' from their album, *Destroyer of the Void*.

A sense of play is what drove this story. Like many other readers, I love trickster tales—the aura of mischief, imminent danger, and naughtiness surrounding these characters is so appealing, I wanted to have fun with one myself. I was aiming for a happy*ish* story—one in which small joys are made sweeter because they are contrasted with moments of loss. The music I listened to while writing this piece was upbeat, grounded in folk tales; cyclical and full of promise.

From the Teeth of Strange Children

ALBUM: Over the Rhine, *Drunkard's Prayer*. SONGS: Cowboy Junkies, 'Lungs' (from *One Soul Now*); 'Hurt' by Johnny Cash (remake of the Nine Inch Nails song by the same title, on *Cash: The Man Comes Around*).

I never wanted to write a vampire story. After reading Richard Matheson's *I Am Legend* a few years ago, I decided that every chilling and heart-wrenching thing that could be accomplished with a vampire narrative had officially been achieved, and I was satisfied to leave it at that. (Let's be clear here: I'm talking about the novel; not the film with its weird CGI zombie things.) Soon thereafter the world was inundated by sparkly night creatures, and I was even less inclined to venture into the crypts and faux-gothic settings of the *vampyr* in my own work.
And then.

Last year I wrote not one, but *two* stories focused on vampires because I realised there was something still to be said. Or, perhaps, something that needed re-saying. What worked best, from my perspective, about Matheson's book was the uncanny human/not-human nature of his monsters. And they were *monstrous*—there would be no secret picnics in the forest, no loving gazes across the high school cafeteria for these beasts. Their ability to scare was incredible because they were simultaneously *just like us* and *not like us at all*. They were flawed, human-like beings with alien motivations. Selfish in ways only creatures without a conscience can be. Disturbing in their fixations. Vampires should make us feel helpless; drained (emotionally, if not physically); and anything but comfortable. They should do things that make us squirm, that make us wish never to see them again.

Encounters with vampires should leave us afraid of the dark.

The Wager and the Hourglass

SONGS: Hem, 'The Cuckoo' (from *Rabbit Songs*); Gillian Welch, 'Wichita' and 'Red Clay Halo' (both from *Music from the Revelator Collection*); Carolina Chocolate Drops, 'Cornbread and Butterbeans' (from *Genuine Negro Jig*).

Dreams rarely produce good stories. Though whimsical or spooky or outlandish in content, their logic is not really that of literature. Nevertheless, we can draw on them for inspiration—even if we can't rely on them for plot—which is how this story came to be. Nothing in "The Wager and the Hourglass" has anything to do with the dream I had in the wee hours of the morning before I began working on this piece. Sure, there was a boy and there was a girl. They were in love. The boy was in danger and the girl had to save him. That's where the similarities end. I woke up on the verge of tears, and felt weepy for much of the day. Luckily, I got some sage advice (thanks, Brain) and opted to try and capture the misery I was feeling in writing. The result? A fast-paced clever-girl story which isn't sad at all. See what I mean? Dreams just don't look on paper as they do in our sleeping heads.

The Short Go: A Future in Eight Seconds

SONGS: Gillian Welch 'Barroom Girls' (from *Revival*); Amy Millan, 'Ruby II', 'Hard Hearted (Ode to Thoreau)' and 'Pour Me Up Another' (from *Honey From the Tombs*).

Rodeos are fascinating and horrible spectacles, much like new love. Make one mistake and you could be done for before you even get a good grip; trampled instead of triumphant. But hang on tight, make the right moves, and you should come up a winner. (*Should.*) So I wanted to explore the highs and lows of young love; to dabble in restrictions that belong in fables; and to see why people might feel justified in clinging to superstition. The tone of the piece had to resonate with oral storytelling and folklore—it was important that our narrator knew more than us while he spun his yarn. And it was just as important that there were hints of Greek mythology in the setting because I had visions of wrangling Minotaurs.

To Snuff a Flame

SONGS: Loretta Lynn: 'Coal Miner's Daughter' (title track of the 1970 album); Joanna Newsom, 'Soft as Chalk' and 'Does Not Suffice' (from *Have One on Me*); The Avett Brothers, 'I and Love and You' and 'Head Full of Doubt/Road Full of Promise' (from *I and Love and You*); Orealis, 'L'Hiver Sur Richelieu/Miss B's Dreams' (from *Musique Celtique*).

This story started life as a 1,200 word foray into the story of Red Riding Hood, told from the path's perspective. The path was obsessed with Little Red and more than a little bit jealous of the wolf who'd wooed and won her. If he could have peeled himself off the forest floor, the path would have stalked her—no doubt about it. Although the original version of this tale was too short (and consequently unresolved), I remained interested in the ideas that drove me to write it. Doolittle took on some of the path's characteristics, but brought his own memories and motivations to the story. Lola Mae echoes some of her predecessor's traits, but is neither as valiant as my first Little Red, nor is she quite like her traditional antecedents. She's simultaneously devious, smart, and innocent; she wins and also loses. In both of its incarnations, the story focuses on clever girls as viewed from a male perspective; but though these girls are desired, their actions and decisions prevent them from being seen as mindless objects. They interact with hungry wolves-in-men-suits and inspire impossible obsession. Yet Lola Mae isn't the real focus of 'To Snuff a Flame', despite her prominence in the tale. Shape-shifting drives this narrative: how people change, physically and emotionally, and the prices they'll pay to undo what's been done.

Depot to Depot

SONGS: Gillian Welch, 'One More Dollar' (*Revival*); and 'White Freightliner Blues' (*Music from the Revelator Collection*).

It amazes me how many car accidents there are on Australian roads. Growing up in Canada, I learned what treacherous driving conditions were: blizzards, black ice, freezing rain, drops the size of grapefruits pummelling the windshield during midsummer storms. Once, driving no faster than 30kms an hour, I slid into a ditch in the dead of winter because a thin carpet of snow had drifted across the asphalt, caught my tires, and let me know—in no uncertain terms—that I was no longer the one in charge of the vehicle's direction. Sure, Canadian winters produced tonnes of accidents; but, as frightening as the statistics were, they at least kind of made sense. Since moving to Adelaide, I have been sometimes bewildered, sometimes bemused at how the lightest shower sends drivers into a panic. How, lacking the blinding snows and ice-slicks, too many Australian drivers rely on speed to send them into early graves.

But this isn't a public service announcement. Instead, it's a recreation of the thoughts that were running through my mind when, at the end of a long weekend not too many months ago, I watched an all-too-familiar news broadcast in which the reporter tallied up the holiday road toll. So many deaths on perfectly clear highways. And I wondered how long it would take the police to find cars that had slammed into trees out on lonely country roads. How the numbers in the newscaster's story were once people. How the next motorist who drove past would feel upon seeing the mess; upon finding the bodies. Which led me to think about what kind of people might be on those night-dark roads—and then, though I hadn't intended it, I found myself writing a story about a fat old trucker named Haros.

Commonplace Sacrifices

ALBUM: Josh Pyke, *Memories & Dust*.

Written in 2008, this is the oldest story included here and the only one that sprouted, fully-formed, in my mind. The idea came to me thanks to a scorching South Australian heatwave and a line in one of James Joyce's *Dubliners* stories. I can't remember which story it was. Due to the heat, a second floor apartment (with west-facing aspect), and my intolerance of temperatures above 18 degrees, I was camped out on the living room floor trying my damnedest to catch every draught of cool air our crummy air conditioner deigned to release. And, to be honest, I was reading Joyce to help me fall asleep ... when my eyes lit on a passage describing mundane things in a mundane Irish setting in a mundane narrator's voice as "sacrifices". The word dropped like a rainbow spark in a sentence of grey ideas. The juxtaposition of a boring narrative (sorry, James) with such an evocative act—I had visions of Saint Sebastian, and Catherine Wheels, and martyrs roasted on pyres—shook me awake. My heart pounded. How could everyday actions match the medieval sacrifices in my imagination? Magic, I thought, had to be involved. And so the narrator immediately came to life. But as the story unfolded, I knew that magic wasn't what made the sacrifices within it special. It was the realisation that they were familiar—commonplace, even—that gave this tale shape. The original version of "Commonplace Sacrifices" was published in *On Spec*, Vol.21, No.4 (Winter 2009).

Wires Uncrossed

ALBUMS: Hem, *Eveningland* and *Rabbit Songs*.

I tend to get lots of ideas while being driven around. There's little else to do while sitting on a bus or in the car but think, so I try to take advantage of the free-brain time and let my thoughts go where they will. One time, when we were coming home from Burra, South Australia, I was gazing out the passenger-side window at brown fields and low golden hills. For hours, few trees interrupted the landscape. Everything was low, dry, isolated. Except, that is, for the telephone towers jutting here and there out of the hot earth. At first I imagined them as great metallic Ents, and imagined where they were slowly going, tethered to each other with their drooping, skipping-rope wires. Then I thought of Wells' *The War of the Worlds* (which may or may not have had something to do with the fact that we were listening to an old radio adaptation of the novel that Chad had picked up at an op-shop) and hoped the telephone-aliens would take off soon. And then I thought, *What if the telephone poles sprouted from below?* For a split second, I pictured a field of telephone poles marking the graves of children buried underneath them. I tucked this image away, not sure what to do with it. Later, I picked up a book about vampires at a second-hand sale. It mentioned a once-held belief that vampires were born not from blood, but from adultery. But at this stage, I still refused to write a vampire story. So I tucked that idea next to the image of the telephone-pole children. These ideas chatted to each other while I was daydreaming, staring out the bus window on my way to work. A few drafts later they actually started to communicate.

Forever, Miss Tapekwa County

SONGS: Johnny Cash, 'Folsom Prison Blues' (from *With His Hot and Blue Guitar*); Gillian Welch, 'Only One and Only' (*Revival*) and 'Look at Miss Ohio' (*Soul Journey*).

Long before I'd heard of feminism; long before people teased beauty queens for their dreams of world peace; long before JonBenet Ramsey became a headline; there were three sisters, not yet in junior high, who loved watching the annual Miss Teen U.S.A. pageant. All of whom wished that Canadians could enter so they too could wear the glamorous gowns, the satin sashes with State (or, in their case, Province) names running diagonally across perfect torsos. They wanted to win the car, the college scholarship, the trip to Hawaii. Don't get me started on how much we—ahem, *they*—wanted that sparkly crown. Nowadays, my opinions of pageants are far from positive, but *then*. Oh, *then* was a different story. And, in a way, *then* is part of this story. However, the *now* of this tale revolves around my thoughts about superficial beauty and the artificial means by which we try to preserve it. If people are willing to go under the knife for the sake of appearances, would they, if they could, volunteer to be pickled in human-sized jars if it meant they'd stay forever young?

Afterword

SONGS: Shearwater, 'Hidden Lakes', 'Missing Islands', and 'Castaways' (from *The Golden Archipelago*); and 'Palo Santo' and 'Sing, Little Birdie' (from *Palo Santo (Extended Version)*). Loreena McKennitt, 'The Star of the County Down' and 'As I Roved Out' (from *The Wind That Shakes the Barley*). And one final go-round of Gillian Welch's greatest, for old time's sake.

Acknowledgements

"Commonplace Sacrifices" copyright © 2009 Lisa L. Hannett. First published in *On Spec*, vol. 21, no. 4, Winter 2009. Appears here in a revised form.

Everything else appears here for the first time, ever.

ALSO AVAILABLE FROM TICONDEROGA PUBLICATIONS

978-0-9586856-6-5   TROY by Simon Brown (TPB)
978-0-9586856-7-2   THE WORKERS' PARADISE eds Farr & Evans (TPB)
978-0-9586856-8-9   FANTASTIC WONDER STORIES ed. Russell B Farr (TPB)
978-0-9586856-9-6   LOVE IN VAIN by Lewis Shiner (LIMITED HC)
978-0-9803531-0-5   LOVE IN VAIN by Lewis Shiner (TPB)
978-0-9803531-1-2   BELONG ed Russell B Farr (LIMITED HC)
978-0-9803531-2-9   BELONG ed Russell B Farr (TPB)
978-0-9803531-3-6   GHOST SEAS by Steven Utley (HC)
978-0-9803531-4-3   GHOST SEAS by Steven Utley (TPB)
978-0-9803531-5-0   GHOST SEAS by Steven Utley (EBOOK)
978-0-9803531-6-7   MAGIC DIRT: THE BEST OF Sean Williams (TPB)
978-0-9803531-7-4   THE LADY OF SITUATIONS by Stephen Dedman (HC)
978-0-9803531-8-1   THE LADY OF SITUATIONS by Stephen Dedman (TPB)
978-0-9803531-9-8   BASIC BLACK by Terry Dowling (LIMITED HC)
978-0-9806288-2-1   BASIC BLACK by Terry Dowling (TPB)
978-0-9806288-0-7   MAKE BELIEVE by Terry Dowling (LIMITED HC)
978-0-9806288-3-8   MAKE BELIEVE by Terry Dowling (TPB)
978-0-9806288-1-4   THE INFERNAL by Kim Wilkins (LIMITED HC)
978-0-9806288-4-5   SCARY KISSES ed Liz Grzyb (TPB)
978-0-9806288-5-2   DEAD SEA FRUIT by Kaaron Warren (LIMITED HC)
978-0-9806288-6-9   DEAD SEA FRUIT by Kaaron Warren (TPB)
978-0-9806288-7-6   THE GIRL WITH NO HANDS by Angela Slatter (LIMITED HC)
978-0-9806288-8-3   THE GIRL WITH NO HANDS by Angela Slatter (TPB)
978-0-9807813-0-4   DEAD RED HEART ed Russell B Farr (LIMITED HC)
978-0-9807813-1-1   DEAD RED HEART ed Russell B Farr (TPB)
978-1-921857-99-7   DEAD RED HEART ed Russell B Farr (EBOOK)
978-0-9807813-2-8   MORE SCARY KISSES ed Liz Grzyb (TPB)
978-1-921857-94-2   MORE SCARY KISSES ed Liz Grzyb (EBOOK)
978-0-9807813-3-5   HELIOTROPE by Justina Robson (LIMITED HC)
978-0-9807813-4-2   HELIOTROPE by Justina Robson (TPB)
978-0-9807813-5-9   HELIOTROPE by Justina Robson (EBOOK)
978-0-9807813-6-6   MATILDA TOLD SUCH DREADFUL LIES by Lucy Sussex (L/HC)
978-0-9807813-7-3   MATILDA TOLD SUCH DREADFUL LIES by Lucy Sussex (TPB)
978-0-9807813-8-0   YEAR'S BEST AUSTRALIAN F&H eds Grzyb & Helene (HC)
978-0-9807813-9-7   YEAR'S BEST AUSTRALIAN F&H eds Grzyb & Helene (TPB)
978-1-921857-98-0   YEAR'S BEST AUSTRALIAN F&H eds Grzyb and Helene (EBK)
978-1-921857-00-3   BLUEGRASS SYMPHONY by Lisa L Hannett (LIMITED HC)
978-1-921857-01-0   BLUEGRASS SYMPHONY by Lisa L Hannett (TPB)
978-1-921857-97-3   BLUEGRASS SYMPHONY by Lisa L Hannett (EBOOK)

www.ticonderogapublications.com

THANK YOU

The publisher would sincerely like to thank:

Elizabeth Grzyb, Lisa L Hannett, Ann Vandermeer, Jeff Vandermeer, Robert Shearman, Angela Slatter, Lisa Bennett, Simon Brown, Jonathan Strahan, Peter McNamara, Ellen Datlow, Grant Stone, Jeremy G. Byrne, Lucy Sussex, Sean Williams, Garth Nix, David Cake, Simon Oxwell, Grant Watson, Sue Manning, Steven Utley, Bill Congreve, Talie Helene, Jack Dann, Kirstyn McDermott, Stephen Dedman, the Mt Lawley Mafia, the Nedlands Yakuza, Amanda Pillar, Shane Jiraiya Cummings, Angela Challis, Donna Maree Hanson, Kate Williams, Kathryn Linge, Andrew Williams, Al Chan, Alisa Krasnostein, Mel & Phil, Hayley Lane, Georgina Walpole, everyone we've missed . . .

. . . and you.

In memory of Eve Johnson (1945–2011)

Lightning Source UK Ltd.
Milton Keynes UK
UKOW050632141111

182027UK00001B/20/P